BLOOD

OF THE

ASSASSIN

BILL BREWER

Dedicated to you, the reader.

Thank you for choosing this book.
I hope you enjoy the story.

Praise for Bill Brewer

"Action, on fire! With danger lurking from enemies on all sides, and a lone female CIA operative, his only confidante, David Diegert must bring on the action as he dives into the fray once more in the non-stop sequel, *Blood of the Assassin!*"
Lt. Colonel Rip Rawlings (USMC) Co-Author of *Red Metal*

Jeffrey Miller
★★★★★ A Real Page-Turner!
As soon as I started reading, I couldn't put it down. Bill Brewer delivers a hard-hitting, story that's as much cerebral as visceral. If you like your reading fast and powerful, you don't want to pass this one up!

Grady Harp
HALL OF FAME TOP 100 REVIEWER

★★★★★ 'You mean I'll be assigned to kill more people'
Solid, colorful writing that produces an intensely satisfying thriller. This is a very solid start of a most promising series and an introduction to a new writer of considerable skill.

JMabie
★★★★★ Looking forward to Mr. Brewer's next
I think what I liked best was the pace of this book. To call this book an action/adventure is to put it mildly! It is a book I read at warp speed, and one that left me wishing for more.

Amy Williams
★★★★★ A promising series
Brewer is excellent at creating realistic scenarios that keep you immersed in the story, and make it really hard to put down. By the time the story ended, I was out of breath!

Chapter 1

Sherriff Michael Lowery pulled his Ford Explorer
Interceptor into the parking lot of the Moose Jaw Inn,
Broward Minneosta's most popular bar. The colored
lights of his vehicle remained off as he parked the white,
black and gold SUV next to the rusted Toyota Camry of
Tom Diegert. Watching the door of an establishment
which over the years had more than enough run ins with
the law, he waited for the last customers to leave at 2 am
on a Wednesday. Sherriff Lowery knew where to find the
men he was looking for.

Standing with the bar door open, Tom Diegert leaned
back and shouted past his son Jake, "Hey Brad."

The bartender looked up from cleaning glasses.

"Hey, thanks for a really great time," slurred Mr. Diegert.

"Right, Fuck you Tom, just pay your tab next time."

"Hey, I gave ya what I could…"

"Come on Dad, let's go," said Jake as he directed his
father out the door and down the stairs.

"Christ, it was only one or two beers, I paid for the rest,"
bitched the man in whose home David Diegert, the
world's most sought after assassin, had grown up.

Jake tapped his father's shoulder when he noticed the
police truck parked next to their car.

"Judas, what the fuck is he doing here? He knows we're going to be drunk. What the hell's he doing, check'n on us?"

Straightening their gaits, the two inebriated men continued approaching their bedraggled Camry. The paint had dulled to a tarnished beige with rust on the wheel wells and doorjambs. Sheriff Lowery stepped out of the Interceptor. "Hello, Tom."

"Evening Officer."

"It's morning, Tom."

Tom nodded. He stood with his hands folded in front of him like a pious Quaker.

"I was hoping I could have a word with you two about David."

"David?! I got two words for ya, Fuckin Bastard. That punk ass bitch up and left the family. We don't even know where the fuck he is."

Lowery looked from Tom to Jake, who nodded.

"What the hell's going on?" blurted Tom. "Why the hell are you out here in the middle of the night asking about that fucker?"

Lowery found himself a bit off guard, but he had to ask. "Did you know that David joined the Army?"

Tom's ruddy red cheeks blanched. He stammered to say, "No fuck'n way. He left a note saying he was leaving. He didn't want to live with us no more. He never said he was joining the Army." Looking at Jake, they both nodded as Jake said, "He would've told me something like that. He's my brother."

Lowery let that sappy line pass. He knew neither of these two douche bags ever gave David any reason to trust them. He regretted asking the question, but the investigation into a violent incident in Austin required him to collect background information. He had to ascertain if these guys might be hiding the man wanted for questioning in the murder of a Mexican citizen outside a bar in Austin Texas.

"When was the last time you saw him?"

Jake replied, "February."

"Yeah right, it was cold as a bitch. Fuck'n snow everywhere," added Tom.

Pushing for more information, Lowery asked, "What were the circumstances when you last saw him?"

"Aah, he was taking Denise to the doctor. He dropped her off and was long gone when she came out," stammered Tom, swaying on his feet as he scratched the patch of hair above his ears and below his dirty ball cap.

Lowery's suspicion intensified in the red glow of the Moose Jaw's neon sign.

"He did leave that note," added Jake.

"Yeah, it said he was sorry for being a fuck-up, and he was going away," said Tom. "He didn't say where, so I suppose he could've joined the Army once he ran outta money."

"But you haven't spoken to him since February?"

"Nope," said Tom, shaking his head.

Lowery wanted to cut his losses with these losers, but Tom started asking questions.

"What kinda trouble is he in?"

"What makes you think he's in trouble?"

"HA, you do. You're not going to hang out here and talk to us in the dark unless something serious has happened."

Lowery held his tongue, but he couldn't pull his gaze away. He knew what an abusive man Tom Diegert was, and Jake was complicit in the domestic dystopia of the Diegert household.

"Sherriff, did David kill somebody?"

The stoic lawman struggled to control his reaction to this blunt question. He also reasoned if they knew something, he might as well get it out of them now.

"A man was murdered in Texas, and David is a person of interest wanted for questioning."

"Texas? He ain't never been to Texas before," exclaimed Tom.

"Who did he kill?" asked Jake.

"We aren't sure he killed anyone. We just want to speak to him."

"Down in Texas, is the dead guy a spick?"

Lowery's glare was made all the more intimidating by the flow of red neon over his craggy face.

Tom retreated, "I mean if he killed a spick, that's different then if it was a white guy, right?"

Lowery could barely contain himself as he listened to the ignorant bigotry of Tom, reinforced by the head nodding of Jake.

Bringing his 6 foot 4-inch frame closer to the squat man and his chubby son, Lowery handed them each a card.

"The taking of any human life is murder. Please call me if he contacts you, we need to talk with him."

"OK, Sherriff," said Tom, "but if that bastard shows up, I'll save Texas the trouble and just shoot him myself."

Lowery's anger popped as he turned on the shabby man. "You're a pathetic excuse for a father. Whatever David may have done, you are culpable." Stepping closer, his eyelids narrowed. "The hateful way you treated him sickens me. I should've arrested you a long time ago."

A sadistic smile crept across Tom's face. "But you can't, and you know it. You can't do shit to me. Besides Jake here, is a fine son." Broward's local drug dealer smiled at the Sherriff as his father patted him on the back.

Looking at the pair with disgust, Lowery realized Tom was right.

"Get in your car and drive home. I'll be following you." Tom gave the Sherriff an awkward salute before climbing in the Camry, letting Jake take the wheel.

Driving the deserted streets of Broward with Lowery right behind him Jake thought back to when David was, maybe 12 years old. They had a chicken coop out back that was regularly raided by a clever vixen. Tom wanted to kill the fox, but the persistent canid always eluded his 12 gauge attacks. Staying up late one night Jake sat in a blind near the coop. He watched as the bright red killer stole a chicken and ran into the woods. Following the thief, he discovered the lair where this young mother had a litter of kits.

Six baby foxes waddled out of a hole under a log and shared the bounty of chicken their mother had provided. Waiting until the mother left to hunt again, Jake dug out the pups, stuffing them in a canvas bag. In the morning he showed his father what he had. Tom was so proud of Jake. He beamed his yellowed tooth smile as he gave the 16-year-old a can of beer for breakfast.

"You know what we're going to have to do with them don't ya?" asked Tom.

Jake slowly nodded his head.

"I think you've done enough," said Tom, "it's your brother's turn."

Tom called David out to the barn. The kits had been dumped into a cardboard box. David looked in and saw the cutest little creatures he'd ever seen. The six of them huddled together, frightened in this strange place as they tried to comfort one another. Their big dark eyes peered from their tiny little faces with tense, fearful curiosity. David knelt down, reached in and picked one up. The soft, warm body felt so small as it trembled in his hands. He gently stroked the fur on the top of its head as the bright orange bundle, with its little black paws, filled his palm.

Tom stepped forward slapping David's arms, sending the kit tumbling back into the box.

"These aren't fucking pets."

Falling back on the barn floor, David looked up at the rage on his father's face.

"They're our enemy." Pointing across the barn at Jake who sat impassively, Tom continued. "Jake captured 'em. He did an important thing for this family. You know the mother of these little runts has been killing our chickens. The fox is stealing our livelihood," shouted Tom as he thrust his fingers at the box of babies. "Now we're going to even the odds and reclaim our power by eliminating the enemy." Striding between his two sons, Tom took center stage as he barked, " Protecting the things your family needs to survive is the job of a warrior. Being strong, and not letting others take what you have requires guts and toughness," said Tom his beer belly shaking whenever he thrust his fist in the air. "Jake stayed up all night to find the home of the thief and capture these, vicious threats." Tom leaned forward as he glared at David. "It's now your turn to protect this family."

Tom reached into the box grabbing each kit and stuffing them, squeaking and yelping, into a canvas bag.

"You're going to kill 'em," he commanded as he placed in front of David the bag with the wriggling little bodies desperately clambering over one another. Their pitiful yelps emanated through the fabric.

"You can either drown them in the rain barrel like a pussy, or you can use the sledge on them."

Tom hefted the sledgehammer and dropped it on the barn floor next to David.

"A warrior makes sure his enemy is destroyed. He takes the life of those who steal from him with brute force. Those little pups will grow into thieving foxes. We stop that right now. Smash 'em and prove that you deserve to be part of this family."

Jake felt sorry for his brother, David loved animals, he studied nature and knew way more about it than either he or his father. Killing animals was all Tom Diegert knew, his greatest pride was being a hunter. The Warrior stuff he was blabbering about always came out whenever they so much as shot a squirrel. Still Jake was on the upside, and he remembered how there was no way he was going to let any sympathy for his brother cause him to act against his father.

"Stand up," shouted Tom. David rose from the floor, quivering. The bag of wriggling little fox kits at his feet. "Pick up the hammer and smash 'em," ordered his father. David hesitated, looking from the bag to the hammer. "Don't be a pussy like your Mom. These fuckers need to die."

David placed his hand on the hammer. The sledge had a 36-inch wooden handle with a 10-pound octagonal head. He closed his fist around it, lifting it very slowly. Tom's eyes widened with delight. David held the tool turned weapon in both hands. He looked at his father and saw wretched anticipation in the ugly man's face. He saw the thirst for violence and the bloodlust the old man held for these infants of the forest. Broadening his stance, as he had been taught to do when chopping wood, David lifted the hammer, looking at the canvas bag with its little bodies struggling within. Holding the hammer aloft, he started to tremble.

"Do it," shouted Tom.

David's tears broke over his lids, falling to the barn floor like the first drops of a sudden rain storm. Turning away from the bag of pups, he dropped the hammer and broke into uncontrollable sobbing.

"Oh no you don't, you wuss. You pick up that hammer, and you finish the job."

David collapsed to the floor curling into a fetal position.

"Oh my fucking God," exclaimed Tom. Turning to Jake, he said, "Can you believe this fucking pussy is crying like a little girl over these foxes?"

Jake recalled how bad he felt for David, but he just nodded his head.

"He is not the son of a Warrior. He's an injun bastard, who doesn't have the strength to protect his own family." Tom drew close to David, "You're a no good pussy who doesn't have the guts to kill his enemies. Well, you just keep your fucking eyes open."

Tom stepped back grabbed the hammer swung it high and brought the ten-pound maul on to the canvas bag. The yips and mews turned into screeches of terror as blood stained the fabric. Tom swung the hammer, again and again, each blow ceasing the wriggling of the little bodies. After striking the bag a dozen times, the short, ruddy man panted. Seeing one body still moving he swung the hammer again, flattening the bag, staining the canvas with more blood.

David watched the massacre from eye level as he remained on the floor throughout the ordeal. Struggling to catch his breath Tom said, "You don't deserve to be in this family since you aren't willing to fight for it. I won't forget that."

Dropping a shovel in front of David, Tom said, "Since you're so fucking broke up about these runts, you bury 'em."

Leaving the barn with his father, Jake recalled feeling like shit, but glad that he was not the one his father hated. David took the shovel and the grisly cloth bag and disappeared into the woods, for three days. Their mother, Denise went crazy not knowing where he was, but Tom didn't care.

When he eventually returned, Tom didn't say a thing, and Jake remembered David never confided in him ever again. As the years passed and David grew bigger and stronger, Tom always sided with Jake, isolating David, so he had only the friendship of his Mother.

Reaching their driveway, Jake parked in front of the garage. He watched Lowery's Explorer pass on by. Tom had passed out, so Jake reclined the seat and covered his father with the blanket they kept in the car for just such occasions. At the kitchen door, he stopped to look at the barn and thought of David. He wondered if his father had really made a killer out of his brother.

Chapter 2

Shining through the tall windows of Klaus Panzer's London office, the steepening angle of the sun's rays annoyed the world's most powerful tycoon of global commerce. Stroking a screen built into his desk, the curtains descent began, casting a shadow over the large video monitor upon which Mr. Panzer gazed at his three partners in economic world dominance.

These four wealthy men, are the members of the Board of Crepusculous. Together for two decades, they've gradually amassed tremendous wealth and, more importantly, significant power. All were born into wealth and worked to expand their fortunes. Together they are interdependent, cooperative, and fabulously successful. They keep very low profiles, never appearing in any media. Remaining invisible, they control the factors that affect the majority of the world's population. They are the one percent of the one percent. Rarely are they ever in the same location, but they frequently use video conferencing to discuss business, politics, and world events as they strategically plan to increase their possessions, profits, and power.

"Good morning, gentlemen," began Klaus Panzer. "You are all looking well."

Panzer could see Dean Kellerman, Julio Perez, and Chin Liu Wei. The video screens facilitated complete communication; not only words, but moods and emotions were visually displayed.

Panzer continued, "We do have business to discuss, but first I want to acknowledge the results of our most recent tournament at the Proving Grounds." The Proving Grounds is part of a Board owned paramilitary base, known as Headquarters, located outside Vidale Romania. At Headquarters, the Board houses and trains special operations forces for use in covert corporate actions necessary to protect the interests of Omnisphere. Maintaining their own army gave the Board the capacity to thwart any attempt to interrupt or undermine their business practices. Special Operations also included the capability of carrying out sanctioned direct actions against targeted individuals; corporate assassinations. The assassins needed to possess superior skills and abilities, allowing them to operate alone carrying out clandestine kill orders with ruthless efficiency, undetected violence and absolute secrecy. Three times a year Headquarters holds a tournament in the Proving Grounds where a number of potential Crepusculous assassins are pitted against each other. The kill or be killed requirement of the competition leaves only one person alive. The successful individual becomes an asset to be deployed when a political, corporate or personal target is chosen to be eliminated.

Both Wei and Perez turned their heads, uncomfortably looking away from the camera.

"It seems the American won the contest and will become our newest asset. Well done, Dean," announced Panzer.

"Thank you. He certainly has proven to be a tough bugger. He made a hostage rescue all by himself back in December. I believe he will be useful to all of us."

Perez exhaled a lungful of smoke before saying, "The man I sent was a last-minute submission. I had lost track of the date of the tournament; I'll send a better man next time. But my man fared no worse than yours, Klaus."

Kellerman replied, "Yes, Klaus, I was quite surprised you sent a family man."

"He had gambling debts."

"I regret the loss of Shioki Wong," offered Wei. "But the next man will be better prepared."

"Very well, our selection process is complete. We now have a new operative for mission assignments, Mr. David Diegert," concluded Panzer.

"One last thing," said Perez. "This David Diegert, is he the man who carried out my sanctions in Miami and Paris?"

Panzer nodded, adding, "He also eliminated Farroq Arindi, the man who was complicating our land purchases in Somalia and threatening the shipping lanes through the Indian Ocean."

A wry smile crept out from under the mustache of Perez, followed by a concentrated plume of smoke. "He has chosen a life of death."

Kellerman changed the subject. "Mr. Wei, I'm concerned with the disparity in the interest rates being charged to the US Federal government."

"What is your concern?" asked the surprised Chinese banker.

"Are rates going up across the board or are different branches getting different rates?"

"Different rates for different customers results in better payment compliance."

"That may be so, but rates should be universal across the government so that the economic readjustment plan we've been developing will have a greater impact."

"Different rates create more profits in the short term."

Panzer spoke on the subject. "Common rates will definitely facilitate more damage to the US government. I think what we need to do is recommit to the economic readjustment plan, our plan, and realize that the time for action is upon us. All of our individual efforts should be focused on making this long-range plan a success."

Wei replied, "I realize the devaluation of the US dollar will benefit us all. I did not realize the timeline was so aggressive. I will regulate one common interest rate and align all government borrowers. I am committed to the plan."

"Excellent. Are there any other questions regarding the plan for US economic disruption?"

"From readjustment to disruption just like that?" questioned the aging Spaniard.

"The downfall of the US dollar will create an economic opportunity the likes of which has never been seen before. Our digital currency, Digival, which is based on the value of our collective wealth, will improve the world's economic mechanisms and the Board's position of power."

The men eyed each other, searching for signs of reassurance that each of them was committed to the plan. Once the process of devaluing the dollar, and thus weakening the US government, was underway, there could be no turning back. These men had to trust one another to follow through with their portion of the plan.

After looking at each other for a quiet moment, Panzer spoke. "At this point in time, I am asking that each of you indicate your commitment to the plan or express any concerns that you have."

The men looked at one another with affirming nods, which was all that was needed to communicate their commitment within the intimate brotherhood of the elite group.

"Very well," said Panzer. "I do believe we have covered our agenda, and I move to close the meeting."

Each man agreed, and the video screens went dark.

***

Klaus picked up the phone and called Kellerman. "I'm glad you brought that issue up with Wei. I think he will comply."

"I hope so. We need to have the branches of the US Federal government on equal footings for the plan to have its full effect."

"I know, and I think Wei knows as well, but it's hard for him to take even a temporary loss."

"Yes, but in the end, the man will own California!"

"The readjustment will work. We've been planning too long for it to fail. Besides, the US just keeps ignoring its problems and making the situation inevitable."

"We're just pushing the train over the hill, so it runs away and destroys their ridiculous way of financing their lives."

"Very well, my friend, their indebtedness will be our next source of wealth."

It was the huge indebtedness of the United States that stimulated Panzer and Kellerman to develop the plan for economic readjustment. Kellerman, the actuary, calculated the unsustainable nature of US economic policy. The whole system operated on a promissory note.

A use-it-now, pay-for-it-later mentality that guided car purchases, home purchases, and in the case of the Federal government, almost all purchases. The entire country was leveraged, and a requirement to pay back even a portion of the total debt would bring to a halt the system of economic figments that fueled America's system of overspending.

When Kellerman shared his beliefs with Panzer, the German saw the vulnerability and an opportunity to correct the balance of power. The Board held a global perspective, and even though American assets like the New York Stock Exchange were important, distributing their assets across the globe was more valuable than a "Strong America" propped up by a foolishly financed system of borrowed dollars and unpaid debt.

Ironically, the US dollar remained the strongest currency upon which the value of all other currencies, and several critical commodities, including oil, was determined. Panzer sought to seize the opportunity created by the fact that the world's economy was based on a currency backed only by a promise. He determined that a currency based on the vast wealth of Crepusculous's worldwide assets, a true corporate currency, would be a better way for the world to operate. It was also determined that eliminating physical money, cash, and coins, and distributing the currency in a digital-only format, would be more efficient and secure. He successfully convinced the other Board members of his views, and they formed a plan to take down the dollar.

The plan had four phases: First, create a vacuum of leadership with a significant assassination. Second, upset the stock market by moving assets out of US holdings, tanking stock prices. Third, produce chaos and destruction the likes of which the US had never seen.

This phase would make the population feel the impact of the failure of the Federal government, making it ripe for readjustment. Fourth, call in the debt. Mr. Wei held 60 percent of US Federal debt financed through China. He would call in the loan, which would trigger a run on US debt obligations, and the government would go bankrupt. This wouldn't be one of those congressional showdown shutdowns. This time the government would be so insolvent that it would not be able to function, and Federal services would vanish.

A period of chaos, civil unrest, and lawlessness would take place. The value of the US dollar would evaporate, eliminating the basis for the worldwide system of governmental currency. Into this vacuum, Crepusculous's public corporation, Ominsphere, would continue to promote Digival, making it a global currency with a common value throughout the world, no exchange rates based on geographic location or political ideology. It would make the globe one common market. All commerce would occur as digital transactions. The world may hesitate to adjust, but quickly those who do not participate would be left in a barter-only economy. Omnisphere's power in the global market would be unprecedented, and Crepusculous would enjoy absolute power from its position in the shadows. When things settled down, a new corporate structure would replace the US Federal government. As the saying went, "Out of chaos, opportunity appears." America was still the best real estate on the planet, and this plan would allow the Board to acquire it at rock-bottom prices. The US would become the de facto Corporate States of America.

"Dean, I want to ask you about something else?" began Panzer. "Aaron shared with me the story of the Cambridge boy's rescue back in December."

"Yes, what of it?"

"What concerns me is that Michka Barovitz, a two-bit hoodlum, loan shark, and mobster, dared to extort an associate of ours and then kidnap his son. Such audacity cannot be tolerated without a response."

"We did respond. We acquired the boy right under his nose, and he lost several men in the process. David Diegert accomplished the rescue singlehandedly."

"Of course I appreciate all of that, but what I mean is that Barovitz must be dealt with directly and eliminated, or such brashness will undermine our position."

"How can such a lowly crook be of any concern to us?"

"Aboveground, you're right, we can't be hurt, but underground, the community has a harsher code. Arms dealing and covert actions occur in the shadows, and your reputation is the only credential you carry. We are well known in the dark world. Our reputation is stark; it guarantees us full payment for deliveries. Barovitz just challenged that."

"What are you suggesting?"

"The assassination of Barovitz."

"Oh my, you are taking the hard road."

"I believe a strike team can take him out on his island in the Aegean."

"And you're seeking Board approval?"

"No, but I am letting my one true friend and confidant know I'm ordering the mission.

Pulling the receiver from his ear and giving it a look of consternation, Kellerman said, "Why did you not bring this up before the Board?"

"I did not wish to explain my reasoning to the entire group; plus, a covert mission is by its very nature secret."

"Well, I appreciate your confidence. I wish you success, and I hope your underground reputation is enhanced."

"I'll keep you better informed of the mission's progress than you did me back in December. Have a good day, Dean."

As he replaced the receiver in its cradle, Kellerman reflected on the percentage of their wealth that was derived from illegal, unethical, and morally depraved activities. The figure was at least 20 percent. Between the arms, drugs, unregulated harvesting of raw materials, corporations that employed low-wage workshops, and hiring out operators for contracted covert actions, Kellerman acknowledged to himself that he was the direct beneficiary of heinous and entrenched criminal activity. The realization left him with a nauseous ache in his stomach, and an unsettling question as to what he would do about it.

Chapter 3

Drinking the black, bitter coffee he preferred, Aaron Blevinsky, Director of the Crepusculous paramilitary base, known as Headquarters, started his morning by sending a text to Fatima Hussain: *Meet me in my office at 0900 for a mission briefing.* Fatima, a woman of Pakistani descent who was the best female operator in Crepusculous, resided in Headquarters and served as both a superb operator and a trainer of recruits. When she arrived at Belvinsky's office, she found a tense man cursing at his computer. Fatima knocked on the open door. "Yeah, Come in," he said.

The bald, mustached man briefly looked up over his computer screen, saying, "If you want coffee, it's right there."

"No, thanks." Fatima took a seat facing Blevinsky's desk.

"I'll be right with you," he said and went back to pounding on his keyboard.

After several minutes, Fatima asked, "When is the mission?"

"Hang on, I have to finish this."

Fatima stood up. "Call me when you're really ready to meet with me."

Looking up at her from under a furrowed brow, he said, "Your time is mine. If I say wait for me, then you will wait. Now sit back down."

He stared intensely at her as she avoided his eyes and sat back in the chair. Blevinsky returned to his keyboard. Fatima fumed at being ignored in spite of being called to this meeting. After several more minutes, Fatima could see that Blevinsky's anger was growing. Whatever he was working on wasn't going very well. Suddenly, he slammed his fist on the desk, saying, "Dammit, this isn't going to work!" He pushed himself away from the desk and directed his attention to Fatima.

They both smiled at each other, their smiles being anything but genuine. "I apologize for the way this meeting began," said Blevinsky.

"You seem to be having some troubles. Is there anything I can do to help?"

Looking back at the computer on his desk, Blevinsky slowly said, "With that project, no." Turning to face her, he continued, "But I have another mission for you." Fatima focused her attention on him. "We have a CIA-directed contract to eliminate a target in Germany. I have a full dossier with mission specifics, but what I want to discuss with you is, I would like you to work with a partner on this mission."

Uncomfortable with this idea right from the beginning, Fatima protested. "Why do I need a partner? What is the danger?"

"I have a feeling that this job may involve a counterstrike on the operator." Fatima remained quiet as Blevinsky explained. "First, the longer I stay in this business, the less I trust anybody. Second, the CIA rep who set this up is the guy we usually deal with, and when I tried to contact him to verify the job, all his numbers and addresses were no longer functioning. Third, three months ago, a contract guy I worked with in the past took a CIA job and was killed after completing the hit by a counterstrike. It all adds up to a situation that makes me very nervous."

"And why are we taking the job at all?"

"There's a Board member who wants us to be cozier with the CIA and is insisting that we do the job."

"No matter what the risk?"

"Correct. So I want to send you with another operator who will be able to watch your back and expedite your safe extraction."

"Let me guess, you're sending Strakov with me?"

"No, actually, I was going to send Diegert."

"Diegert! He's fresh out of training; I don't think he could handle it."

"Oh, cut the crap! You know as well as I that he's a better operator than anyone else we've got. He's especially good at improvising during dynamic situations."

"He's careless and risky."

"He's determined and resourceful, and if you weren't so hung up on him being so good in spite of your torturing him, you would stop with this façade and start planning the mission."

"What if I refuse?"

"Refuse a mission?"

Blevinsky slid forward to the edge of his seat and lowered his voice. "If you refuse this mission, I'll send you out of the facility and have Strakov's strike team track you down and eliminate you for practice."

He leaned back in his chair and folded his arms over his chest, saying, "In the process, you might even get to find out if Alexi is actually bisexual."

Fatima looked at him with the fire in her eyes that made everyone uncomfortable. She picked up the dossier, turning as she left, and said, "I'll tell Diegert myself."

***

Fatima found Diegert target shooting on the range. She saw he was sighting in the sniper rifle she had used to rescue Andrew Cambridge, the one he had brought with him in a custom case. He was shooting at targets with tiny human silhouettes that conveyed the relative proportions of long distances. His results were impressive. She waited until he had emptied his magazine before tapping on his ear covers. Pulling off the ear protectors, Diegert said, "What do you want?"

"I need to meet with you about a mission."

"Right now? Damn, you know how much it hurts to tap on these things. When's the mission?"

"In two days."

"I'll be done here in half an hour. You could've sent a text."

"I wanted to make sure we met as soon as possible."

"We will . . . in half an hour, in the cafeteria."

She spun on her heels and left.

Diegert ejected the magazine, disconnected the stock, and unscrewed the rifle's barrel. He placed each part in its foam cutout within the case. While putting the stock in, he noticed a rectangular cutout in the wall of the foam. Pulling at the piece of foam, it separated from the wall, and from inside the rectangle, Diegert extracted a USB storage device. The only marking was its twenty GB capacity. He slipped the little piece of plastic into his pocket and replaced the piece of foam. At the armory, he handed the case back to Lindstrom, who said,

"It's a pretty accurate rifle, isn't it?"

"Yeah, and the scope was easy to sight in."

"Everything's in the case?"

Diegert was slow to answer. Studying Lindstrom's face, he wondered if the armorer knew about the USB. When he saw Lindstrom's gaze intensify, he snapped the hesitation out of his response.

"Oh yeah, everything's there. Thanks for letting me shoot it. I gotta go."

Walking away from the armory, Diegert's curiosity grew as he fingered the cool piece of plastic in his pocket.

American food has become ubiquitous; every lunch offered a choice of hamburgers, chicken nuggets, or macaroni and cheese. Although there were others choices, Diegert usually found himself drawn to one of these. Today, however, the menu included pizza. One of the pies featured sausage, mushrooms, and broccoli. Diegert ordered two slices. At the table, Fatima's disgust was not hidden.

"What? It has vegetables," Diegert said as the melted cheese stretched from his mouth. He hungrily chewed the warm, cheesy slice. "Tell me about the mission."

Fatima leaned forward, even though they were sitting away from other diners.

"It's a contract hit for the CIA. The target is selling some secrets. I'm posing as a representative of a Pakistani customer and will take him out at the meeting in the hotel."

"So why am I part of this?"

"You're to help with extraction."

"Why would you need my help?"

"Blevinsky's nervous about a counterstrike."

"What do you mean?"

"I mean, after the hit, somebody puts a hit on me."

"So I make sure that doesn't happen."

"Correct."

Diegert's face grew smooth as the wrinkles in his brow disappeared while he contemplated Fatima's revelation.

"OK, when do we leave?"

"Tonight."

"I'm on it. It will be worth it just to get out of this stinking place."

Back in his room, Diegert inserted the USB into his computer. The device loaded but required a password. What would Shamus McGee use for a password? Diegert started with IRISH, then IRELAND, DUBLIN, BELFAST, SHAMROCK, LEPRECHAUN, ST. PATRICK, BLARNEY STONE. Attempting access again was denied after so many password fails. While waiting out the time lock, Diegert remembered Barney telling him, "Shamus was a good Irishman, he loved his Guinness." When the computer allowed him to try passwords again, he put in GUINNESS. Nothing DARK PORTER, DRY STOUT, No access. Bringing up Guinness on Google, Diegert studied the simple banner with the familiar name in its distinctive font followed by the logo of the golden harp. Diegert typed GOLDEN HARP in the password bar, and the device opened to reveal a series of folders. The ones labeled "Crep. Profiles" and "Crep. Plans" drew his attention. The first file he opened was titled "General Information on the Board of Crepusculous."

The Crepusculous Board of Directors consists of four men. I have been able to identify and profile two of them, and I continue to investigate the other two members. There is no doubt that they will be as wealthy, powerful, and as secretive as the men profiled in this report. Suffice it to say, they are the upper echelon of the world's powerful elite.   *Shamus McGee*

Diegert's immediate suspicions upon finding the device were confirmed; Shamus McGee was a double agent. He opened the file titled "K. Panzer."

Klaus Panzer is sixty-two years old and very healthy and fit. He exercises regularly and challenges himself to take adventure trips to some of the most remote places on earth. Klaus is a driven man. He's the de facto chairman of the Board, exerting his influence with his lack of hesitation to forcefully speak his mind. His family's empire began when the Panzers became the primary arms supplier to the Nazis. Operations moved to Switzerland after the war, and the company became the world's top supplier of high-quality military armaments. Engineering and design of new weapons led them to the development of all manner of defense products, from guns and ammunition to missile defense systems, as well as digital control and communications equipment. Panzer continues to oversee a research and development program from which I have had great difficulty gaining specific operational information. I can report that the personnel are top scientists in physiology, neurology, nanotechnology, engineering, and genetics.

Panzer has never married. He does, however, have children: two daughters by two different women. Thirty-four-year-old Gretchen is an accomplished businesswoman who handles the family's real estate. The other daughter is ten years younger. Sashi has completed a liberal arts degree but has not used it; instead, she has been paid handsomely to model activewear and rep numerous adventure sports products. Klaus Panzer has no son.
The Panzer home is a huge mansion in Innsbruck, Austria. They possess other residences including a townhome in London.
S. M.

It wasn't hard for Diegert to imagine the strong, outspoken German leading this band of wealthy men to further acquisition of wealth and power. The next file was labeled "D. Kellerman."

Dean Kellerman is a sixty-year-old Englishman. He's in good health and remains active and fit. His money comes from insurance companies; however, he has also established hedge funds capable of tipping the market with the movement of money. Commodities, including oil, agricultural products, and minerals, are also controlled by the Englishmen. Through the manipulation of the price of these basic raw materials, Kellerman impacts the price the world pays for everything. Kellerman's holdings also include large sections of European real estate and media companies that provide television and Internet service to most of the world.

Kellerman's wife, Felicity, passed away two years ago from pancreatic cancer. He has two children, Michael and Colleen. Michael is thirty years old and is a drug addict. Rehab programs and addiction management treatments have failed, and the goal is now to keep Michael out of jail.

His daughter, twenty-five-year-old Colleen, graduated summa cum laude from Oxford's business school. She currently manages the philanthropic activities of the family, which donates hundreds of millions of dollars each year.

The Kellerman family has several residences, but they consider Rosethorn, a 130-acre estate ten miles outside of London, to be their home. Kellerman conducts his business from his office suite there, while Colleen orchestrates many gatherings and social fundraisers at Rosethorn, so the family is never socially isolated.
S. M.

Kellerman's profile depicted a more traditional man of wealth who enjoyed his station and played the part of a British aristocrat. Diegert's opinion, though, was not swayed by this impression. This man was part of Crepusculous, so his money had blood on it.

In the folder labeled "Crep. Plans," there was only one file:

Through questioning personnel and intercepting communications, I have determined that Crepusculous has a plan for what they are calling "economic readjustment." It is a four-stage plan to disrupt and destroy a country's economy. I believe these men feel they can manipulate markets and destabilize the political structure of a vulnerable country in order to control the economy and the resources of such a nation. This disregard for social order and political process makes them more dangerous than originally perceived. It will be my priority to determine which third-world country is the target of their ruthless power-seeking.
I have also discovered evidence of widespread corruption within law enforcement agencies throughout Europe, Asia, the Middle East, and the United States. Crepusculous uses its leverage within law enforcement to control the actions of agents who are moving against their interests and directs law enforcement to act against their rivals. Their influence is malignant and metastatic.
S. M.

Diegert closed the file and the folder before removing the device from his computer. He placed the device in his pocket while he thought back to Barney's story about the death of Shamus McGee. The list of possible governments, and rivals for whom McGee could've been working as a double agent was huge, but clearly the data he'd collected could prove fatal to others as well.

As Diegert packed his bag for the upcoming mission, he remembered that since winning the tournament he was allowed to make outside calls. It had been so long since he had spoken with his family, so he called his mother.

"Hello, David."

"Mom, how ya doing?"

"I'm doing very well, dear. I want to thank you for the money."

"You're welcome. Is the bank happy now that the mortgage is all paid off?"

"Well . . . not quite yet."

"Whaddya mean?"

"Your dad hasn't paid them yet."

Turning his head toward the ceiling and dropping the phone from his ear, he grimaced and felt like an idiot for not having transferred the money directly to the bank to satisfy the debt. Diegert bit his lip as he placed the phone back to his ear.

"Why didn't you pay them? I put the money in your account."

"Dad has access to that account, and he says that since we have two months to pay, we should hold on to the money and earn some interest."

Slowly shaking his head from side to side, he could see his dad saying something that sounded sensible but was, in fact, a ruse for him to do something stupid.

"Mom, if there is any way you can just go to the bank and give them the money to pay off the mortgage, I beg you to do it. Don't let Dad screw with that money."

"Oh, David, things are never easy, you know that."

"Yeah, I know I also worked very hard for that money, and I want it to be used to pay off the house, and if that doesn't happen, I'll be very upset."

"I understand, but I'm amazed you got that much money so quickly. How did you do it?"

"Good luck and hard work, Mom, two things Dad and Jake have never had or done."

"I'm sure it'll all work out for the best. Dad just wants to utilize all the financial time we have."

"Financial time? Mom, that sounds like Dad's bullshit. Please, I gotta go but do me the favor of making sure the house's debt is paid. I gave you that money for that and no other reason. I want you to be secure in that house."

"Thanks. David, you're so wonderful. I miss you, and I love you."

"I love you too, Mom, good-bye."

"Good-bye, honey."

After disconnecting, Diegert finished packing for the mission, grateful he would soon be focusing on something other than his fucked-up family.

Chapter 4

The Gulfstream streaked west, chasing the setting sun as it carried Fatima and Diegert to their first official mission together. Fatima explained what lay before them in a bit more detail.

"The target's name is Hans Klemmler. He's an executive at Zeidler-Roche, a company that contracts with the US Department of Defense to handle communications. He's selling encryption codes on the black market. Posing as the front person for a Pakistani customer, I'll be meeting him to pay him in cash. I'll be dressed in traditional Pakistani attire, covered head to toe in order to facilitate infiltration. The hit will take place in the meeting room, and then I must be extracted."

"We'll dupe them. We'll leave that counterstrike team with no idea how they lost us."

Handing Diegert a sheet of photos, Fatima continued, "Blevinsky's mole in the CIA provided us with these photos of operatives who are tasked with being active in Frankfurt tomorrow."

Reviewing the photos, Diegert noted two women and three men. The women both looked to be in their twenties, one blonde, the other brunette. The guys were a wider range of ages. The oldest looked to be in his fifties, with gray hair and a beard. The other two were in their twenties or thirties. One had dark-black hair and dark features. The last guy had a thick, athletic neck, shoulder-length blond hair, and a very piercing gaze for an ID headshot.

Diegert folded the photos, tucking them away. He felt even more confident now that he could identify the CIA by sight.

"We've got at least another hour in the air. I brought a bottle of wine." Her voice was very seductive, but then again Diegert readily perceived everything she said as seductive.

"Is it white?"

"Of course not; it's Cabernet Sauvignon."

Fatima handed him the bottle and the corkscrew while she retrieved two glasses. Once poured, Fatima asked, "To what should we toast?"

"To the success of this mission."

"I don't like toasting the future. We should acknowledge something that has already happened."

"Like?"

"I raise my glass to you for completing your training and becoming an operator."

"Thank you," said Diegert, raising his glass, clinking hers, and then taking a sip of the deep-red wine. Feeling a bit obligated, Diegert raised his glass and said, "I want to toast you and thank you for the support you gave me. You helped me to succeed."

Glasses clinked again, and they each took a sip. Diegert couldn't hold her eye contact, and she wouldn't look away from him. "I'm not certain you believe your own words, but I thank you."

"Your methods were . . . unorthodox, but here I am."

Fatima's gaze had a questioning quality that Diegert acknowledged by taking a satisfactory sip, setting down his wineglass, and then making direct eye contact.

"Is there a woman in your life, out there somewhere?" she asked.

Diegert was surprised by the question. "No . . . No, there's not."

"Why not?"

"Because I live at headquarters. As you know, there's very little opportunity to meet eligible women."

"Ah, but what of the past? Is there no girl at home wishing you had married her?"

"Uhh . . . No, there is no one waiting for me. My profile at home was not exactly marriage material."

"The passionate heart looks beyond, sees the man, and feels only desire."

Looking at her, he picked up his glass and took another sip of wine.

Fatima continued, "I'd think a handsome man like you would have a woman somewhere in the world who feels that way about him."

"If she exists, I haven't met her."

"You may not have recognized her feelings."

"Or no girl has ever felt that way."

"I look at you, and I know that in your hometown there were girls who dreamed of you, talked about you, and desired you."

"You've never been to Broward, Minnesota."

"I know, but I have been in the heart of a teenage girl who became a woman, who recognizes the attractive qualities of a man."

"OK, I get what you're saying, but the answer is no. I don't have a secret girl waiting for me to come home and marry her. What about you? What about Hamni? Hamni is your son, correct?"

Fatima's Cabernet-induced relaxation vanished, and her fire-and-ice face returned. Diegert was not surprised. He fully expected her to react angrily, but up here in the airplane, he figured he might actually get her to reveal what he already believed.

"Who told you this?" spat the furious woman.

"You just did," replied the relaxed man.

"I told you nothing."

"Oh, but that's not true. We speak with more than words. Tell me about Hamni, you must love him very much."

"I'm saying nothing."

"Then he's in danger. Is he being held so you'll do this work?"

Fatima's anger grew, but it started to mix with a sadness that she found increasingly difficult to control. The combination made her feel vulnerable. A feeling she would not tolerate. She looked at the confident young man and hated the fact he seemed not to have the same emotional vulnerability. She stood, picked up the bottle of wine saying, "Finish the extraction plans before we land." She walked into the private quarters of the plane, closing the door behind her.

Chapter 5

The Gulfstream landed as darkness fell upon the Frankfurt airport. Leaving the private terminal, Diegert drove the Mercedes E350 with Fatima beside him dressed in a fashionable jilbab that draped her entire body. She wore a scarf over her head and neck, and her face was covered by a veil. All the garments were color coordinated in deep red with an embroidered border of gold around the entire suit. The veil she wore didn't disguise the intensity of her eyes.

Diegert said, "Before we go to the hotel, we've got something to pick up."

"What?"

"I'll show you."

Diegert drove to the Sachsenhausen section of Frankfurt and slowed the car to a prowl. When he stopped at an intersection and rolled down the window, three young women ran to him. He indicated he wanted to speak to the one with dark hair and eyes who appeared South Asian.

"You want to get in and come with us?"

The young lady lowered her gaze to see Fatima, covered in Islamic dress in the passenger seat.

"Don't be fooled," said Diegert. "She's totally into it. Five hundred euros."

The dark-haired streetwalker climbed into the back. Fatima's glare burned on Diegert, who said, "You'll be glad we did this."

The Westin Grand Hotel in Frankfurt was an impressive modern structure, that looked distinctly out of place amid the antique buildings that surrounded it. A block from the hotel, Diegert pulled over. Turning to the streetwalker, he handed her a hundred euros. "Go to the Westin Grand and sit outside the Danube Room on the second floor. We will meet you there in fifteen minutes."

The experienced pleasure provider was not unaccustomed to clandestine meetings, and her nods of certainty gave Diegert confidence as she stepped out of the car.

At the Westin, Fatima exited the Mercedes carrying a briefcase and proceeded into the lobby. She made her way to the Danube Room for the meeting with Klemmler. She followed the posted directions and spoke to no one on the hotel staff.

Diegert drove the Mercedes out the driveway of the hotel's covered entrance, crossed the street, and parked twenty meters away on the opposite side of the road. He sat in the car looking for the faces of the CIA observation team. Unfolding his sheet of photos, he quickly picked out the blonde woman and the dark-haired man sitting outside together in an elevated café across from the hotel. Diegert had to accept that the beard was a little longer and the man was wearing a cap, but he recognized the oldest member of the team in the window of a Brauhaus next to the hotel.

Search as he did, he couldn't find the other two observers and deduced they were inside the hotel.

The Danube Room could accommodate up to twelve people, so there was plenty of space for Fatima and Hans Klemmler to conduct their business. Klemmler had two armed bodyguards occupying the room with him. When Fatima entered, Klemmler introduced himself. "Greetings, Fräulein, I am Hans Klemmler," said the tall, balding German, extending his hand.

She ignored his hand, stepping around him to avoid contact. Klemmler dropped his hand to his side. From behind her veil, Fatima said, "Good day, sir, shall we proceed with the transaction?"

"Yes, of course. However, I would appreciate the indulgence if you would allow my associate to ascertain that you are in fact unarmed."

Klemmler graciously opened his palm, indicating the way was clear for her to enter the restroom attached to the meeting space. The dour-faced, heavyset female guard followed Fatima into the restroom. Once inside, Fatima quickly undid the front of her jilbab, opening it to reveal a formfitting full-length black body suit. The curve of her hips, the outline of her breasts, and the narrowness of her waist were all obvious yet completely covered. The guard was at first surprised at the sudden revelation of Fatima's undergarments, but she realized it made the task less embarrassing. As the woman stepped forward to frisk her, Fatima tugged on a tab that released a silenced Walther PPK that slid down the length of her sleeve into her hand barrel first.

The guard was so intent on feeling for weapons, she did not see the arrival of the pistol. When she realized there was a barrel pressed against the base of her skull, the thought lasted less than one second before Fatima pulled the trigger. With the suppressor pressed tightly against its target, the report of the discharge was heavily muffled. Blood splattered across the room but not on Fatima. She caught the weight of the woman and guided the body quietly to the floor. She did up the front of her jilbab and stepped carefully across the floor, avoiding the puddle of blood.

Outside, Diegert stepped out of the car wearing a dark jacket and a navy-blue baseball cap. He pulled a pack of cigarettes from his pocket, shaking the pack only to realize it was empty. He played it up, appearing annoyed at being unable to smoke. After several minutes of acting frustrated, he crumpled the empty cigarette pack, threw it in a garbage can, and marched off.

When Fatima stepped out of the restroom, the male guard glanced at her. He looked perplexed when she raised her hand and fired a bullet in his face. The shot twisted his head. Fatima fired again, striking him just behind the ear and dropping him to the floor. Klemmler sat dumbfounded when he saw that the weapon was now pointing at him. So amazed was he that when the first bullet hit the right side of his chest, he still couldn't believe what was happening. The second bullet, piercing the other side of his chest, carried less surprise but more damage as it ruptured the left ventricle of his heart. His body fell back in his chair, which tipped over, dumping his bleeding chest onto the floor. Fatima stepped to him and watched the painful grimace on his face turn to the flaccid expression and dilated pupils of death. Assured her target was deceased, Fatima placed the gun into the briefcase and exited the Danube Room.

Having convinced the CIA he was searching for his nicotine fix, Diegert turned the corner and began running to the back of the hotel. He entered through the loading dock and met Fatima outside the Danube Room. She removed her jilbab and gave it to Diegert.

Diegert stepped over to the hired lover. "Here, now is the next part of the fantasy." Diegert handed the young lady the jilbab.

"Put this on and return to the Mercedes, which is parked across the street. We will meet you in ten minutes."

The girl looked a little surprised, but Diegert reasoned it probably wasn't the strangest thing she'd ever been asked to do. With the jilbab on, she wrapped the scarf around her head and drew the veil over her face.

"Excellent," said Diegert. "We'll see you at the car in ten minutes."

Diegert removed the dark jacket he was wearing, reversed it to tan, and gave it to Fatima. He took off his navy-blue cap, reversed it to white with a red Fiat emblem, and put it on Fatima's head.

From his seat in the Brauhaus, the gray-bearded man thought it had been a long time for the driver to get a pack of cigarettes. He contacted his CIA team inside the hotel. "Status?"

"Moving to the second floor now," replied the man with long blond hair.

"Clear in the kitchen," said the brunette.

Diegert went to the hotel lobby. He watched the prostitute cross the street and approach the Mercedes. When she reached the car, a Chevy pickup screeched to a halt, and a band of neo-Nazi skinheads unloaded and began harassing her. The skinheads pushed, shoved, and punched the woman in the jilbab. When they pulled off the scarf, the terrified prostitute started screaming about not being the person they wanted, but her looks were convincing enough, and the beating continued.

Diegert knocked on the women's room door where Fatima was waiting. They fell into step as they traversed the second-floor hall.

The blonde agent, dressed in a dull blue maintenance suit with a tool belt, turned the corner and strode down the same hall as Diegert and Fatima. They all recognized each other instantly, but none gave away that fact. Immediately after passing in the middle of the hall, they all whirled around to attack. Only the big blond man was surprised.

Diegert lashed out with a series of kicks to the lower leg. The best kick forced the blond operative to stumble forward. Fatima took advantage of his awkward movement, driving a knee into his chest and striking the back of his neck. The big guy fell forward, tackling Diegert. Diegert felt his nose gushing blood after the blond guy's forehead collided with his face. The CIA agent raised his head for another strike, and Diegert blocked it with his right forearm. With his left, Diegert pulled a screwdriver from the man's tool belt and stabbed him in the rib cage. Fatima grabbed the power drill from the other side of the tool belt and drilled holes in the back of his thighs.

The torquing and tearing of flesh forced a frightening scream as the man rolled off Diegert, grabbing his wounded leg. Fatima, eyeing his vulnerable chest, drove the full length of the bit through his right pectoral. The suction of puncturing his lung held the drill in place, and Fatima had to pull hard to rip the power tool from the dying man's thorax.

Diegert got to his feet, calculating the guy was in his final moments as blood flowed out of his mouth with each breath. Grabbing Fatima's hand, he said, "Let's go."

Dropping the drill as they ran down the hall, Fatima pulled her hand from Diegert's, accelerating ahead of him.

With two final strikes to the face from a sawed-off baseball bat, the prostitute's body went fatally limp. The skinhead dropped her to the ground where she crumpled into a lifeless heap. Gray Beard contacted his team. "It's over, target is neutralized."

The blond man uttered his final words over his comm device. "Wrong person . . . target in hotel."

Gray Beard spoke to the brunette in the kitchen. "Confirm target."

The brunette inverted the kitchen knife in her hand, so the blade was parallel with her forearm as she exited the kitchen.

When they arrived at the rear loading dock, Diegert saw a large truck filled with potted plants, flower boxes, and floral displays. The worker was just about to begin unloading when Diegert approached him wearing a small oronasal respirator. He sprayed the plant man with a concentrated chloroform mist known as Trank. He caught the unconscious man before he hit the floor and loaded him into the back of the truck. He motioned for Fatima to get in the driver's side. She climbed across the cab to the passenger's side, and Diegert started up the truck.

The brunette arrived at the loading dock just in time to observe the loading of the driver and a woman in tight black pants climbing into the flower truck.

She contacted the team. "Target escaping in a flower truck. I'm in pursuit."

Diegert had the truck in gear and moving out of the loading dock when the brunette woman leaped on the open doorstep, reached in and cutting his right arm with her knife. He struggled to keep the truck straight as his attacker drew her arm back for another strike. Fatima's hand caught the woman's forearm, impeding her second stab, and held her fast. Diegert accelerated, swerving the truck toward the alley wall. Sparks flew as the bumper ground against the brick wall. Diegert straightened the steering so the entire side of the truck was scraping against the alley wall. When the sliding driver's door was hit by the wall, it shot forward into its closed position, trapping the woman by her arms. The brunette was now compressed between the truck and the wall, pinned by the door and pushed against the side-view mirror. The force of the truck abraded her back against the wall, and she was disemboweled as the mirror bracket gave way, tearing through her chest and abdomen. Her body fell to the alley floor in large, shredded pieces over a forty-foot distance. The truck passed out of the alley and onto the street with blood and gore-streaked across the side panel.

Seeing Fatima's face in the truck as it passed the Brauhaus, Gray Beard ordered the couple in the café into action. "Get moving after the flower truck."

The blonde woman and the dark-haired man pulled their Opel Astra onto the street and weaved through traffic to catch up with the truck as it moved toward the autobahn.

Gray Beard got on the phone with the skinheads.

"You have made a mistake. The actual target is getting away in a flower truck. Stop them, or you won't be paid."

Diegert headed for the highway as fast as traffic would allow the big truck to move. The Opel chased the truck, making progress through traffic with its nimble handling.

Accelerating onto the autobahn entrance, Diegert moved immediately to the fast lane. The Opel and the skinhead's Chevy followed them onto the highway. Once on the expressway, Diegert could see the CIA couple right behind them. He did not want to battle them at the airport. "We're going to switch places. You ready to drive?"

Fatima nodded while climbing over the center console. Diegert let her slip under him, relinquishing the truck. Stepping into the back, Diegert was careful not to step on the unconscious plant man. He made his way to the rear of the van and slid the door up into the ceiling. The Opel was right there, and the two CIA agents looked directly at him. Diegert also saw the big Chevy truck in the midst of the traffic on the highway. The blonde woman stretched outside the passenger window, firing her pistol. Her shots were wild, sparking and ricocheting off the van. Diegert ducked back.

Racks of flowers and plants were lined up inside the van. The wheeled racks were locked down for transport. Diegert unlocked two racks of plants each ten feet long and eight feet high with a dozen shelves of potted plants. He pushed the racks out the back of the truck, sending them flying off the deck of the van and onto the CIA Opel. The racks landed on the hood, smashing the windshield, spraying dirt and foliage all over the highway and causing the CIA vehicle to spin out of control and crash into a Volvo, setting off a chain-reaction catastrophe. The skinhead's Chevy swerved to the shoulder and rough-rode the margin of the highway to avoid the pileup forming around them.

Diegert shouted for Fatima to speed it up and get to the airport. He looked back to see the highway clear except for the skinheads. The truck carried four guys, two in the cab and two in the back. They looked like the original Road Warriors with their outrageous urban tough guy costumes and tattooed bodies.

One of the guys in the back leveled a shotgun across the roll bar and fired at the truck. The slug hit a rack of plants, spraying dirt in Diegert's eyes and lacerating his cheek with ceramic shrapnel. With his nose already bleeding and a cut on his arm, he had to take a moment to wipe the dirt and blood from his face. Up in the front of the van's cargo area, Diegert located a large bronze planter filled with dirt and a small, dying tree. The planter was on a wheeled moving cart, which Diegert unlocked. He positioned himself to push the heavy bronze ball-shaped planter, shouting for Fatima to speed it up.

When he felt the truck accelerating, he pushed with all his might, and the giant planter rolled down the floor of the van and out the back end. The heavy spherical pot hit the pavement and started bouncing toward the Chevy truck. The pickup's driver was frozen with indecision, and the planter crashed onto the truck's hood, smashed the cabin, and rolled over the roof, crushing two skinheads. The driver was blinded by the smashed glass. He lost control of the vehicle, which spun sideways, tipped perpendicular to the road, and rolled several times before coming to a halt with four very dead neo-Nazis.

Diegert saw nothing of what happened to the skinhead's truck. The momentum with which he'd pushed the planter had carried him right off the back of the deck. He would've been a smear of roadkill had he not caught the edge of one of the locked-in plant racks with the toe of his right boot. His entire body dangled in the slipstream of the van. He was millimeters from having his face, hands, and arms abraded to red mist by the asphalt below him.

Fatima watched the planter knock the pickup off the road through her mirrors, but she had no idea Diegert was in trouble; she couldn't see him at all. Using the strength of his leg and abdomen, Diegert contorted himself such that he was able to grasp the edge of the van's deck with his right hand. Fatima saw the exit for the airport and turned the van onto the ramp. The centrifugal force gave Diegert the chance to grasp a vertical handle on the upright edge of the van's back end. With both hands having a grip, Diegert began to pull himself into the van. Fatima was traveling so fast that when she hit a speed bump in the road, it violently jostled the entire vehicle. Diegert went airborne when the van hit the bump.

Both his legs shot out behind him, and his right hand lost its grip on the edge of the deck. With only his left hand gripping the uphaul handle, the assassin was once again dangling off the back end, this time with his boots dragging on the road. Like a belt sander, the pavement was grinding the leather of his boots to dust. With all the strength that remained in his left arm, Diegert pulled on the handle. He got his right hand to the edge of the deck and hauled himself up. With a twist from his waist and a kick of his right leg, he pulled himself off the road and onto the floor of the van.

He took one full breath, and the van came to a stop. Fatima jumped out of the cab, came around to the back, and found Diegert sitting on the floor of the van. "Quite a show with those skinheads, eh? Come on, don't just sit there, we've gotta go."

Diegert stepped down off the van and boarded the waiting Gulfstream. The jet made an immediate departure, and the two operators were in the air when the police, with their lights and sirens wailing, surrounded the flower truck and took the groggy plant man into custody.

"That was too close," said Fatima, feeling quite satisfied with her driving. "What happened to your boots?"

"Abrasion. Hey, is there any of that wine left?"

Fatima went to the private cabin and came back with the bottle and tumblers. "I hope you'll still drink it out of these glasses?"

"Anything that holds liquid is fine with me."

Diegert gulped the first glass, and with raised eyebrows, Fatima filled it again. "I'm going to clean you up."

Diegert took a big swig of wine.

Fatima sat with her legs curled up under her while she cleaned his wounds and face. "How did you know the flower truck would be there?"

"I didn't."

"It was just luck?"

"It was improvisation. I figured some kind of vehicle would be back there. Maybe a laundry truck or food delivery, but flowers, I didn't expect that, and it didn't matter."

"Well, it certainly worked," said Fatima as she wiped away the black potting soil. "That was pretty clever of you to use that girl as a decoy."

"Yeah, more fortunate for us than her."

"I like working with you. This mission wouldn't have worked if we weren't together."

"You're right, being a team is important, and I'm going to ask you about something I think we can work on together. Tell me about Hamni, and don't go locking yourself in the back."

The fire and ice began to form on her face.

"You have a son, and he does not have his mother. I can tell you that my mother was very important to me when I was young. I relied on her way more than my father, and I was able to grow up OK because she was there."

Diegert slid forward on his seat, deepening his voice and looking into her eyes.

"You're important to him, and I want to help you get him back."

"By inserting yourself into this situation, you can only make things worse."

"Crepusculous has him, don't they? They have him, and they make you work for them."

"The best thing you can do is drop this and stop trying to be the hero to a little boy you've never met."

"I'm not trying to be a hero, but I am trying to help. Tell me what you know about the Board members of Crepusculous."

"I don't have anything to tell you."

"I can tell you two of their members: Dean Kellerman and Klaus Panzer."

"Good for you. I'm sure you'll have a seat at their table just as soon as you make a trillion dollars."

Chuckling, Diegert said, "That shouldn't take long."

"That will never happen," Fatima snapped. "These men were rich before they were born. Their power and money make us all their servants. You can deceive yourself into believing that you can do something to affect them, but the truth is, you're powerless. Hamni won't be back with me until I fulfill my obligations."

"And what are your obligations?"

Fatima took a long sip from her glass and struggled with her answer. "The requirements are always changing. First I am led to believe one thing, and then I'm told another. All the while there is threat to my son if I do not comply. I love my son!" shouted Fatima. "By doing what is asked of me, I'm protecting him. If I fail, he dies."

Diegert remained silent for a moment. "I can see the devotion you have for him. But I can also see how Headquarters is manipulating you. Your strength and your determination are admirable, but they are also allowing you to endure this unfair situation too long while Hamni grows up without you. He won't know you if this continues. When did you last see him?"

Fatima was now choking back tears. She hated displaying her vulnerability and was torn between her belief of superiority and her feeling of camaraderie. She answered his question matter-of-factly. "I last saw him four years ago."

"How old was he then?"

"Five years old."

Diegert paused, thinking of the years. "We had better get that boy back soon."

Fatima fired, "Do you think I don't consider that every day?" She looked away from him. "I have him in my mind and in my heart every minute of every day until it becomes so heavy a burden I collapse under its weight. I sit and cry under its force, but I do not want the burden removed for fear I will then feel nothing for my son, and he will be totally lost to me."

Fatima's eyelids could no longer contain the tears that now streamed down her face. She did not sob, bellow, or blubber, but the tears rolled down her cheeks and dripped off her chin. Diegert handed her a napkin, witnessing the emotional turmoil with which Fatima lived.

She dried her tears, saying, "These men are light-years ahead of you. There is nothing you can do."

"I do not think like you. They are men, they arc human, and they have weaknesses."

"Oh, cut the crap, men who crave and amass power cannot be stopped by their servants."

"You can't know how to defeat them if you do not know who they are. Tell me who you know on the Board, and we'll learn things about them."

"What do you mean you will learn things about them?" asked the skeptical lady.

"I can tell you that Dean Kellerman resides in a hundred-thirty-acre English estate. His son is a drug addict, and his daughter runs a family-funded charity foundation. Klaus Panzer is not married but has two daughters. He's the true leader of the Board. I look at him like the kingpin in a drug cartel. Both of those guys are well protected and censor any media profiles. Kellerman always comes across as a devoted philanthropist, although his name is not on any buildings. Panzer is never in the media, but if we want to influence the Board, he's the one to be manipulated."

"How did you get this information and how do you know it's accurate? Anyone could post that bullshit on the Web to smear these guys."

Diegert felt the USB device in his pocket. He hesitated as he thought about trusting Fatima with the source he held between his fingers. He started this, so he figured he had to press forward.

"You're right, but this information comes from an insider."

Diegert pulled out the USB.

"What's that? You want to impress me with a piece of plastic?"

"On this device is the work of a mole who is no longer active. I have read the files, and this person was collecting data on the Board members and their plans."

"So what does it reveal?"

"I just shared with you two identities you would otherwise have never known. Now it is your turn to share something with me. Who do you know on the Board?"

Diegert could see her hesitation and waited while she struggled with her words until finally, she spit out a name. "Julio Perez," she said, nearly choking as the name she'd shared with no one fell out of her lips. "He practically owns South and Central America."

"Very well, then, we'll see what we can learn about Mr. Perez and start the process of recovering your son."

Diegert relaxed back in his chair stretched out his legs and took another swallow of wine. He'd finally gotten her to crack, and he could now help her. Fatima looked surprised and disappointed. "Well, what do we do now?"

From his position of repose, Diegert said, "Whoa, there, cowgirl. We can't search for Board members at thirty thousand feet on my smartphone. It requires proprietary software, which I have on my computer in my room but not up here."

Leaning over and smiling at her, he said, "Don't worry—in my room I'll show you everything."

"In your room, you will show me only what I want to see, and that's the use of intelligence rather than bullets to get Hamni back, so he won't grow up without me."

Chapter 6

"We may have a problem here," said Jake Diegert after reading a news story in the Bemidji Pioneer about the establishment of a digital currency by the corporate giant Omnisphere.

"What? What's wrong?" asked his father Tom.

Jake read part of the article, "Digival is a new corporate currency being introduced around the world as an alternative to traditional government-issued money. It's independent of all governments and is sponsored by the world's largest and wealthiest corporation. Available in a digital-only format, it supplants the need for cash while also creating a digital record of every purchase."

"Dad, this new Digival is a digital-only means of buying stuff."

"You mean like a credit card."

"Well, yeah, but it's not the card—it's the money behind the card. Instead of dollars, the thing of value will be Digival. Digital units that you have in an account that you shift to whoever you're buying stuff from."

"So?"

"So . . . when people buy drugs from us, they pay us cash. That way there is no record and people are anonymous. That's kinda important for what we sell."

"When does this stuff go into use?"

"It's already in use. So far, not too many people are using it, but the news says they expect use to grow quickly because Omnisphere is promoting Digival with huge incentives."

"Like what?"

"They'll increase your money ten percent when you switch from dollars to Digival."

"Wow, maybe we should change some of our cash."

"Negative. We are not changing to any form of money that can be tracked. We are so far under the radar that our business is practically invisible until we start making digital records of every purchase with every customer. No way are we going Digival."

"Do you have to buy a machine to do Digival?"

"No, it's all handled through an app on a smartphone."

Tom Diegert grabbed the chain connected to the belt loop on his pants and pulled his fat wallet from his pocket. Opening the thick black leather fold, he pulled out a wad of bills and flipped them with his finger saying, "Well, then, fuck them. It's cold hard cash for me. Fuck them and their digital bullshit. As long as I have dollars, they will have to accept them, cuz they're backed by the US government, and nobody can take that away."

Jake, watching this display of patriotic delusion, deepened his frown as he said, "Yeah right . . . whatever, Dad."

***

In his room back at Headquarters, Diegert fired up Tor on his computer, input the required passwords, and began searching the darknet. The darknet shielded the accessing computer from network detection. This convenience allowed Diegert to search through it without arousing the attention of Headquarters' IT specialists. Julio Perez had

an information file on the darknet, which meant
facilitators had collected information on him, but no
contracts had been activated. Julio had a son named Julio
Jr., who was born in 1963 but had died in 2003 at the age
of forty when he'd crashed a Ferrari F430 in the
countryside of Spain. Julio's first wife had divorced him
when he was thirty-seven years old, and he remarried at
age forty-five. He had two more children with his second
wife: a daughter, Gabrielle, and a second son, Javier.
Both of these children were living.

To find more about the two Perez children did not
require the darknet. Instead, access to Facebook was
granted through an intrusive app called frenemy. The
program provided access as a friend on Facebook without
having to ask. Both of the Perez children were clearly
enamored with Facebook and Instagram. In fact,
Gabrielle Perez had her own You Tube channel where
she interviewed celebrities and other people she found
interesting. She posted the videos and had enough of a
following to have some advertising mixed in. She wore
fashionable clothes and drove expensive cars, as a rich
girl, what else would she drive? After watching some
interviews on her channel, Diegert found her not as
annoying as he'd expected. Her interview questions were
interesting, and she let the people answer without
interrupting. Not all the topics were significant, but she
didn't seem as shallow as he'd anticipated.

Javier's Instagram, however, painted the perfect
picture of the rich partying playboy. The locations were
exotic, the vehicles were big and fast, and everything was
expensive. Cars, SUVs, yachts, he had them all, and he
photographed everything. His pictures were organized
under "Places," "Parties," "Toys," and "Girls." Diegert
scrolled through the "Girls" gallery. All the women were

young, sexy, and gorgeous. There were literally hundreds of beautiful women. He seemed to have a penchant for Asian beauties. Diegert scrolled down into pictures from several years ago. He suddenly stopped at a picture with Javier at a party, smiling and looking a little drunk, with his arms wrapped around a strikingly beautiful dark-haired, spaghetti strap–dressed Fatima Hussain. Her face was unmistakable. He leaned back in his chair, saying to himself, "Fatima, you naughty girl."

Chapter 7

Returning to her room from a workout, Fatima was approached by Blevinsky. "Excuse me, I would like to speak with you," he said.

Fatima stopped and stood at attention, ready to listen to the Headquarters' director. Blevinsky recognized the respectful posture and told her, "Relax. Please walk with me."

They went outside to the grounds in the rear of the building. "I see the mission in Germany was a success."

"Collateral fatalities notwithstanding, I agree, we succeeded."

"Diegert was helpful?"

"Yes, he's an effective operator and has a keen capacity to improvise."

"What do you mean?"

"He turns obstacles into opportunities, and he has the skill and guts to try dangerous things and succeed. All traits which I believe are prerequisites for this type of work."

"Do you believe he's ready for a solo mission?"

"Is it an assassination?"

Blevinsky nodded his head, and turned heading back toward Headquarters.

"Yes, I believe he is, and I'm confident he will accomplish the task and extract himself no matter what the circumstances."

"Thanks, I appreciate your candor and the training you have given him."

"Thank you, sir, I intend to fulfill my obligations."

At the entrance to the building, Blevinsky made one last remark. "Oh, by the way, I have heard from London, and Hamni has learned to ride a bike."

He smiled when he said it as if he were some loving uncle bringing news from a summer vacation. Brooding on the false kindness in his voice, Fatima's mood soured as she walked back to her quarters. She burst into her room and slammed the door. She paced frantically and looked in the mirror at her angry reflection. She saw her own pain, her frustration, her maternal love withering on the vine. She was exhausted. The hurt turned into sadness, and the crying took control of her. She fell to the floor sobbing, convulsing and releasing years of pain as she grieved the undelivered love for her son.

***

Much later that night, Blevinsky received a call from Klaus Panzer. "Aaron, are we ready to enact the initial phase of the plan?"

"Yes, sir, we are prepared."

"Indeed. How are the preparations for the third phase progressing?"

Blevinsky was afraid this question was coming. The third phase consisted of thermobaric explosives detonating simultaneously in several US cities. It required a single source of ignition that was free from the Internet yet operated by remote signaling from Europe. The ignition system had to be one that couldn't be interrupted or jammed by electronic countermeasures. A single source of satellite detonation was risky, but if implemented properly, it would undermine the electronic safety net upon which the US government relied. It was an audacious plan that would be devastating to the United States, but the logistics, the technology, the communication, and the coordination were all proving very difficult and time-consuming. Blevinsky found himself constantly tied to his computer and often having to come up with alternate plans when the originals failed. Worst of all, though, was the fact that the Board had put this project in the hands of an up-and-coming new member, the son of Julio Perez, Javier.

Blevinsky hadn't disliked the thirty-year-old playboy until he didn't answer his communications for days and any request for a phone conversation received only a text. Javier had a sense that being in charge meant you touched something once and it was done. The complexity of the explosives and the placement of them by confederates whose silence was absolutely necessary, as well as the sophistication of the signaling and detonation process, meant that this project had to be addressed and handled on a daily basis. Blevinsky was doing all the heavy lifting, but Javier had to be involved regarding expenses and major plan alterations. When these issues interrupted Javier's pursuit of fucking forty women in forty days, Blevinsky lost patience with the irresponsible son of a man who failed to instill any discipline in his heir apparent.

With all that in mind, Blevinsky responded to Panzer, "The project is proving very difficult, and changes are constantly being made to accommodate necessary adjustments."

"Are we on schedule? Now that we have begun, we must be ready to carry out each phase in a timely manner."

"Yes, of course. We are still on schedule, but, frankly, one of my biggest frustrations is with the man in charge of the finances."

"Javier," said an unsurprised Panzer.

"Yes, sir. He proves himself less interested in the business of the Board than the pleasures of his prick! If you will excuse my expression?"

"No . . . that's fine," replied Panzer. "Like many young men, that guy is distracted by sexual pursuits. He is the future leader of the southern hemisphere, though, so we do want him to develop."

"Sir, the success of the whole third phase hangs in the balance."

"I appreciate your concerns, Aaron, but I want Javier not only committed and responsible but culpable as well. I want his skin in the game when his father dies, and power passes to him."

"Now I see, sir."

"With him activating the single-source detonation device, I'll have the kind of control that makes me welcome him to the Board of Crepusculous."

"Yes, sir," said Blevinsky, realizing once again that Klaus Panzer's actions always fulfilled a manipulative goal.

"If we start to fall behind, you let me know. Otherwise, take full charge. I'll see to it that all expenses are covered."

"Thank you, sir. It is a relief to have you aware of the situation and to have your support."

"Excellent! Proceed with the plan. One more thing, Aaron. I'd like to set up another job."

Blevinsky froze on the phone as he listened to Panzer.

"I'd like you to task a team with killing Michka Barovitz. I believe he's on his island in the Aegean this time of year."

Blevinsky still had no words as he contemplated the audacity of this man to ask for another job in the middle of preparing for this long-awaited primary mission.

"Do you think we have a window of opportunity now?" asked the German.

Going against his best tactical judgment, yet following his sense of Panzer politics, he replied, "Yes, of course, sir, we can carry out this sanction."

"This operation is not sanctioned by the Board. You're to carry it out directly under my orders and to keep the whole mission and all its information completely black."

"I understand. I'll gather the intelligence and put together the team. I'll inform you when the mission has been completed."

"Thank you, Aaron. I knew I could rely on you," Panzer said before disconnecting the call.

Although he presented a confident and reassuring demeanor to Panzer, Blevinsky knew that completing this mission without interfering with the other would require immediate action. He called Strakov.

"Da."

"Alexi, I've just received orders for a priority sanction. Assemble a four-man team and report to the armory."

"Da."

Blevinsky e-mailed Carl Lindstrom a directive indicating the kit required for each operator, as well as the vehicles the team would need. The knock on the doorjamb of his open office drew his gaze to Diegert standing on the threshold. Neither man spoke for a moment until Blevinsky said, "You knocked, so why are you here?"

"I have something to ask you."

"What is it?"

"As a full operator, I believe I'm supposed to be paid for missions."

Directing his full attention on Diegert, Belvinsky asked, "Where'd you hear that?"

"Fatima."

Throwing his body back in his chair, Blevinsky said, "She's right, but so are you. If you don't ask, I won't pay you. It's a Balkan custom."

"Then I'm asking for a hundred grand."

Chuckling as he leaned forward, Blevinsky maintained eye contact with Diegert. "That's a little steep."

"That's what I got before I was brought here for training."

"Yes, but as a contractor, many of your expenses are your own. Now we are providing everything. You're not getting that much, try again."

"Seventy-five thousand dollars."

"Too much . . . again."

"Fifty thousand, and that's going low."

Blevinsky looked down at his desk and started speaking to the wood grain, "I'll pay you fifty thousand, but you have to do something more." Turning up to Diegert, he continued, "I have a mission that's taking form right now with Strakov leading a team. You join them, and fifty thousand dollars will be in your account when you return."

"If I don't?"

"You'll only get five thousand for pissing me off."

Diegert leaned against the doorjamb with his arms crossed over his chest.

"And I imagine Strakov doesn't know I will be on his team."

"He doesn't yet, but I'll take care of that."

"What's the mission?"

"If I tell you, you'll know before Strakov."

"I feel sooo special."

Blevinsky's brow wrinkled at Diegert's wisecrack, making his forehead look like a wide staircase leading to a bald spot.

"You're going to assassinate Michka Barovitz."

Diegert remained stoically still as his eyes narrowed at the mention of the Romanian mobster.

"Why didn't we kill him when we rescued the kid?"

"We didn't have orders."

"You want me on this because I know the casino?"

"No, Barovitz has a private island in the Aegean. We'll hit him there."

"Then why do you want me on this?"

"Because you proved to be resourceful in Germany, and you're the best fifth man I've got."

"Being on mission with Strakov and his gang, he'll probably take me out."

"Listen, you can't be afraid of anyone. This business requires bravery like no other. You have to bypass the fear and find a way to get the job done. Strakov will stay on mission. He isn't going to fuck around with you."

"Strakov makes decisions with a head full of hate. Your reassurance gives me no confidence. If he fucks with me, then he doesn't come back, agreed?"

Curling his lips into a bemused smile, Blevinsky replied, "It's a deal, and you two will both come back still hating each other."

Chapter 8

At the armory, Strakov arrived with Jaeger, Pierre, and
Enrique. Lindstrom had their kits ready. Each man was
outfitted in the latest generation of body armor. The suits
incorporate RDP-composite materials, which *React* to
forces, *Dissipating* energy to provide *Protection* against
trauma: RDP. The fabric was as comfortable to wear as
cotton and could be fashioned into clothing of any design.
When the fabric was exposed to sudden trauma, such as a
bullet, it would stiffen by a factor of three hundred,
providing projectile penetration protection. The four men
were dressed in identical suits. The pants had kneepads
built into them, as well as integrated thigh straps for the
attachment of gun holsters and knife scabbards. The
upper body jacket provided extra protection at the
shoulders, and the sleeves had integrated gauntlets
covering the forearms. The clothing was sleek and
formfitting, not baggy or binding. Each man buckled on a
utility belt with pouches carrying extra ammunition,
explosives, mini cams, listening devices, and infrared
infiltrative viewing mechanisms. Black tactical boots and
gloves completed the outfit, complementing the
thundercloud gray and black trim color scheme of the rest
of the uniform. The weapons Lindstrom issued were
H&K MP5 submachine guns with integrated laser sights.
The weapons were outfitted with sound suppressors and
extra-large magazines. An additional Glock 9 mm

occupied the thigh holsters, so each operator was armed with a second weapon.

When Diegert walked into the armory with Blevinsky, the room turned silent as eyes looked at the American with surprise, curiosity, and disdain. Diegert could feel the derision with which his presence was being judged. He hoped that Blevinsky could see what a bad idea this was; instead, the operations director instructed Lindstrom, "Carl, I need you to put together one more kit for Diegert here."

Strakov exploded. "No fucking way! We're not adding him to the team now; we leave in thirty minutes."

Blevinsky's hands went up as he approached Strakov. The heavy bald man wrapped his arm around the big guy's shoulder and walked with him to the back of the armory. Away from the others, he told Strakov, "Relax, Diegert is good, you know that. You're going to assault with a four-man team; you'll need someone to guard the boat."

"We've got other men who could be added to the team."

"There's not enough time now. Diegert is it, and I want you to lead him like any other operator. Treat him as a team member and bring him home safe."

"You've really pissed me off."

Blevinsky's hand snapped out, grabbing a section of Strakov's beard between his thumb and forefinger, and he pulled the taller man's face down to his.

"You will treat him with respect or I'll have the next class of recruits hunt down your naked ass in the Proving Grounds."

Blevinsky slapped Strakov across the face with his other hand. "I don't care if you're my nephew, you will conduct yourself as a professional when you are on a mission. You will follow orders as they are issued and operate with the team that is assigned."

"Da," offered Strakov, who was still bent forward with his beard in Blevinsky's grasp.

"Good, now get back over there and get ready to go," said Blevinsky as he released Strakov's chin.

Strakov and Blevinsky returned to the staging area just as Lindstrom unzipped a black cloth bag and extracted a set of clothing for Diegert. The pants were black canvas with cargo pockets on both thighs. The shirt was a black Under Armour compression garment, and the vest was a Kevlar model that looked like it had already stopped several bullets.

Diegert's thoughts were spoken by Blevinsky's words, "Hey, where's Diegert's RDP suit?"

"We only have four of the new suits," replied the disappointed armorer. "This is the best we have. Just last month, we would have sent the whole team out in these."

Blevinsky's face softened, but Diegert's annoyed and disappointed expression deepened.

Strakov approached Lindstrom, Blevinsky, and Diegert. "Mr. Lindstrom," said the big Russian as he raised his hand to reveal a tactical night-vision scope. "Can I put this on Diegert's weapon?"

"You think he'll need night vision?"

"Yeah, I think it will be best for him to be prepared for any contingency."

"Alright, you can install it on his rifle over on the bench."

Diegert turned his head to watch Strakov walk to the workbench. Blevinsky slapped him on the back. "Go get changed; you're leaving right away."

At the workbench, Strakov installed the NV scope on the rifle's rail system. He sighted it and was able to see targets in the darkness. Then he opened the breach of the chamber and extracted the firing pin. This act of sabotage rendered the weapon useless in spite of the cool NV scope. He left the weapon on the bench as he stepped away with the small metal firing pin tucked in his pocket.

Wearing the black outfit, Diegert joined the others as they boarded the Sikorsky X2 helicopter. The aircraft had a dual rotor design overhead that provided tremendous stability and hovering capacity. A perpendicularly mounted rear rotor provided exceptional pushing power, making the X2 the fastest helicopter in the world. With a capacity for six passengers, all five of the operators were accommodated in the cabin. Once the team was secured, the craft took off. One and a half hours later, the helicopter delivered the team to the Aegean coastal port of Keramoti, Greece. There they loaded into a Zodiac for the thirty-minute ride to the island of Thesalonas, which Barovitz owned. The Zodiac had a unique seating system specially designed for riding through rough seas. The seats were designed to be straddled. They looked like little horses with a grip handle in front and a padded backrest. The boat could accommodate a crew of nine, so the team easily fit into the craft.

On board the Zodiac, Enrique stepped to the controls of the craft and fired up the 225 hp Honda outboard engine. For such a big, powerful engine, it was amazingly quiet, especially at low rpms.

The sky had darkened about an hour before, allowing the team to depart into the blackness of the night. As the boat progressed, a light rain began to fall.

The island of Thesalonas had a history of being owned by criminals. Slave traders, pirates, opium merchants, and now a mobster had all laid claim to the beautiful and secluded retreat. The exchange of the island had never occurred through a sale but rather a change of possession to fulfill a debt. Barovitz had gained control through the indebtedness of a particularly unlucky Greek gambler. To keep it protected, he had two guards occupying the island at all times, along with a full-time caretaker. When he traveled there, two additional guards accompanied him, along with two to three young women. Blevinsky shared this information with the team, preparing them to take out four men along with Barovitz.

Enrique slowed the engine to a quiet purr as they approached the dock at Thesalonas. The rain was falling harder, but the lack of guards at the boat dock was a welcomed surprise. Barovitz had traveled to the island on a twenty-five-foot yacht, which was secured to the dock and currently unoccupied. As the Zodiac pulled up to the dock, Diegert jumped out and tied the ropes to the mooring cleats. The four Crepusculous operators immediately formed into two-man attack teams and proceed to the island. Diegert, with his assault rifle slung from his shoulder, prowled up the dock to inspect Barovitz's yacht.

The unguarded vessel beckoned exploration. Stepping onto the gangplank, he crossed the threshold and stole into the hold. Passing by the luxury seating, bar, and bedrooms, he made his way to the engine compartment. The big boat was powered by a truck engine, which Diegert disabled by removing the distributor cap, leaving the spark plugs without the capacity for ignition. Back up on deck, he tossed the distributor cap overboard, ensuring the vessel could not be used for an escape. With the rain persisting, Diegert decided to stay on board the yacht under the second-floor overhang.

Approaching the big house, Enrique and Pierre went north as Strakov and Jaeger proceeded to the south. When the teams could no longer see each other, they checked their comms.

"Bravo, this is Alpha," said Strakov.

"Copy," replied Pierre.

The main entrance to the house was to the south, and Strakov grew nervous when they were able to creep right up to the landscaped foliage and not encounter any guards. *Could we have been detected?* he thought. He was concerned their cover was blown, and they would be walking into a trap. "Bravo, talk to me."

"I see two tables, four Tangos per table. Barovitz is here; they're playing cards."

Strakov realized that eight men were more than they had expected but not more than they could handle. "Execute the plan."

"Copy."

Pierre and Enrique drew blocks of C-4 from their utility pouches and pasted it to the doorknob and the hinges. Igniting the volatile dough sent the door crashing inward, blowing the north entrance wide open.

The first table of card players was hit by the shock wave as well as wood shrapnel and metal hinges. All four men were knocked to the ground. Enrique fired his weapon, ending their lives with four precision shots, before squatting on the floor, closing his eyes, and covering his ears.

The second table suffered ear-splitting decibels and sudden blindness when the flashbang Pierre tossed detonated among the pot of poker chips. Uncovering his ears and opening his eyes, Pierre took aim at the disoriented men. He took down two with bullets to the head and neck. The third man raised his gun, firing at

Enrique and striking him in the chest and shoulder. It was the third bullet, though, that pierced Enrique's neck, spraying blood across the room. Pierre saw Enrique fall as he shot the man who had wounded his comrade.

Barovitz recovered enough of his bearings to see that Enrique was down and that Pierre was moving toward the injured man. Stumbling to his feet, the mob boss awkwardly ran out through the north entrance around the west end of the house toward the dock.

Pierre called on the comm, "Man down, requiring medical assistance."

Strakov called back. "Target status?"

"Barovitz is mobile, moving in your direction."

"Copy," said Strakov as he and Jaeger crept closer to the south entrance, anticipating Barovitz's exit onto the veranda where they would lay waste to the arrogant mobster. As they trained their attention in front of them, Barovitz ran behind them toward the dock.

Being the team medic, Pierre rushed to Enrique in time to see a stream of blood pumping out of his neck. As he moved closer, he could see that the distance the blood spurted was declining with each beat. Enrique's life was exiting his body as Pierre pulled open his medical pack and stuffed the wound with gauze. Adhesive tape and manual pressure were not enough, though, to overcome the lacerated trachea and the torn carotid artery and jugular vein. Enrique's life was ending, but Pierre held pressure against the wound and fought death's pull on his comrade's soul.

From under the rain-protected overhang on the yacht, Diegert heard the flashbang and saw the shooting. After the violent firefight, he expected the strike team to return. The man who came running onto the dock was quite unexpected. Dressed in black pants and a white silk shirt, Barovitz was soaked by the rain, which had intensified as the attack ensued. Diegert ducked down behind the bulkhead of the galley, leveled his weapon, and focused on the target of Barovitz's chest through his NV scope. As the man came closer to the yacht, Diegert's confidence grew. When he pulled the trigger, he expected to see Barovitz go down, but instead, he only felt the compression of the mechanism with no reaction. With the target still in the scope, he tried to fire the weapon again, only to once again have the system fail. He unslung the weapon and checked its functions.

Arriving at the yacht's side, Barovitz moved his formerly athletic body as quickly as he could, untying the moorings and jumping onto the deck. He climbed the stairs to the second floor, making his way into the control room. Turning the key produced only an unproductive run of the starter motor. "Fuck!" shouted the frustrated man as he turned the key again, hoping to hear the ignition of the engine. *"Shisa,"* he cursed to no one but Diegert, who had crept up the stairs without his ineffective weapon and approached the doorway of the control room undetected. As Diegert looked in the entrance, Barovitz noticed the break in the line of the doorway and kicked the door. Diegert pulled back and blocked the door with his foot. He pushed the door back in with such force that it hit Barovitz in the head, lacerating his forehead.

Bleeding, Barovitz turned to face Diegert, who was ready to fight. He circled Barovitz, sizing him up, looking for vulnerability. Barovitz stepped past the boat's controls, reached his hand alongside the console, releasing the fire extinguisher, which he flung at Diegert. The heavy canister struck the forearm and the forehead of the American. Diegert staggered back but regained his composure only to see Barovitz extract a pistol from a drawer. The bullets whizzed past Diegert as he exited from the control room with the most evasive movements his instincts could produce.

Diegert sprinted to the top of the stairs. He grabbed the rails and slid down to the first floor. Barovitz rushed to the stairs, firing down. One of the bullets struck Diegert in the left shoulder, knocking him to the floor where he crawled under the overhang. Barovitz descended the stairs with his gun in front of him.

Strakov and Jaeger, hearing the gunshots from the yacht, sprinted to the dock, arriving in a joint tactical approach. Strakov signaled Jaeger to reattach the yacht's ropes.

Barovitz searched the first floor. The blood trail was difficult to follow in the darkness, but he knew this boat better than anybody. He stepped into the luxurious quarters, turned on the lights, and fired into the front wall of the polished cherry bar. Splinters flew as bullets pockmarked the finish. Having spent half a clip, Barovitz stepped to the bar and peered over the heavily lacquered top. Diegert, grateful for the solid construction of the handsome bar, swung a liquor bottle from his hiding place below the bar's surface. The bottle smashed on Barovitz head, showering him with glass and expensive liquor. As the stunned mobster stumbled back, Diegert vaulted over the bar, only to land on the piercing base of the broken bottle. The upward-projecting shards of glass tore into his boot and ripped through his foot. Diegert bellowed as the unexpected injury radiated pain throughout his lower leg.

Strakov and Jaeger entered the room. Barovitz grabbed Diegert, stepped behind him, and pointed his pistol at the two arrivals.

"Drop your guns and move the fuck back."

Strakov and Jaeger stood their ground, pointing their MP5s at Barovitz.

Moving the barrel of his pistol to the base of Diegert's jaw and shoving it hard enough to twist the American's head, Barovitz said, "Get the fuck out of here or I blow his head off."

Strakov fired two bullets into Diegert's chest, sending him backward and spinning out of Barovitz's grasp. Jaeger fired at Barovitz, hitting him in the forehead and imploding his skull, nose, and eye sockets. Barovitz fell back on the floor. Blood began to pool in the concavity that had replaced his handsome face.

Pierre appeared at the entrance. Strakov spun, turning his weapon on the man.

Raising his hands defensively, Pierre said, "Hold on, it's me, brother."

As Strakov lowered his barrel, Pierre stepped forward. "Enrique is dead." The Frenchman could see that Barovitz's wound was fatal since his face looked like a bowl of sangria. Diegert was on the floor gasping for breath next to the bullet-blasted bar. Pierre assessed his medical condition, determining that the bleeding shoulder needed attention first; the foot required dressing, as well, but the worst thing affecting Diegert was his traumatic pneumothorax.

"How is he?" asked Strakov.

"He's bad. He's got at least one collapsed lung. I need the first-aid kit from the Zodiac."

Strakov remained impassive, looking directly at Pierre. "Well, then, you better go get it." Pierre held the stare as he stood up and left the yacht.

Strakov felt the hate he had for the hotshot fucking American coalesce with the adrenaline pumping through his body as he placed his laser sight on Diegert's head. His finger trembled on the trigger as the desire to kill fought with what little sense of team cohesion he had. As he stiffened his arm and tilted his head to focus on the laser point, Jaeger stepped forward, placing his hand on Strakov's arm, saying, "Come on, let's go get Enrique."

Pierre passed his departing teammates as he returned to the yacht. At Diegert's side, he opened the kit and dressed both of his wounds, stopping the bleeding. Pierre looked at the white-and-black leather amulet with the footprint spanning both halves that was around Diegert's neck. Examining the reverse side, he was perplexed by the Ojibwa inscription. In spite of being fluent in French, English, Spanish, and German, he could find no meaning in the unfamiliar letters.

The force of Strakov's bullets had collapsed Diegert's lungs. The Kevlar vest had stopped them from penetrating, but the concussive force separated the lung tissue from the inside of the chest wall. Tears in the lungs allowed air into the chest space that was compressing the lungs so they could no longer ventilate. Diegert was slowly suffocating as his lungs continued to deteriorate. Pierre knew he had to act fast.

Chapter 9

At the big house, Strakov and Jaeger surveyed the dead and realized there was a lot of money on the floor. Some of it was stained with blood, but it was all valuable and unaccounted for. Both men picked up bills, folded them into wads, and placed them in their pockets.

Strakov noticed the door movement first. Jaeger picked up on the sudden weariness of his partner, who signaled him to train his attention on the door to their right. Both men quickly stepped to opposite sides of the door. Strakov was on the entrance side. He could see a descending stairway beyond the door. Signaling Jaeger to pull the door open, he trained his rifle to shoot into the stairwell. When Jaeger pulled the door open, a woman's shriek blasted into the room. Strakov fired his weapon, but the bullet went high as he diverted the aim at the last second. The screaming continued down the stairs as the woman retreated, while more screaming echoed up from the building's basement.

The two baffled men looked at each other with relieved smiles as they stepped into the stairwell. The women were huddled in a back storage room. A woman of medium height with a shock of dyed pink hair stepped out from the storeroom, while a taller woman with shoulder-length dark hair and defiant dark eyes took a position in the storage room doorway.

"How many more of you are there?" asked Strakov as he flipped a glowing switch that turned on the hall lights.

Squinting against the sudden brightness, the woman with pink hair replied, "There's no need to hurt us. We're not the type to speak to the police."

Strakov leaned closer to her and peered beyond the taller one. "How many?"

The defiance slackened as Strakov's infectious menace diluted their bravery.

"There are five of us all together," stated the tall, dark-haired one.

"Get them all out here."

The women responded, and Strakov lined them up along the wall in the harsh light. They were all in their twenties with trim bodies featuring ample T & A.

"Do any of you have a weapon?"

Several said no, while others just shook their heads for fear that any speech would overwhelm their emotions, bringing on fits of crying.

"Give me your phones," ordered Strakov as he held out his hands and collected all five devices.

"You're the girlfriends of the men upstairs, aren't you?"

"We would've been . . . at least for tonight," answered the tall one with dark hair.

A sardonic smile crept over Strakov's lips.

"My partner and I'll be leaving this island. I don't want any of you coming out of this basement for two hours. You got that?"

The two invading tough guys turned to climb the stairs.

"You can't just leave us here," said the girl with pink hair.

Strakov stopped on the third step, turned back, and placed his laser sight on the girl's cleavage, saying, "You can stay down here and live or come upstairs and die."

The girl looked to the floor and stepped back in line against the wall.

Reaching the top of the stairs, Strakov directed Jaeger, "Set the charges."

Strakov reinvestigated the corpses by the overturned card tables. Looking at their firearms, he picked up a Taurus 24/7 tactical .45. The grip felt right in his hand, and a full magazine was an extra bonus. The next man's weapon was an HK P2000. This weapon was commonly carried by police officers. Digging into the dead man's coat pocket, Strakov pulled out his wallet to find his police badge. Officer Hiro Eliglanis, Athens Police. Strakov pocketed the weapon and the badge.

"The charges are all set," announced Jaeger upon his return. The two men walked out the south entrance, stepping onto the veranda where their attention was drawn to the field in front of the docks. They both looked up as the whirling rotors of the X2 helicopter lifted it off the island and turned north, heading back to Greece. "What the . . ." was all Strakov could manage to say.

Pierre had acted fast; he knew Diegert was tough, but even the toughest would die without sufficient oxygen. Calling the helicopter to evacuate them back to Headquarters seemed like the most prudent and appropriate action. Diegert was unconscious, and his breathing was becoming more shallow and irregular. He needed the staff and equipment of a true medical facility. *Fuck Strakov,* thought Pierre.

Chapter 10

In flight, Diegert's skin began to turn grayish blue. His
life was ebbing away as the helicopter sped toward
Headquarters. Although he lay on a stretcher
unconscious, a dark, cold sensation ran over Diegert,
making him aware of someone's presence. He looked
around in the darkness and could see no one. He couldn't
see or feel his own body, but he was able to move and
look in all directions. The darkness seemed to be in front
of him, but it had a distant, faded aura around it that made
him feel like there was a huge black circle in front of
him. *What is this?* he questioned. *What's going on?*
Where am I? From the left, he saw a man appear. Dressed
in black clothing, the man's face and body emerged as he
walked right by Diegert without acknowledging him. The
face was old and lined in deep crevices, but the walk was
brisk and powerful.

"You're a conflicted man, David Diegert," said a
voice from behind him. Turning to the right, Diegert was
startled to be spoken to, yet now he saw nothing but
darkness. "You're blinded by greed and obstinacy."
Diegert turned to the voice immediately in front of him
and looked into the dark eyes and skin framed by thick
gray hair parted in the middle and pulled back into a
ponytail. The face was aged, but the energy of this man
radiated into Diegert and commanded his attention. The
mouth did not move, but the message was as audible and

clear to Diegert as any words ever spoken. "You have a spirit you do not recognize, and it is fighting for you. It will not give up on you, but you are pushing it away and challenging its loyalty."

Confused and angry, Diegert shouted, "Fuck this spirit bullshit, what does it want?"

Pierre looked at Diegert, surprised to hear him speaking while he remained unconscious.

The motionless face answered Diegert's question. "Acceptance is what the spirit has always sought. You must ask it into your life."

"I don't want it," retorted Diegert. "Who the hell are you?"

"I am the Anishinaabe, and I can only guide those who are willing to follow."

The face faded into blackness and spoke to Diegert again from behind.

"I'm afraid you have many dark deeds ahead of you, David."

"Does that mean I'm not going to die?" asked Diegert.

"Not today, but if you die as you are, living in darkness, your spirit will never find the light, never join the Anishinaabe."

Diegert turned to the voice behind him, but the face was not to be seen.

"Your amulet's inscription, 'A man must travel through the darkness to find the light,' implies that you must seek the light and not get lost in the darkness.

"Show me the light, then, give me the directions," demanded Diegert.

The voice replied, "You have been given all you need, but you must accept and look through eyes of hope rather than fear. *Ondaas minawaa*."

Diegert opened his eyes into the blindingly bright light of the cabin interior. The sound of the rotors and the movement of the helicopter entered his sensory neurons, informing him he was still alive and inside an aircraft. Turning his head, he saw Pierre, who placed a reassuring hand on his shoulder. "You're going to be alright. Did you have a bad dream?"

Diegert nodded and laid his head back down for the rest of the flight.

***

On the dock at Barovitz's island, the zipper pulled together the sides of the body bag enclosing Enrique's remains. Grasping the bag's handles, Strakov and Jaeger lifted their fallen comrade into the Zodiac. Before setting off for Keramoti, Strakov ignited the charges Jaeger had set around the house. The explosions blew out the critical support structures of the first floor, collapsing the entire second floor and roof. Several fires broke out, and soon the once grand house was a conflagration of flames and smoke.

The Zodiac's engine accelerated, and the inflated boat pulled away from the island, leaving behind the dead and dying. Strakov radioed Lindstrom and ordered a van to be sent to the port. He and Jaeger would drive back to Headquarters transporting Enrique.

***

In medical, Diegert was recovering under the care of Physician's Assistant Henry Bellsworth, whose supervising physician was in London and communicated with Henry only when absolutely necessary. Henry enjoyed his job because he got to practice as a doctor and only had to go to school for four years.

"How are you doing today, Mr. Diegert?"

Opening his eyes to a groggy sense of awareness, Diegert squinted as he adjusted to being conscious.

"I'm alright."

"Your vitals are looking good, how's your ventilation?"

Taking a careful breath, Diegert replied, "I can breathe, if that's what you mean."

Placing his stethoscope in his ears, Henry instructed Diegert, "I want you to sit up so I can listen to your lungs."

Diegert slowly rose to a seated position while Henry placed the bell of the stethoscope on his back. "Take a deep breath for me."

Diegert drew in a deep breath, and when he began to exhale, he started coughing so violently that Henry had to help him lay back down, and it took several minutes until his breathing returned to normal.

"Mr. Diegert, you've suffered two collapsed lungs, a dual pneumothorax. I have corrected the immediate condition, but your lungs are not yet healed. You also have a gunshot wound to your left shoulder and lacerations to your right foot. The healing challenges you face are substantial."

"You mean, I'm going to be here awhile," Diegert croaked.

"In a normal situation, that would be true, but we have treatments not available to the typical patient. Crepusculous funds a venture called Creation Labs. It is a biotech facility specializing in the science of human enhancement."

Diegert nodded.

"I'll be administering a treatment called Healix. This medication is a form of rapid reactive stem-cell therapy. You have heard of stem cells, right?"

Diegert nodded again, although he really knew very little about cells.

"The stem cells are sensitive to cytokinetic signals your body is releasing from all the injured tissues. Reacting to these signals, the stem cells differentiate into the type of proteins necessary to complete the healing process. Having stem cells turn into the right kind of cells right at the site where they are needed speeds up the healing process tremendously. The quicker you heal, the quicker you're back to normal without so much down time for recovery."

Diegert shrugged his shoulders and gave an affirming nod but not a smile.

Henry continued, "Creation Labs makes the kind of medicines everyone could have if people weren't so bunged up about stem cells. Crepusculous has enough resources that it funds its research without any government money. You're lucky to be on the right side of this issue, and you'll see how good you're gonna feel when Healix has done its job."

Healix hadn't started its job just yet, and Diegert felt like shit. "Hey, until Heal-afix starts working, you got something to take off the edge?"

Henry administered a dose of morphine into Diegert's IV, and within minutes the pain and discomfort disappeared and the aching man fell fast asleep.

***

In Blevinsky's office, Pierre sat waiting for ten minutes. He contemplated the conversation he was about to have and realized the truth was on his side and Strakov was the one who'd fucked up. Although he knew Strakov had shot Diegert, he had no evidence, so he would share only the facts. Blevinsky walked in and took his seat behind his desk. He pulled up Pierre's report on his screen and began. "So tell me in your own words what happened at the island that led you to request the helicopter?"

"While still at the house, I heard shots coming from Barovitz's yacht. I arrived to find Barovitz dead and Diegert injured."

"Injured by gunshots?"

"Yes, and he also had a lacerated foot."

"Who shot Diegert?"

"I do not know; perhaps it was Barovitz."

Blevinsky cast a doubtful look, but Pierre refrained from reaction.

"Then what?"

"I administered medical treatment to Diegert, dressing his wounds and stabilizing his collapsed lungs as best I could."

"Collapsed lung?"

"Yes, both lungs, actually. The bullet strikes to his chest were not penetrating, but they damaged the underlying lung tissue and he was suffocating."

"Where were Strakov and Jaeger?"

"They'd returned to the house, and I was unable to contact them. Diegert was dying, and I knew he wouldn't survive a boat ride. I radioed the helicopter, which arrived in minutes, loaded Diegert, and if we'd not flown straight here I'm certain he would've died."

"But you did leave your teammates on the island."

"They had the Zodiac, and I know the two of them to be very capable men who can adjust to circumstances and succeed no matter what the challenge."

"That's quite an endorsement."

"I hope they would say the same about me, and if similar circumstances ever require it, I would gladly stay behind in order to save an injured comrade."

"Diegert is a comrade, now is he?"

Pierre looked at Blevinsky with quizzical surprise. "Of course he is; he was on the mission with us, and I believe he was the first to confront Barovitz, and he suffered for it."

"Well, I'm glad teamwork is the name of the game, and I'll be sure Diegert knows who he has to thank for his life. That'll be all. You've got no duty call tomorrow. Take it easy."

"Thank you." Pierre rose out of his seat and asked Blevinsky one more thing. "Has there been any contact from Strakov and Jaeger?"

"That's nice of you to ask. Mr. Lindstrom sent a van to the port at Keramoti; the two of them'll be driving back with Enrique's body. I imagine they'll be here tomorrow."

Pierre nodded as he left the office, walked down the hall, and pulled out his phone. He texted Strakov: *You're in the clear with Blevinsky. Diegert has survived, drive safe.*

Strakov replied: *Thanx and FU.*

***

After a good night's sleep, Diegert woke up feeling surprisingly better. While he'd slept, the pluripotent stem cells contained in the dose of Healix responded to the chemotactic signals released by the injured cells in his body. Following the trail of signals, the stem cells traveled to the areas of injury and transformed into the specific cells needed for damage repair. The specificity of this process allowed Diegert to heal at a rate ten times faster than he would have in an untreated state. His muscles, blood vessels, and skin were repairing themselves in an accelerated fashion. Even the inside lining of his lungs, damaged by the concussive force of the bullets, was reattaching itself to the chest wall, improving his breathing by the hour. When Henry Bellsworth checked in on him, he was very impressed. "Damn, boy, you are healing fast. The stuff I gave you is good, but you're going to be up and active in record time."

"Not fast enough for me."

"You really have no clue, but today you're staying here in medical. Is there anything I can get for you?"

"I'd like a phone to make a long-distance call."

"*Long distance?* I never took you for being that old. I'll get you a phone."

When Henry returned and gave him the phone, he also gave him privacy by closing the door to his room.

After failing several times to get his mom on her phone, Diegert reluctantly called his brother. "Yeah?"

"Hey, Jake, it's me, David."

"David Dipshit, David Douche Bag, David Dickhead. What the fuck you doing calling me?"

"Look I tried to reach Mom, but she isn't answering. Where is she?'

"You're such a fuckup. How do you think it's going here in this town with my dishonorably discharged brother on the news for murder and running from the law, huh?"

"Screw you, you fat fuck. Where's Mom?"

"It's killing Dad, ya know. He can't go anywhere without people asking him about you or just plain avoiding him. The tow-truck business is drying up because of you."

"Look, are you going tell me where Mom is or what?"

"She's not here."

"Shit . . . when will she be back?"

"We don't know because . . . . we don't know where she is."

"What do you mean you don't know where she is?"

"She didn't come home from work three days ago, and we haven't heard from her."

"Three days! You've called the police, right?"

"We reported it late yesterday, but believe me, the mother of America's Most Wanted isn't a high priority with the Broward County cops. You're a real selfish bastard to call her."

"Don't call me that."

"I'll call you whatever the fuck I want, but a bastard is what you really, are and now the half-breed whore from whom you spawned is probably out getting knocked up again."

Diegert remained silent as the urge to crush the throat of his idiot brother boiled inside him.

"Hey, David . . . David Dog Shit . . . You still there? I'm sure the county sheriff would be very happy to hear from you about this case. In fact, it might be kind of suspicious not to hear from you regarding your missing mother. I guess you'll just have to keep an eye on the news and learn what happened to the slut when everybody else does. I'll let Dad know you called, and fuck you, you bastard."

Diegert heard the call disconnect, and he slid his phone away from him across the top of the bedside table.

Holding his forehead in his palm, he scratched his scalp and gripped a handful of hair. He tugged on it till it hurt and then slammed his fists onto the bed frame. Staring across the room, he realized how little he could do. His mother was smart. His mother was resilient. But what if Jake or his father had harmed her? Jake called her such awful names. Could they have hurt her? He accessed the Internet on his phone and searched for the Broward County police blotter, but there was no report of a missing woman. Why would her disappearance remain unreported? Had they really called the police? He couldn't call the police himself; they would trace his call and track him down. It was frustrating to have the one person he really cared about, and who cared about him, missing, her whereabouts unknown. That good feeling he'd had when he'd woken up quickly dissipated.

After twenty-four hours of resting in bed and worrying about his mother, Diegert had a visitor. Fatima strode into the hospital room dressed in black, looking strong and fit.

"I heard you were cleared for visitors."

Diegert couldn't keep from smiling, and his lips cracked a bit since he hadn't curled them up in such a long time.

"Thanks for coming," his unused voice croaked.

"You're looking better than I thought you would . . . physically, anyway."

"Yeah, they've got great medicine here."

"Well, then, what's bothering you?"

"What do you mean? I'm fine."

"You sure there isn't something bothering you?"

Being revealed by her made him uncomfortable, which she quickly picked up on.

"If you don't tell me what's wrong, I can't help you."

Diegert struggled with what to say while Fatima waited patiently.

"Alright, you know how important my mother is to me."

Fatima nodded her head.

"She's missing, and I can't find anything about where she might be, and I'm afraid my dad and brother might have hurt her."

Fatima pulled out her smartphone. "Denise, right?"

"Yeah."

Fatima tapped and stroked her screen. "Minnesota?"

"Uh-huh."

"What's her cell phone number?"

Diegert gave it to her. Quiet and focused for the next several minutes, Fatima concentrated on her screen. Diegert was restless with anticipation. He wanted to know where his mother was, but he feared the only thing Fatima would find was a report of a dead body.

"I can see a lot of activity on her phone in Broward County."

"Right, that's where she lives."

"The last recorded activity was in Minneapolis."

"Minneapolis? That doesn't make sense; she would never go there."

"If your father and brother were going to hurt her, would they have taken her there?"

"No way; the two of them would never go to the cities."

"Well, then, they probably didn't do anything to her."

"Probably."

"What do you think happened?"

"I don't know, but it's weird for her to be in Minneapolis. Can you see who she called? Can you tell how long she was there?"

"No, this software is not that sophisticated. It only traces the GPS locator on her phone. It can't tell if she's there, but her phone is."

Diegert leaned back against the pillow, brought his fist to his chin, and thought that, while Fatima was very helpful, he really couldn't draw any conclusions from what she had discovered.

"Thanks, I appreciate your help. I think I'm going to get out of here in two more days."

"Good. It'll be good for you to get back on your feet, back in the game."

Diegert nodded as Fatima squeezed his hand gave him a little smile and left. As she exited the room, he couldn't help but think how unlike a game this all was.

***

Two days of driving brought Strakov and Jaeger back to Headquarters. They turned over the van to Lindstrom, who also took care of disposing of Enrique's body. The muscular Spaniard's death would go unreported and unrecorded outside of the compound. The industrial furnaces that provided the complex with heat also served as a crematorium where the temperatures were so hot that there would be no remains to scatter.

After submitting his after-action report and eating a good dinner, Strakov was relaxing in his room. The big Russian's room was larger than the one Diegert occupied. The extra space afforded Strakov room for a couch and a large screen TV. The TV was connected to the Internet so that entertainment was not limited to just a laptop. As Strakov streamed his favorite show, he was interrupted by a knock on the door.

Through the narrow space created when opening the door, Strakov was perturbed to see Blevinsky's face. Blevinsky pushed the door open, pressing his hand into Strakov's chest as he entered the room.

"What are you doing here?"

"Just a welcome-back visit. Actually, I've read your report and I'm just seeking clarification," said the round, bald man as he looked around the room. Strakov hated the way this intruder was tacitly inspecting his private quarters.

"I'd like you to tell me what happened on the yacht."

"Jaeger shot Barovitz."

"Did you provide any assistance?"

"Like it says in my report, I removed the shield the coward was hiding behind."

"How did you remove this shield?"

Strakov bent his elbow, pointing his hand like a gun, saying, "With propulsive force."

Blevinsky tilted his head, put a smirk on his face, and bore down on the bigger man with his unflinching eyes.

"Look, I knew he had Kevlar," admitted Strakov.

"It's only thanks to Pierre that he's not dead," Blevinsky said.

"If he had died, I would happily consider the mission a complete success."

Blevinsky straightened his gaze and narrowed his eyes. "We've been planning an important mission for a long time now, and in this folder"—Blevinsky raised his hand, in which he held a manila folder—"is your briefing." As he handed the folder to Strakov, he stepped over to a small table at the side of the couch. Blevinsky picked up the Taurus pistol and the HK P2000. "What are these doing here? There are no weapons in the complex outside of the armory. You know that."

Strakov averted his vision to the ceiling, rolling his eyes and sighing.

"Where did these come from?"

Strakov brought his head down but kept his eyes diverted from Blevinsky's.

"Collateral acquisitions."

"You mean the guns of dead men."

Blevinsky pulled back the slide on the Taurus, emptying the chamber, and snapped out the clip. "Fully loaded as well."

Strakov closed his lids, slowly turning his head while reopening his eyes to direct his gaze on Blevinsky, but said nothing.

"The rules of engagement inside Headquarters disallow fratricide."

"I don't consider him a brother."

Leaning in, Blevinsky replied, "I don't care." Pointing his finger into his own chest, he continued, "You are in my house and will follow my rules."

Tilting his head back and looking down on his upset uncle, Strakov asked, "What about outside of your house?"

Picking up the two pistols, Blevinsky crossed the room, saying, "Read your mission briefing and be ready." At the door he stopped to say, "And stay off the gay porn."

Chapter 11

After being released from medical, Diegert returned to his small room, slept in his narrow bed, ate in the cafeteria, worked out in the gym, and presently was shooting on the target range. He was assuming the role of a trained operative without a mission. It was strangely satisfying and frustrating at the same time. All the training was fun but had little meaning without a mission, but having a mission meant he was going to have to kill someone. Damned, both ways. He distracted himself by rattling off three round bursts on the MP5. Later that night before falling asleep, Diegert got a text from Blevinsky.

Meet me in my office tomorrow morning 0800.

Diegert got up at 0530, which gave him time to exercise and eat breakfast. When he arrived on time, Fatima was already sitting across from Blevinsky. "Good morning," began the director.

Diegert just nodded and sat down. Perturbed, Blevinsky chastised him, "It is customary to return a greeting."

"Oh . . . good morning, sir."

"Thank you."

Looking at Fatima and back at Diegert, Blevinsky continued, "I am assigning you a mission that is crucial to the Crepusculous business plan, and requires your skills and abilities."

"OK, what's the plan?"

"That's on a need-to-know basis."

"Yeah . . . but aren't we the ones who need to know?"

"You are, but you only need to know when it's necessary."

Quickly deciphering what Blevinsky was saying, Diegert replied, "You mean, I don't get the whole picture. I only get to know what to do just before I do it?"

Blevinsky smiled, realizing he wasn't going to have to explain it to him. "Correct. Fatima will be accompanying you, and you will have to see the armorer and go to medical for special equipment. One piece is particularly interesting." Blevinsky was excited to tell Diegert about whatever it was. "You will be fitted with a tympanic transponder. This nanotechnology communication device is a microparticle that, when affixed to the tympanic membrane, your eardrum, can transmit waves directly into the ear without an audible signal to be heard by others. The transponder can also transmit your voice through the interpretation of bone vibrations."

Blevinsky looked like a kid with a new game app. "Medical will fit you with the device, and we will be in constant communication."

"Great."

"You will leave the day after tomorrow, and remember, when you're operational, it is always mission first."

"Yes, sir, you got that last line right off the cob didn't you?"

"Forget the wiseass shit, you were brought here and put through this training specifically for this mission. It is your destiny here, and I expect you to perform with excellence. Now you're scheduled in medical at 1030 and at the armory at 1300. Get going and have a good day."

Walking with Fatima from the office, Diegert asked, "So what do you know that I don't?"

"I know that you won't know until I tell you. That is all I'll tell you." She smiled with obvious satisfaction.

He rolled his eyes, turned the corner, and walked away from her. At the cafeteria, he got a hot cup of coffee and walked down to the armory. Lindstrom was reloading bullets.

"I have you scheduled for 1300."

"Well, here I am, and here's a hot one for ya."

Diegert put the coffee down on the bench next to the skinny gray-haired man.

"I'll take over the bullets if you tell me what you've got for me."

"Deal. You get started. I'll get the hardware."

Diegert had reloaded nearly a hundred bullets before Lindstrom came back. "That took a while."

Lindstrom, holding a hard plastic case in hand, looked at Diegert's production. "Oh . . . I thought you'd be further along."

"What's in the case?"

Lindstrom opened the cover, revealing a Desert Eagle .50-caliber pistol cushioned in custom foam. Immersed in the surrounding foam were ammunition magazines and another piece that Lindstrom extracted first.

"This sighting mechanism is a computerized decision maker. It calculates all the data regarding the probability of a projectile to strike a target, and it chooses the time to fire the bullet. All we need is an agent to get in range of the target."

"I've actually used this sort of thing before, but it was controlled remotely from a tablet."

"Oh, yes, the True-Shot system," said Lindstrom. "We have that, but it has not been deemed functional for this mission. This works similarly, but you will have to aim at the target. Once locked on, the computer will alert you when it's time to take the shot." The armorer handed Diegert the device. Holding it by the mounting clip, he looked through the small optical lens next to the cube-shaped plastic box that housed the computer. Lindstrom continued, "The ammunition is unique as well. Inside the projectile is a guidance chip that seeks the target. Both the gun and the bullet are guided by an invisible laser. The laser is so small that human eyes can't see it, but its signal can be detected by the computer and the chip in the bullet."

Lindstrom looked up at Diegert. "Lasers, computers, microchips; you can't miss with this thing, and the force of the .50 cal will completely destroy any human target."

"Do I get to practice?"

Lindstrom tilted his head down and looked at Diegert from above his glasses. "Practice what? All I'm going to do is show you how to assemble it, activate it, and point it; the thing does the rest."

Diegert brought the sighting mechanism back to his eye and pointed it at a drill press across the room. The computer indicated a lock on the target, and when Diegert moved the mechanism, the reticle in the telescopic sight remained aimed on the drill press. After watching it function through the eyepiece, he looked up at Lindstrom.

"Any questions?"

"Is this the unit I'll be using?"

"No, a duplicate will be supplied to you when you need it."

Lindstrom returned the sight to the case and closed it up. "Back to bullets, please."

Diegert stood up from the reloading station. "Sorry, I've got an appointment in medical. Thanks for seeing me early. Enjoy the coffee."

"Hey . . . Good luck on your mission."

In medical, the insertion of the transponder only took a couple minutes. The medic tested the reception, and Diegert could hear incoming communication easily, and his voice was heard by the technician with no difficulty. "Hey, how do I turn this thing off?"

"You don't."

"Is there some kind of a program that controls its transmissions?"

The medic thought for a moment and then looked at his tablet. "Well, yeah, there's an app here that I use to measure and adjust things."

"Great," said Diegert. "Please send the app to my phone."

When the app popped up, Diegert scrolled through it. With a satisfied look on his face, he thanked the medic and left.

Unlike other missions when they left with all their gear and flew on the Gulfstream, Diegert and Fatima boarded a commercial flight and flew to London. At Heathrow, they boarded a flight to Montreal. Diegert's passport identified him as Jacques Le'Pruc, resident of Chibougamau, Quebec. He had to practice the town's name a few times in case he was asked. Fatima had made certain they were not sitting together on either of the flights, but avoiding Diegert wouldn't be so easy on the next leg of their journey, a nine-hour drive to Windsor, Ontario.

Diegert didn't understand why they hadn't just flown to Windsor, but then again, each leg of this entire mission was not revealed until he needed to know about it. He'd only found out they were going to Windsor because Fatima hadn't shut off the voice on the GPS system fast enough. They shared the driving, switching every couple of hours. During Fatima's stretch between Kingston and Toronto, Diegert began, "When we were discussing Hamni the other day, I failed to ask you one very important question."

Fatima looked at him, saying nothing.

He continued, "I didn't ask who Hamni's father was?"

It seemed as though Fatima anticipated this question, because she had no reaction at all. She had learned that Diegert got information by asking probing questions and relying on emotional reactions for answers. So this time she gave none.

Diegert tried another angle. "When I was in school, seventh grade, one day I stayed late working on a science project or something. Anyway, I was waiting for my ride home outside the school and these older boys, high school seniors, were there. They started picking on me. There were four or five of them, and they were having fun bullying me. The biggest one suggested a wedgie. Do you know what that is?"

Fatima shook her head.

"It's when someone grabs the back of your underwear and pulls it up out of your pants and over your head."

Fatima squirmed uncomfortably at the thought. Picking up on her reaction, Diegert said, "Yeah . . . it hurts. But it's also humiliating."

Diegert was quiet for a moment as he relived the memory. "There I was, though, other kids coming around laughing or scurrying away so they wouldn't be next. I was all alone with my tormentors. Then my mom pulls up. She sees what's going on, and she marches up to the biggest one, who was yanking on my pants. She yells at him to stop and pushes him away from me and slaps him across the face. Not just once, but, like, four times. The other kids were in shock, and so was I. The big guy ran away and we drove home. That night she took me to the YMCA and signed me up for a karate class. I was so grateful. She gave me the opportunity to develop the skills to defend myself, and that really boosted my confidence. I hadn't even realized what a scared little person I was until I took those classes and learned what it meant to face my fears."

Fatima asked, "Where was your father during all this?"

"My father really didn't like me. I didn't know why until years later, but I always knew he didn't. He preferred my brother, and his dislike for me was demonstrated on a regular basis. Neither my mom nor I ever mentioned the incident. He didn't care about the YMCA thing as long as I got all my chores done. She was my protector. She was my parent, and I owe a lot to her for making sure I survived my childhood."

Both of the car's occupants were quiet and contemplative. Diegert thought of the fact that his mother was now missing and there wasn't much he could do about it. He had faith in her resilience, but he doubted his brother's and his father's innocence in her disappearance.

The conflict gnawed at him, but he knew that soon he would have to focus on his mission.

Fatima broke the quiet. "Hamni was born premature. Four weeks early. He may not have gotten the best prenatal care, so out he came not quite ready for the world. In the emergency room, they put him in a special box so he could breathe and gave him medicine to help his lungs. The doctor in charge knew I didn't have insurance or any money. He suggested that I consider the baby's future. Would I like to just hold him and let him pass peacefully?"

The determination began to show on Fatima's face. "I told him I had a mother's love and that he had better do everything possible to save my child's life. That if my child died, I would not only sue him but track his family down and hurt them."

She felt the strength of that long-ago threat and realized now how outrageous it was, as well as how desperate. "That doctor's eyes popped open, and he went right to work ordering medicines and procedures and everything they had to help Hamni."

She smiled and almost giggled thinking back to her feisty younger self. "I was there every day at the hospital. Taking care of him and making sure he got what he needed."

"Giving him his mother's love."

"He ended up with some developmental delays and continued to need medical care after we were discharged from the hospital."

"Where was his father during all this?"

Fatima could feel the manipulation, and she could see what Diegert had done to ease into getting the information he wanted. She wondered to herself if he had ever had a wedgie. Still, it felt good to talk about Hamni and the challenges of his early days. "He was out where he always was, with a hundred other women. He was a very irresponsible man and was completely unaware of Hamni's birth. I know you want me to tell you who he is, but I suspect you already know. The world no longer allows the keeping of secrets."

Diegert could see there was no advantage to continuing the ruse. "Javier Perez," he said. "How did you meet him?"

"At a wild frat party. He was so handsome, so attractive, and every girl in the place wanted him. It becomes an unconscious competition when a man that desirable is in the presence of several women. You begin pursuing him just so you get him before the other girls do. It's stupid, and you will do stupid things, but you want to win. I won that night. We had sex upstairs in someone's bedroom. He was good. He would come and get hard again and fuck me again and again. I had never been with a man who could recover so quickly and get hard again, you know?"

Diegert barely nodded.

"When he was finally done, that was it, he said good-bye and walked out. He left me undressed in some stranger's bed. I realized right then what a mistake I had made. I wanted to forget the whole thing. I wanted to pretend it hadn't happened. As I dressed, I noticed a watch on the nightstand next to the bed. It was engraved on the back: *To my dear son Javier, may time always be on your side. Love, Julio.* The watch was a Rolex, of course. I put it in my pocket and left the party. A month later, I realize I'm pregnant, and soon my parents are furious with me. They are not strict Muslims, but Pakistani culture does not tolerate promiscuous sexuality, and an unwed pregnancy was absolutely shameful. My father wanted to perform an abortion himself. I had to leave. I lived with friends until the birth, and then I lived in a shelter. It was awful being homeless with Hamni, and his special needs were very expensive. Debts were mounting. I had to do something. Javier lived in a grand home in Sussex. It was fenced, guarded, and under camera surveillance. I got past all of that and into his private quarters. I told him we had sex, I got pregnant, and he now had a son. I showed him pictures of Hamni. He laughed and said it was all a lie, and that's when I quoted his watch: 'May time always be on your side. Love, Julio.'"

He realized I wasn't lying and asked what I wanted. I told him I needed money for his son's medical bills. I didn't tell him how troubled Hamni was, but I figured this guy had no clue about medical expenses or the needs of a special child. I told him how much money I needed, and only then did he ask how I got into his place. He was amazed that I was able to bypass all his security and get to him. He agreed to help me, but I would have to do something for him. We agreed to meet the next day, but he insisted I leave and exit his home without being detected. Which I did. The next day we met, he had set up an account I could use for Hamni, and he introduced me to Blevinsky. Headquarters had been looking for female operatives. Blevinsky gave me some trials to perform and had me shoot at a range, and soon I was recruited into service. Hamni was placed in a home where he receives the special care he requires."

"A deal made with the devil."

"Maybe, but, you see, I had to do what was necessary for my son."

"How about Javier? Do you have any communication with him?"

"Not very often, but at least he knows who I am now."

"Julio's the man, though. He's the member of the Board you told me about."

"Yes, but he is old and in poor health. Javier is the one who will take over the business."

"Business? It's more like an empire. Is he up to the job?"

"Hopefully he has matured; otherwise it will be a mess."

"Somehow I don't think the other Board members are going to let things become a mess." After pausing, Diegert asked, "Does he ever visit Hamni? Does Hamni know who his father is?"

"For your first question, I don't know. He does know where Hamni is, and it's not that far from his home in London, but whether he ever visits I don't know. I have never told Hamni who his father is. I'm not certain he understands the concept."

"I see."

"Look, we've got a couple more hours before Windsor; let's switch, I want to sleep."

Taking over the wheel, Diegert thought about his concept of a father. Tom Diegert represented the worst, he wondered how good of a father he would be. If he was fortunate to have a child he hoped he would love that little person as his Mother loved him.

Chapter 12

Diegert finished driving the last hour and a half from
Dutton, Ontario, to Windsor. He followed the GPS
coordinates precisely, arriving at Riverside Park. Fatima
woke up when the car's engine turned off. Diegert smiled
at her sleepy face, and she made a cute crinkle with her
nose as she had a little yawn and stretched her stiff body.
Diegert's phone rang. Blevinsky was on the other end.
"I'm going to activate the device in your ear." Diegert
heard a small electronic tone, then, "Diegert, do you read
me?"

"Yeah, I hear you.

"Remove the black bag from the trunk."

Diegert got out and found the bag in the car's
trunk.

"Change into the black clothes."

Diegert put on the black combat fatigue pants like
they had at Headquarters. He put on a black turtleneck
and laced up a pair of black tactical boots. There was a
small black toque for his head. A black jacket with a dark
diamond-patterned exterior was also included. Curious,
Diegert read the inside label to learn that the jacket was a
thermal suppression garment. The jacket would reduce
his heat signature so he could avoid the thermal scanners
used to secure the border. "All right, sir, I'm dressed."

"Proceed to the water's edge near a grove of large willow trees. You will find a tarp covering a kayak. Inform me when you locate it."

As he walked down to the river, Diegert looked at the ragged skyline of Detroit, Michigan. He was going back to the USA. It was quite puzzling to him that he was going to assassinate somebody in this recently bankrupt city. Glancing back at Fatima, he waved good-bye. She nodded her head slightly. Diegert found the kayak; it, too, was black. "Got it, sir."

"Launch the vessel, paddle across the river, and land at the William G. Milliken State Park. Conceal the vessel and inform me when you have crossed."

Diegert had been in a kayak a few times in Minnesota, so he wasn't worried. At the moment he launched, a large container ship slowly passed by. Diegert paddled next to the vessel, then tucked in behind it, finally paddling into its wake lines on the opposite side to complete his crossing. In the late-afternoon darkness, his movements were unobserved, and he found a grove of trees to stash the kayak. He had stuffed the black tarp into the storage hold and now used it to conceal the kayak's presence. He informed Blevinsky, "I'm in the US."

"Good. Proceed to the parking area on the east side of the park and locate a white van with the markings 'Motor City Electric.' You will be expected."

Diegert saw the van. As he approached, the side door slid open. He stepped inside. The man in the back of the van introduced himself "I am Abraham."

Indicating the driver, he said, "He's Mohammed."

"Right," said Diegert.

The van started moving, but Diegert could see no landmarks or street signs from the back of the solid-sided van. Blevinsky came back on. "Open the black bag."

Diegert saw a big black bag and unzipped it. Inside was a navy-blue nylon jacket with "Event Security" written across the back in big yellow letters. The coat had a smaller version of the same statement on the left chest. He would also be wearing a baseball cap of the same colors with the same identifier emblazoned across the front brow. His credentials were on a laminated magnetic strip card with his picture. The card was on a lanyard, and it identified him as Matthew Wilcox, an employee of Eagle Talon Security.

Sewn into the left panel of the jacket was a holster with the Desert Eagle pistol Lindstrom had shown him. Diegert took a moment to look over the weapon. Abraham's curiosity couldn't be contained, and he watched Diegert intensely as the gun was being inspected. Satisfied the weapon would operate, Diegert placed it back in the holster. He slipped the jacket on and zipped it up. He donned the cap and the lanyard just as they arrived at his insertion point. The van came to a stop, and Blevinsky was back in his ear.

"You will exit the vehicle and walk north on Concord Street. Blend in with the other security guards who are manning an outer perimeter."

While listening to the instructions, Diegert slipped his finger under the phone in Abraham's belt holster, pushing the phone up and into his hand.

Diegert stepped out into a very strange environment. The urban landscape was dominated by the decaying edifice of an old industrial facility that had been abandoned long ago. The surrounding area was comprised of vacant lots with weeds, small trees, and windblown trash entangled in the unmanaged growth. There were small buildings that suffered the same blight as the mammoth-old factory. Diegert took all this in with a brief turn of his head. What was so strange was all the people, bright lights, security, television broadcast towers, limousines, and activity. The juxtaposition of desertion and occupation was striking and intriguing. Something big was going on in a place where nothing good had happened for at least a decade. He walked toward the building and saw other security people dressed like him and started acting like them.

Blevinsky instructed him, "Proceed to the third floor on the northeast side of the main structure."

Diegert thought it very strange that he might be here to put a hit on a rock star or some other urban performer. As he moved through the abandoned factory, he noted all the destroyed interior materials hanging in loops and shreds, making it look like a rotten urban jungle. He couldn't understand why a big event would be put on in such an unsafe and unkempt area. Diegert felt a buzzing in his right jacket pocket. He hadn't realized he had a company-issue walkie-talkie. When he pulled it out, a voice message instructed him, "Arrival in fifteen minutes. Please take your final positions."

Diegert found the third floor and was on the northeast side in an area where there were stairs to the ground just behind him.

Blevinsky came on again in his ear. "Proceed forward to the support structure in front of you."

Diegert looked about. He stood behind a stained support structure where he had an unobstructed line of sight to the central platform.

"Remain in position and await my instructions," Blevinsky directed.

Fatima, sitting in the car across the river in Canada, received a text from Blevinsky. *Drive to Toronto, catch Flight 485 to Heathrow. Communicate with no one.* This was strange, but she reasoned that there must have been a change in the extraction plan for Diegert. Another three hours of driving; at least she didn't have to go all the way back to Montreal.

Diegert really didn't think about what he was about to do. Instead he was planning his route back to the van and his extraction once the deed was done. It never made him feel good to think about the target except as a mission to be completed. He heard fast-moving, powerful footsteps coming in his direction. He stepped out from behind the concrete support pillar and startled the big man he heard coming.

"Oh shit . . . you scared me, man. I was afraid no one was guarding this stairwell."

Diegert noticed the "Supervisor" title on the right chest of his navy-blue jacket.

"Don't let anyone up or down it. No one should be using those stairs, you got it?"

"Yes, sir," replied Diegert before the big guy enthusiastically walked on, continuing his rounds.

"Arrival in two minutes, look sharp, people," crackled the walkie-talkie. Diegert returned to his position where he was able to see the central platform around which everyone's attention was focused. The platform was covered by a tent with an awning extended out over an area where a car would arrive.

"Arrival," the walkie-talkie chirped. "The president has arrived."

As Diegert was listening to the walkie-talkie, he thought he heard "the president," but he wasn't sure. Looking out on the scene in front of him, a big black limousine had arrived under the awning. After a minute, the limousine drove out from under the tent awning. The canvas that covered the driveway and the platform was pulled back. Revealed to everyone was a stage with a podium upon which was affixed the seal of the president of the United States. Standing at the podium was President Peter Carson.

Diegert was the only one in the building, perhaps the only one in the entire world, to be surprised to see the president in this venue. The leader of the free world stood on a stage in a dilapidated Detroit factory to deliver a speech. Diegert's predicament was now clear to him. He thought about all that the Board had on him, the killings in Miami, Paris, and Mogadishu. He reasoned he didn't have to do this. He could avoid capture and evade the law; hell, he had done that before. He could paddle back to Canada and live in the mountains. Yes, the Board had an expectation that he would complete this mission, but that didn't mean he had to carry it out. Blevinsky spoke, "Look at the video on your phone."

Diegert looked at his phone, and on the screen was his mother with a gag in her mouth and a gun to her head. The realization that Crepusculous had kidnapped his mother flashed across his mind.

"We won't hurt her as long as you fulfill your obligation. But if you don't shoot the president, she will be hurt and humiliated before she dies slowly and painfully. Get ready."

Diegert's head was spinning: kill the president or sentence his mother to rape and torture. He looked out at the man surrounded by Secret Service and speaking on a national broadcast.

"Good evening, ladies and gentlemen, thank you for coming tonight to Detroit! Motor City!" the president said with enthusiasm as the audience thundered their applause. "Look where I've brought you" he began. "Look at what has been left behind. The people who built this and ran it are very wealthy. One is a billionaire, and the other has over seven hundred million dollars in personal wealth. The average pensioner from this workplace receives less than twenty thousand dollars a year and no health care. This type of disparity is what I'm calling economic feudalism. When the leader of a company is paid five hundred times what the average employee earns, income disparity grows. America is becoming an imperial feudal system with powerful, wealthy overlords taking indecent incomes for themselves while the hardworking, educated, dutiful employees are paid proportionally less and less each year. The erosion of the middle class means that even well-educated workers are earning salaries that do not allow them to maintain their modest lifestyles."

Carson's style of dynamic speaking captivated audiences, and the theater of this venue made his point even more salient and profound. With emphatic hand gestures and a knack for seeming to address each member of his audience individually, the president carried his point forward.

"Earning five hundred times less than your boss does not represent your economic worth. There is no way one person does five hundred times more work than another. No corporate leader has five hundred times more responsibility than the average worker, and any lifestyle that requires five hundred times more money to sustain is absolutely excessive and morally repugnant. Corporate kings and feudal serfs, that is what America is becoming, and I will address this issue legally, socially, morally, and personally."

"Engage the target," commanded Blevinsky.

Diegert drew the .50-caliber pistol from the holster. He pointed the barrel toward the president.

Looking through the sight, he could see the reticle hovering on the president's head. With the grip firmly in his hand and his index finger extended outside the trigger guard, he steadied the pistol so the reticle remained still. Suddenly, the gun fired.

Diegert hadn't pulled the trigger, but the bullet was on its way. The shot, though sound suppressed, startled Diegert, because he thought the mechanism still required him to pull the trigger. The bullet followed its laser-guided path and struck the president in the head, creating an image of blood and brains exploding off his shoulders like a video-game graphic. The moment of stunned silence didn't last long before the screaming, the hustling of Secret Service agents, and the sirens began to wail. Diegert had to move and follow his extraction protocol. He reholstered his pistol and descended the staircase. On the ground level, many of the other security guards were confused now that something had actually happened. In an authoritarian voice, Diegert shouted, "Stay at your posts. Don't move from your positions. Maintain the security of your designated area."

Diegert said this several times as he moved south toward the point where he was to meet the van. Bewildered guards seemed relieved to be told what to do. It reduced their anxiety and reassured them as the word spread that the president had been shot.

Diegert arrived at Bellevue Street and East Grand Boulevard, but the van wasn't there. Bellevue Street was lined on both sides by decrepit, decaying factory buildings like the ones on Concord Street. While Diegert looked to see if the van had been stopped by the police or had to park elsewhere, his eyes caught sight of the dazzling light of a laser sight. He immediately ducked and rolled on the ground as a round whizzed by and struck the pavement where he had just been. He regained his feet and sprinted into the destroyed interior of another deteriorating factory.

Bullets pockmarked the ground as he ran and then the walls of the building as he continued deeper into its interior. He kept moving until he found cover behind a solid brick interior wall.

The shots stopped, and it remained quiet for several minutes, giving him a moment to think. *Sniper fire? There's no way the Secret Service could be firing at me already. I've been set up.* He realized he was about four miles from the river where the kayak was. *If the kayak is still there,* he thought. *Crepusculous has set me up to take the fall.* He heard footsteps crunching through the dry debris on the building's floor. He was being pursued. The night's darkness made the building's interior a place of shadow and dappled light. He peered around the wall behind which he was hiding and saw two figures moving cautiously toward him. He pulled back behind the wall and reached out his hand, searching for debris. He felt a small pile of broken bricks. Taking a chunk of brick into his hand, he heaved it across the building perpendicular to the direction the pursuers were coming. The brick hit a piece of sheet metal, making a very loud clang. He threw more pieces of brick, making it sound like there was movement. The pursuers crept close to the wall behind which he was hiding. He heard one of them say, "We're getting closer to his signal."

Diegert realized how they had found him. He slipped out his smartphone, activating the app for his tympanic transponder, and shut it down.

"Shit . . . I just lost the signal."

"Let's follow those earlier sounds."

The two men passed the wall behind which Diegert was hiding as he relocated himself around the back side of the wall. He was able to see them moving away from him. As they proceeded, the one in the lead stepped forward and banged into an obstruction.

"Shit."

Together they tried to find a way around the obstacle. Eventually one of them turned on the flashlight attached to his HK45 pistol. Doing so created silhouettes in the ring of light. Diegert drew the Desert Eagle, placed the reticle on the first guy's neck, and pulled the trigger. The bullet ripped through his vertebrae and tore open his throat. The guy's body fell to the floor, and the light beam from his weapon illuminated the building's interior to the west. The second man scurried to the east, leapt through a window space, and crashed through the brush and weeds that grew outside the building.

Diegert sat motionless, listening. He would have to move. Whoever it was that had run off would surely be back, and this old building would be overrun. He could see that the light beam still shined from the fallen man's pistol. He crept down to the body and took the gun and an extra clip of ammunition. He shined the light on the man's face before turning it off, and was both surprised and not surprised to see the dead man was Curtis Jaeger. The Board had a counterstrike team after him, and the presence of Jaeger gave him a pretty good idea as to the other man's identity.

Diegert removed the combat vest from Jaeger and put it on under his jacket. The vest had a communication device clipped to it. He quickly moved to the north, making his way through the debris and clutter of the former factory. The comm unit crackled, and he recognized Strakov's voice. "He's on the run, and he's killed Jaeger."

The reply came from Blevinsky. "Look, we need to button it up. Backup is several minutes away. Continue your pursuit."

At the northernmost end of the factory building, Diegert scrambled through a vacant weed-covered lot and collided with a three-foot granite block. He hit his knee hard on the solid stone and limped a bit before encountering another large block of granite. The weeds were at least three to four feet high, and so were the stones. As he moved about, he realized he was walking on graves. This weed lot was a cemetery. Even the dead in Detroit had been abandoned.

The irony of escaping from being killed by hiding in a graveyard wore off instantly when he was hit in the back of his right shoulder by a shot without sound. The force of the projectile didn't penetrate the vest, but it spun him to his right, knocking him forward into a gravestone. He tumbled and fell in the weeds between two graves.

Strakov saw him go down and quickly advanced with his gun, ready to fire again. Diegert rolled onto his hands and knees and crawled behind a line of gravestones. He peered up and saw Strakov coming. Diegert raised the HK45 and fired. Strakov fell to the ground. Diegert moved immediately, crouching low and running across the graves and between the lines of gravestones, his shoulder throbbing. Shots whizzed by him, ricocheting off the stones. He hit the deck and hugged the ground for a moment, then rolled over and fired. Strakov had to take cover from the bullets sent in his direction. Diegert was the one to escape the game of pistol tag as he burst through a line of bushes that defined the border of the graveyard.

He hopped over a chain-link fence and sprinted through an empty neighborhood of small houses, heading toward the river and a busy street with shops and high-rise apartments. His sense of safety in numbers immediately dissipated when he saw angry mobs of people on the street. The president's assassination had people upset, and they were outside expressing their outrage.

Diegert kept his hat low and his eyes downcast as he walked the streets. He hoped his security jacket would lend some authority to his presence. As he passed a sports bar with a big-screen TV in the front window, he saw that the screen was filled with a picture of his Eagle Talon Security identity card. The card identified him as Matthew Wilcox, but the graphic underneath scrolled his true name: David Terrence Diegert. The scroll indicated he was armed and dangerous and that citizens should report sightings to law enforcement. The manhunt was on. With the technology of Crepusculous and the reach of the Internet, Diegert had suddenly become the world's most wanted man. The president's death was so much bigger than his other jobs, and he realized his chances of escape were growing slim.

Two dudes working the front door of the bar gestured to one another, and one of them got on his phone while the other stepped forward for a better look. "Hey, dude?"

Diegert never looked at him; he just turned and started running. The bouncer shouted out "It's him . . . It's the guy who shot the president."

Diegert caught the looks of people as he sprinted past them. Just running through the streets with a security coat was enough to draw attention, but with the shouting added in, Diegert knew he was in trouble. He ran by a small park with a big graffiti-covered statue. The park was dark and for the moment unoccupied. On his smartphone, he searched for a place he reasoned would provide safe haven from Strakov and the vigilante mobs forming on the angry streets of Detroit. Survival was often achieved by knowing when to avoid a fight you cannot win. His search revealed the address 1300 Beaubien Street, which was only four blocks away.

"Hey, there he is!" Diegert heard the shout and saw a group of people running through the darkness into the park. He bolted from the statue and ran toward Beaubien Street. He sprinted down the middle of whatever street he was on, dodging oncoming traffic and causing cars to slam on their brakes. Angry motorists blew their horns and shouted out their windows. The more fit members of the mob continued their pursuit. Diegert continued down the street until he hit Beaubien Street. He saw an address on a building: 939. As he ran the address numbers increased: 998, 1005. Looking back down the street, the mob was gaining on him. He stopped and as they approached he pointed his gun and fired over their heads. The pursuers ducked for cover and cleared the street. Diegert continued—1180, 125—and at the corner of Beaubien and Clinton was the address he was looking for. Diegert dashed up the steps of the Detroit Police Department station at 1300 Beaubien Street.

Walking through the station doors, it was eerily quiet. Alone in the reception area, he had to call out twice before an older, overweight woman, not dressed in a uniform, approached the counter. "Look, we're kinda busy tonight. Is your problem an emergency?"

"My name is David Terrance Diegert. I'd like to speak to an officer."

"What about? All our officers are on emergency assignment."

"What is your name, ma'am?"

"Helen Mitchell."

"Ms. Mitchell, I'm here to surrender for the assassination of President Carson. Please call in an officer."

Under her breath Helen grumbled, "*Nutjob.*" In a serious tone, she addressed Diegert. "I'm sorry, sir, but you'll just have to have a seat over there and wait for an officer to return."

"Have you been on the Internet tonight?"

"Tonight's events have kept me plenty busy on the radio. I don't have time for Web surfing!"

With a disdainful shake of his head, Diegert walked over to the wooden bench in the lobby and sat down. Over Jaeger's comm unit, he heard Strakov's voice. "I lost him in the city near the river."

Blevinsky said, "He turned off the GPS tracker in his phone, and he somehow turned off his ear implant. Hey, I thought you said Jaeger was dead."

"He's definitely dead. Diegert shot him right through the throat."

"Well, I've got a position on his transponder not far from the river."

"Maybe that fucker took Jaeger's comm unit."

"He's probably listening to us right now."

The moment that last statement was made, the comm unit went silent. Diegert realized his location had been tracked. He pulled off the comm unit, walked to the men's room, and flushed it down the toilet. Walking back into the reception area, he pulled out his phone, dialed

911, and shouted, "They're shooting in the station. The police are being attacked at 1300 Beaubien. Help!"

The 911 dispatcher asked, "Please, sir, may I have your name?" Diegert let out as loud a scream as he could and hung up in the middle of it.

Diegert shouted at Helen, "Where's the interrogation room?"

Perturbed, she looked up at him, replying, "We don't have an interrogation room; it's a secure cell."

"Fine, I want to be put in there."

"You can't go in there until you've been arrested."

Diegert pulled his pistol and pointed it at her. "I don't care if I've been arrested or not; you're going to put me in that cell."

She looked at him stunned and confused.

"Get up, get the keys, and lock me in," demanded Diegert.

Helen walked slowly over to the cell, removed the keys from her pocket, opened the door, and stepped aside.

With the touch of an iron grandmother, Helen laid out the palm of her hand and said, "I'm required to confiscate your weapon."

Looking into her unblinking eyes above her granny glasses, Diegert found himself torn between two conflicting instincts. Submitting to authority was not comfortable, but resisting would result in his death. He slowly turned the pistol over and placed the gun that had shot the president into Helen's hand.

Diegert stepped into the cell and watched as she locked the door, put the keys back in her pocket, and placed the pistol in a drawer of her desk.

***

The president's body was placed in an ambulance and sped off to Detroit Receiving Hospital. Anyone who had seen the images realized they had witnessed a fatal moment. The head injury was so complete, it was obvious the president was dead.

Dick Chambliss, the Secret Service's chief of mobile security, oversaw the prepping of sites and secured the president's environment at his public appearances. Now, in the midst of this catastrophic failure, he was directing the Secret Service's immediate reaction protocol. It surprised him how quickly pictures of the shooter went viral. The shooter's identity and an alias were already scrolling on screens before law enforcement had convened a task force to begin the investigation. No one wanted to catch the culprit more than Chambliss, but he was cautious about the identity of the shooter being so rapidly available and broadcast with such certainty. Dick recalled the false information that was broadcast after the Boston Marathon bombing. Inaccurate identities derailed the investigation and wasted valuable time, which ultimately resulted in more mayhem and death. Due process was still required, even for a presidential assassin.

Chambliss's phone chimed. One of his agent's number appeared.

"Chambliss here,"

"Sir, we're receiving lots reports of sightings of the suspect."

"Whose cataloging the data?"

"The guys at Tech Command."

"Good, prioritize the ones with pictures and videos. I don't want this sucker getting out of Detroit."

Chapter 13

Following the information from Jaeger's comm unit that Blevinsky had extracted, Strakov arrived at 1300 Beaubien Street. Reading the building's sign, Strakov thought Diegert must have been arrested by the police. This complicated things, but he reasoned he might still be able to carry out the Board's plan. Bounding up the stairs, he burst through the doors of the police station and strode into the reception area, booming, "Federal agent. I need to speak to the officer in command."

Helen looked up from her desk just as the phone rang. With an eye on the man at the front counter, she answered the phone, "Detroit Police Department, how may I help you?"

"This is the nine-one-one operator, what is the nature of your emergency?"

"There's no emergency here," replied the confused woman. "Why are you calling me?"

"Ma'am, we received a report of a shooting at the station," stated the emergency services operator.

Frustrated at being ignored, Strakov shouted, "Hey . . . I need to talk to the officer in charge."

Helen, with the phone still to her ear, waved off the shouting man. "I don't know what you're talking about. There is nothing going on here."

"Ma'am, if you're certain there is no need for emergency assistance, I'll cancel the call, but I believe officers are already en route."

"Yeah, yeah . . . cancel the call. Things are fine here."

Hanging up the phone, Helen walked up to the front counter.

Strakov spoke as she approached. "I need to speak to the officer in charge."

"All officers are on emergency assignment this evening. What do you need?"

"I'm a Federal agent, and I'm here to take the assassination suspect into custody."

Helen, whose mind was a lot faster than her body, in spite of her technophobic nature said, "To what suspect are you referring?"

Strakov, feeling the pressure of time and wanting to bully this old lady, said, "A suspect in the presidential assassination is here in this building, and I'm here to take him into custody."

"What makes you think it's a man?"

Strakov showed her a picture of Diegert on his smartphone.

"That doesn't explain why you think he's here," said Helen with her mother-knows-best tone.

Strakov met her with a steely glare. "Are you trying to obstruct me from taking this suspect into custody?"

"I'm neither confirming nor denying that there is anyone in custody here at the station. If I did have someone here, how would I know that you're not an accomplice? You're dressed in that space-age SWAT suit. You say you're a Federal agent, but you show me no

ID. We already have a Federal liaison who is an FBI agent, and he looks and acts nothing like you."

Frustrated with her assessments, Strakov walked around the end of the counter and searched the room signs.

"Hey!" yelled Helen. "You can't come back here."

He saw Diegert through the small pane of thick glass in the door of the secure cell. Turning the doorknob, he found it locked. "Where's the key?" he said as he walked over to her.

"You're not authoriz-" Helen's words were trapped in her throat when Strakov jabbed two fingers into her suprasternal notch. She choked as he continued to apply pressure where the bones of her chest met the base of her throat.

"I want that key."

Helen was terrified and struggling for air but was determined not to give in.

"Hey, Helen, what's going on?" The voice of Ben Hoffman punctured the tension of the moment, and Strakov took his fingers from Helen's chest.

As the scene became clearer, Ben stepped between Helen and Strakov. With genuine concern, he looked Helen in the eyes and asked, "Are you OK?"

Helen nodded while rubbing the base of her throat.

"What the hell's going on?" asked the young officer who had rushed back to the station. "Dispatch put out a frantic call saying there was trouble."

Hoffman looked at Strakov, dressed in his tactical suit with an HK MK 23 in his holster. "Who are you?" he asked.

Helen jumped in. "Says he's a Federal agent, but he sure ain't FBI."

"My name is Brian Stratton, and I'm an agent with the Secret Service."

"Not without ID, you're not," said Hoffman with Helen nodding her head.

"Look, I'm taking the suspect locked in that room into custody . . . now."

At the conclusion of his statement, he drew his MK 23 and pointed it at Hoffman. Reflexively, Hoffman went for his weapon. Strakov fired, piercing the young officer's abdomen, felling him to the floor. A stream of blood poured from his wound. Helen screamed, and Strakov fired at her as well, hitting her in the upper chest. She collapsed across her desk, scattering the clutter that covered the workspace. At that instant, the doors opened and half a dozen officers entered the station. Strakov wasted no time as he exited the office through the rear, descended a back stairway, and made his way to the street through the garage.

The officers entering the station were stunned and began treating Helen and Hoffman. Two of the officers pursued Strakov but were too late to apprehend him. Ben Hoffman's wounds were serious, and he was unable to give an account of what had happened. Helen died on the office floor as a result of the attack, and capturing her killer became a personal cause for the officers of 1300.

Almost an hour had passed before someone realized there was a suspect in the secure cell. Officer Nathan Sawyer looked through the window of the cell and stared in disbelief at the suspect within: David Terrance Diegert.

"Holy shit! Captain, you gotta get over here."

Captain Desmond Thompson joined the younger officer and peered through the window. He was astonished when he saw the man whose face had been broadcast around the world. Here in their cell sat the assassin of the president of the United States.

Trying the locked door, Captain Thompson told Officer Sawyer, "Get the key". While waiting he thought of whom he should contact to deal with this suspect.

"It's not in the cabinet," shouted Sawyer.

"Check Helen's pockets—you know she never put the keys back." Helen's body was still awaiting transport by the medical examiner's office. Sawyer retrieved the keys.

Captain Thompson unlocked the door. Feeling like a monkey in a cage, Diegert rose when the door opened. Thompson began by asking, "Who was your arresting officer?"

"I surrendered myself, and Helen put me in here."

Thompson took a moment to process this surprise before replying, "Helen is now dead, and one of our officers has been shot. Who the hell was that guy who was here when we arrived?"

"Is he in custody?"

"No, he is not, but you better answer my question."

"His name is Alexi Strakov. He's part of a kill team that my former employer has activated to terminate me."

"You're the guy who shot the president."

Diegert held his reply while considering the gravity of his response and the immediate effect it would have on the situation. He realized that, even though he did not actually pull the trigger, only he and whomever was operating the computer that controlled the gun knew that.

"Yes, I am," he said, "and that makes this a Federal case, so I believe you better call in the FBI."

Thompson, repressing the urge to beat the man who had shot the best president this country had ever had, realized the son of a bitch was right. Never softening his hateful glare, the captain stepped out of the cell, instructing Officer Sawyer, "Get Jim Donovan down here."

***

At Pearson International Airport in Toronto, Fatima returned her rental car. She had been listening to music while driving but now realized that there was a lot of security at the airport. Walking through the terminal, she stopped at a TV broadcast of President Peter Carson being shot in the head. Following the graphic image, the video cut to images of David Diegert with a pistol pointing from an elevated position. The next image was the corporate security badge with Diegert's picture and the name "Mathew Wilcox" on the card. Below the image, the graphic read, *AKA—David Terrence Diegert*. The twenty-four-hour news cycle turned the event into a nonstop search for the president's assassin.

On her phone, Fatima called Blevinsky. "Hey, David's in trouble. The hit's gone worldwide, and he's been ID'd. What do you want me to do?"

"Is your flight on time?"

"Yeah, it leaves in forty-five minutes."

"I want you on that plane, and I'll meet you in London. Someone will pick you up at Heathrow. If your flight's on time, you can visit Hamni. Would you like that?"

"Of course, but what about David?"

"Don't worry about Diegert. I know there's been some publicity, but we have his extraction under control. You'll get to see him in London. Have a nice flight."

What bullshit, she thought. *Have a nice flight?* Blevinsky would never say that. *Visit Hamni?* That wasn't an invitation; it was a threat. Watching the television replay, patrons were cursing Diegert's image. In a quiet corner of the gate, she turned her phone camera on herself and recorded. *"Hey, I know you're facing some tough decisions, but I . . . I believe in you. I look forward to seeing you soon."* She sent the video to Diegert and hoped he wouldn't take it the wrong way. As she walked to the board area, she found herself wondering if David Diegert would suffer the same fate as Shamus McGee.

***

The vice president, Lydia Stanwix, was rushed to the White House, where she was secured in the Situation Room. The national security advisor, the joint chiefs, and the directors of both the CIA and the FBI, along with the chief justice of the Supreme Court, were all assembled for the administration of the oath of office. A somber ceremony transferring power to the shocked and grieving vice president was broadcast to a nation reeling from surprise and frazzled with frustration. President Stanwix spoke to the nation from deep below the White House but also from the depth of her very heavy heart.

"My fellow Americans, I grieve with you for the loss of a man who dedicated himself to the well-being and freedom of all Americans. Peter Carson embodied the very best qualities possessed by human beings. His goodness and generosity will stand as a testament to the man he was. I want to express special condolences to his wife, First Lady Mary Carson, and his son, Jason, and daughter, Ashley. Their loss is even more personal than ours. The fact that his life has all too soon become a legacy is a pain we will all have to bear as we progress forward into the world Carson left for us. It has been over fifty years since this great nation faced such a devastating loss of a charismatic and caring leader. For us now, the emotions are raw and the same as those experienced fifty years ago. We, however, have much more sophisticated technology, and we will apprehend this criminal and have him face the justice he deserves. I ask you as a nation to remain calm and vigilant while being cooperative with law enforcement. God bless you all as you grieve this loss and God bless the United States of America."

Jim Donovan was the director of investigation for the FBI in the Detroit area. The fifty-two-year-old had the look of a classic G-man: gray hair cut short, and a slightly soft belly under a midgrade dark suit. He had a reputation within the DPD as a very cordial and cooperative agent who kept his focus on resolving cases instead of controlling turf. The events of this evening had him absolutely overwhelmed. Captain Desmond Thompson had to call him three times before Donovan took the call. "Desmond, what's going on? I'm getting my ass kicked tonight," said the usually polite Donovan.

Thompson replied simply, "We got him. We got Diegert. Come to 1300 but keep it quiet."

***

Strakov called Blevinsky as he walked the streets of Detroit.

"Diegert's in police custody. He's being held in a station house."

"I have a four-man assault team heading to your GPS location. Stay where you are. Their ETA is ten minutes."

"What's the mission?"

Annoyed, Blevinsky retorted, "The mission is the same. There has been no change in the mission just because you've failed three times! Take the assault team and kill Diegert. Leave no loose ends."

Strakov felt like he had just been kicked in the ear. He replied, "Yes, sir, mission first."

"Make certain it is."

After an impatient ten minutes, a white SUV pulled up. Strakov climbed in to find three operators wearing black combat gear including tactical helmets. The driver asked Strakov for directions, and the big Russian placed his smartphone in the tech dock. The GPS-guided route came up on the vehicle's dash screen, and they drove off to Diegert's location.

When Donovan arrived at 1300, Captain Thompson met him and shook his hand. "Where'd you find him?"

"He turned himself in."

Donovan's surprised look and abrupt halt expressed the *holy shit* sentiment he didn't need to say.

"I know," said Thompson as they continued. Donovan was again surprised when he saw the condition of the familiar office. Yellow tape, splattered blood, and busy forensic techs made the office look like so many crime scenes he had worked throughout his career. "What the hell?"

"Helen is dead, and Ben Hoffman is wounded."

Getting the shocked FBI man to focus, Thompson directed him toward the secure cell.

"Diegert's over here. Let's see if we can get some answers."

Donovan was reeling from the news of Helen's death. She was a big old battle-ax of a woman, but she'd had a soft spot for Donovan and had always treated him kindly. He and Thompson entered the secure cell together.

"This is Jim Donovan. He's the FBI agent in charge of Detroit."

"I know who you are, Mr. Diegert, as does everyone in the world with an Internet connection."

Diegert watched the men cross the room. Donovan stood behind him while Thompson circled back to stand by the door. Diegert shifted his chair so he could see them both.

Diegert began, "I realize the pressure you're under to inform the public that the president's assassin has been caught. I'm not denying I am that person, but I believe you should be concerned about the forces behind this and how this event ties to what's coming next."

Donovan and Thompson sat down in hard metal chairs; the FBI agent said, "Go on, Mr. Diegert."

"I am an agent for a group of powerful elites known as Crepusculous. They possess tremendous wealth, and they use it to manipulate governments, markets, and whole economies. Today's assassination is part of a plan to destroy the US economy."

"How the hell do you know that?" asked Thompson.

"At the Crepusculous training facility, I discovered electronic records from a double agent. They revealed a three-part plan to destroy a nation's economy. I figured it was some third-world country, but killing the president was about destroying the United States."

Both lawmen looked at Diegert with a mix of contempt and curiosity.

Diegert continued, "That means there are at least two more actions are planned."

"What are they?" asked Donovan.

"I don't know exactly, but the Board's actions are always multilayered with subsequent missions building on previous successes."

"And why are you telling us this?" interjected Thompson.

"I've been trained by them. When on an operation, the exact nature of the mission or the identity of a target is not revealed until absolutely necessary. I didn't know the target was the president until he stepped out onto that stage."

Diegert looked back and forth, seeing the officer's intense interest before continuing.

"After completing the assignment, there was an extraction plan. When I acted on that plan, two attempts were made on my life. When those failed, my identity was released for worldwide broadcast. It wasn't the police or the FBI that released the information; it was Crepusculous. They want me dead. The man who was here, who shot Helen and the officer, is part of a hit team that will continue to try to kill me." Holding up his smartphone, he said, "The blogosphere is fomenting vigilantes to kill me, and the Board has posted an anonymous reward for my death. The last thing they want is for me to be in custody talking to honest law officers like you."

"Certainly your arrest was a distinct probability," observed Donovan.

"Crepusculous has corrupt agents in every branch of law enforcement. When you announce my custody, the first officers to arrive will be their agents who will assert control, remove me, and terminate me."

Donovan shot a look at Thompson, who, with his chin in his hand, raised his eyebrow. Diegert continued, "The fact that you haven't shot me already convinces me you're not corrupt."

"Don't think that I haven't considered doing exactly that," said Thompson with steely restraint.

Speaking slowly, Diegert said, "Soon they will broadcast fabricated reports identifying me as a radical loner with a vendetta against the president. It will all be disinformation so the Board can control the message and manipulate public perception."

After the two officers sighed and considered what was said, it was Donovan who remarked, "So you're the fall guy, and all this is coming down on you, even though you're the guy who shot the president."

Diegert wanted to explain about the remotely controlled system on the gun, but he could tell these two were looking for a reason not to believe him. He had to keep his story simple so he could convince them that Crepusculous had turned on him and was trying to kill him while also getting them to value him as a source of information regarding the next terrorist attacks.

"Yes, sir, you're right on both accounts, and I want to help you stop the next attack."

Chapter 14

On Beaubien Street, the white SUV pulled up to the police station at 1300 and disgorged its five-man assault team. Alexi Strakov led them up the steps. The four operators, all dressed in black combat gear, carried H&K MP5 submachine guns. Upon entering the office area, Strakov bellowed, "Federal agents." All the cops looked at the black-clad team with tactical helmets, balaclavas, and automatic weapons and felt quite certain these were not Federal agents. Strakov started firing, and the rest of the team opened up as well. Some of the officers dove to the floor and crawled toward the back hall. Others took bullets in their upper bodies and heads, fatally falling to the floor and splattering the squad room with their red, American blood.

The officers, who made it to the back tactical room, grabbed M4 carbines and combat shotguns. In the squad room, Strakov and his team fired their weapons at the secure cell door. Donovan, Thompson, and Diegert backed away from the door as it resisted the barrage of bullets. Donovan looked at Diegert. "This is all because of you?" Diegert tilted his head while shrugging his shoulders.

Strakov called off the futile gunfire and directed two team members to place breaching charges on the door. When the detonators were set, the team converged on the far side of the room. Just before the detonator was engaged, a spate of bullets hit the assault team, killing two of them. The cops were firing from the back hallway. Two of the remaining assault team members moved to cover and returned fire. Strakov saw the detonator in the hand of a dead team member. He crawled from the desk under which he took cover, reached out, and activated the detonator.

The explosion was massive, with the majority of the force directed into the squad room, killing the two remaining assault team members. The cops were blown back into the hall, suffering blast burns and shrapnel wounds. The door of the secure cell was twisted into the room with its top hinge ripped out and the lower hinge still attached by a twisted piece of steel framing. The gaping entrance was clouded in dust and smoke. Inside the cell, all three men coughed and convulsed as they grappled with orienting themselves.

Their ears were deaf and they could hardly breathe with all the dust in the air. Donovan was unseen behind the destroyed door. Thompson took up a position on the left side of the open doorway. Diegert moved to the back right corner and got behind the overturned steel table, using it as a defensive shield.

Strakov rose from his refuge and walked through the dust and smoke, approaching the blasted entrance of the secure cell. With his MK 23 leading the way, he entered the room. Thompson reacted first, firing on Strakov and hitting him in the torso. Strakov's tactical suit prevented the bullets from penetrating, but the force spun the big Russian so he was facing Thompson. Strakov fired on the department captain, striking him with several fatal rounds. Diegert, seeing a service weapon on the floor, grabbed the gun, stood up from behind the table, faced the man he hated, and fired at

Strakov. He first struck him in the hip and then, using automatic fire, progressed up the midsection until he put three bullets in the head of his nemesis. Strakov's big body fell to the floor with a loud thud and a plume of dust. Diegert stepped over to look at the corpse of the man he was so very satisfied to see lying dead.

Diegert pulled back the broken steel door to find Donovan covered in dust with a bleeding cut on his head. He helped the dazed man to his feet, brushing the dust off him. Peering through the clouded air, Donovan saw Strakov's body. Diegert explained, "He's the guy who led the kill team. He was one of the best operators the Board had working for them. I think this is yours," said Diegert as he handed the service weapon to Donovan.

Reaching for his holster and finding it empty, Donovan took the gun and replaced the hot weapon under his suit coat.

"Come on," commanded Diegert.

Before following Diegert into the squad room, Donovan stopped at the corpse of his friend Desmond Thompson. He closed the eyes of one of the best men he had ever worked with, and he thought of how the man's close-knit family would be devastated.

In the squad room, Diegert opened the drawer of Helen's desk and took out the gun that had shot the president.

Diegert placed the gun in Strakov's empty holster.

"What are you doing?" asked Donovan.

"I'm setting up our own disinformation campaign. Let's go," said Diegert.

While crossing the squad room, Diegert removed a helmet and a pistol from one of the assaulters. He and Donovan stepped outside, and the cool night air made both of them cough and spit. The coughing made Donovan's head wound bleed even more.

"Have you got a first-aid kit in your car?" asked Diegert.

Donovan, caught in a spasm of coughing, pointed to a blue Malibu parked across the street. Diegert put on the tactical helmet and led Donovan over to the car. He took the keys from the FBI agent, put him in the passenger seat, and drove off. A few blocks away, he pulled over, got out the kit, and bandaged Donovan's head. With the bleeding stopped, he drove on.

***

Aaron Blevinsky hesitated when he saw Klaus Panzer's name on his phone screen. "Yes, sir."

"What is the status on the elimination of Diegert?"

"I cannot report success at this time, sir, but Strakov's team knows his location and they are assaulting the site as we speak."

"Very well, keep me apprised of developments."

"Yes, sir."

When Panzer concluded the call, Dean Kellerman remarked, "We do seem to be in a bit of a pickle."

"Yes, but we must move forward. Any retraction at this point would be a waste."

"Is Diegert really so important? We've already initiated the media campaign against him. He did it! What could he say that anyone would believe?"

"Ah—you see . . . that's just it. He can't get everyone to believe him, but he might get someone to, and that could do us harm."

"As a dead man, the story is ours to tell."

"Precisely," punctuated Panzer, "We must be the ones to capture and kill him."

Chapter 15

In the deepening night, Diegert drove through Detroit not really knowing where he was going but avoiding the closed roads and traffic control roadblocks by staying on side streets and deserted avenues.

"Hey, you better get on the phone and call some people or do something," he said to Donovan, who sat in the passenger seat recovering from dust and smoke inhalation.

Donovan looked at Diegert, and he wondered how much truth there was in his story. He contemplated what would have happened if Lee Harvey Oswald hadn't been gunned down. Wouldn't we have learned more about the plot behind the JFK assassination? Diegert's story may be just to save his own ass, but as he dialed, Donovan knew he could've easily been killed back at the station, and that hit team was no figment.

"Hello," said a calm, warm female voice when Donovan's call connected.

"Carolyn, it's Jim Donovan. Things are nuts, can we meet at a safe house?"

"Safe house? I was hoping for a cup of coffee."

"No, I need a secure address."

"OK . . . meet me at 2113 Locust Circle in thirty minutes. You gonna tell me more?"

"Trust me, when we meet I'll tell you and show you everything at the center of what happened tonight." Donovan disconnected the call.

"You were smart not to say anything more. Crepusculous owns the means of communication."

Carolyn Fuller was the CIA counterterrorism analyst for the Detroit area and had known Jim Donovan for over ten years. As the senior agent for Detroit, Carolyn had developed a collegial, cooperative, and professional relationship with her FBI counterpart. Their ability to work together proved crucial in 2009 during the underwear bomber incident. The Christmas Day terrorist threat was quickly made safe while the evidence and the suspect were held in an unquestionable chain of legal custody.

Establishing a safe house in Detroit required simply choosing an abandoned structure out of the seventy-eight thousand available, keeping the neighborhood's electricity and water on, and locking it up tight. The house on Locust Circle was a sturdy brick structure on a truly dead-end street. All twenty-four of the houses leading up to it were abandoned. Nature was taking over, with prolific plant growth. Weeds and overgrown trees would one day hide this street's existence. Carolyn had chosen this house specifically because the garage was in the back. The automatic door opener still worked, so once the car was inside, the place retained its abandoned appearance. Inside, the furnishings were sparse and mostly what the previous residents had left behind. The boarded windows denied any natural light, there were, however, enough electric lights to make the place functional. Carolyn hooked up her laptop to the external cameras, checked each view of the property and made some coffee. Looking at the view of the driveway, she wondered why her friend and trusted colleague needed to see her in this place, on this incredible night.

Chapter 16

Dressed in silk pajamas as he paced in bare feet across the soft carpet of his spacious bedroom in London, Panzer wasn't comforted by his thoughts. He found it difficult to imagine the perspective of a person in a powerless position as was David Diegert. He struggled to contemplate the thoughts and actions of a publicly identified criminal on the run from superior adversaries. He could barely stomach the conclusion, but he would have to turn to the authorities. He called Blevinsky and directed him to activate Crepusculous agents in the CIA, NSA, DIA, and FBI. He also reiterated to the director of Headquarters, "It is imperative that we apprehend Diegert." Blevinsky could hear the threat through the airwaves. "Yes, I'm doing everything I can to find him."

Waiting for a response, all Blevinsky heard was the line go dead.

Klaus Panzer placed another call. This one reached Javier Perez in his luxurious town house not far in London. "Javier, I am so pleased you will be ascending to your father's chair on the board soon."

"Thank you, it will be an honor to work with you."

"Change is happening all around us. I trust you've made the necessary arrangements for our third phase of the operation?"

"Yes, I have. All components will be in place in two days."

"Excellent! The trial run of the initiation sequence was successful?"

"Absolutely, single-source satellite initiation worked wonderfully. We had some challenges, but recently Blevinsky and I resolved the barriers, and all our practice runs have been successful."

"The thermobaric charges are ready?"

"Seven of them, yes; the last two are being placed as we speak. Placing the volatile compounds in proximity to each other without spontaneous combustion is a problem our engineers struggled with but solved."

"You have faith in the system now?"

"Certainly. One signal and the compounds activate and ignite."

"Your father will be proud, and I'm glad it's you who'll have the honor of activating the detonation device. It's only right that the next generation of Crepusculous plays that role."

"I'm looking forward to furthering our partnership."

"Very well, we'll speak again soon."

"Good night."

After the call concluded, Javier reflected on a comment his father had made referring to Klaus Panzer as the world's most ruthless man. When he had first heard this, he thought it was a compliment, but now he reconsidered.

Javier also took a moment to reflect on himself. He really did not like thinking very deeply about himself. He found that just under the surface of the success he projected was a man filled with doubt and fear. Fear of failure, fear of exposure, fear of real intimacy. The money, the wealth, the good looks were a façade behind which he hid. He was good at so few things and bad at so many. He lacked the true self-confidence possessed by those who worked hard to develop themselves. He was uncertain as to where his talents lay beyond screwing women.

Women made it so easy for him to feel successful. If the only goal in life was having sex with a woman on the first night, he would be world champion. His relationships, though, were hollow. They always ended with the girl's feelings hurt and him feeling nothing. The intensity of a new sex partner was an emotional sanctuary where he could feel really good for a while, share that with a woman, and then avoid any true commitment. This pattern had worked for him since he was a teenager. Now, at the age of thirty, he was afraid he couldn't relate to a woman in any other way. Seduce, consume, discard was the way he experienced relationships with women. If he was ultimately a failure with women, then he really had no talent at all.

At the conclusion of his third decade, he also had to contemplate the fact that he was a father. He certainly wasn't a good one. He had only been to visit Hamni just once. Rather, he didn't "visit" but went to the facility where Hamni lived and observed. The young boy's special needs were a challenge, but the spirit and perseverance he demonstrated through his activities impressed Javier. His son had guts. The little guy was not going to let his difficulties define him. Why, with so many challenges, was this kid more confident than his father, who had so much and was still capable of so little?

Julio Perez's empire was Javier's destiny, but it felt like a curse. How much does a man need? How far will he go to acquire and retain all that he seeks? Javier really didn't understand why Klaus wanted to destroy the United States and the bombs he was in charge of placing—he had no clue. Blevinsky set it all up, and Javier just nodded and spoke his lines to Panzer. What they were trying to accomplish made no sense, but he was afraid of the consequences if he didn't play his part. He hadn't even bothered to Google thermobaric bombs. Nine cities in the US, though, were going to have one of these things go off. Klaus wanted catastrophic devastation across the country. Javier, as a sign of his commitment to Crepusculous, was to "oversee" the procurement, placement, and activation of the explosive devices. Without Blevinsky, absolutely nothing would've been accomplished. Javier, by position of birth alone, was being credited with setting up an incredibly complex and destructive attack that would bring violent changes to the structure of the United States of America, and he alone possessed the triggering device.

All these thoughts were upsetting, and befuddled his mind. He didn't want to think about these problems; besides, he had a Thai teenager, with bleached blonde hair, upstairs waiting to be fucked.

Chapter 17

Thirty minutes after speaking to Jim Donovan, Carolyn watched his blue Malibu pull into the driveway of the Locust Circle safe house on the camouflaged security camera feed. She activated the garage door, and he parked next to her Honda Accord. With the garage door closed, Donovan stepped out of the passenger side and greeted Carolyn. "Hey, it's good to see you."

"Yeah . . . It's good to see you too. Now what the hell's going on?"

"I have a suspect in the car, and I'd like to get him inside."

"I can see your suspect was driving the car!"

"I know . . . let's get him inside."

Carolyn was taken aback when the suspect stepped out of the car with his helmet on. Donovan grasped the man's left arm and led him up the steps and into the kitchen.

"Take the helmet off," ordered Donovan.

When Diegert removed the helmet, Carolyn recognized him immediately. She struggled to stifle her emotional surprise and relied on her professional stoicism so as not to reveal her reaction.

Donovan said, "I know, I can hardly believe it either, and I know we're in big trouble with this one, but you've got to hear the story."

Donovan and Diegert spent the next thirty minutes telling Carolyn all about the events of the day, and the power of Crepusculous. Listening carefully, Carolyn offered that she was aware of Crepusculous. The Agency had a watch protocol, but what was observed seemed very philanthropic. Nevertheless, the CIA was concerned because the power the Board could wield was significant enough to affect markets and even governments.

"Exactly!" said Donovan. "And that's what they're trying to do in the United States. Diegert here says there's more to come."

"When I was training in Romania at a Crepusculous facility, we planned covert operations that were always multilayered. Each action contributed to the completion of the next, until the final objective was revealed and typically easily achieved because of the preliminary work that had already been done."

"You think the president's assassination was just the first step in a broader plan?" asked Carolyn.

"Yes, I do, and I think the next thing is going to happen very soon. I acquired an electronic record from a mole who was working undercover inside Crepusculous. It revealed a four-stage plan for economic readjustment."

"So what's the next phase of the plan?" asked Carolyn.

"The record doesn't indicate that. I only know that four stages have been planned."

She continued, "I'm aware that the Perez family are members of the Board."

"They are," confirmed Diegert.

"I read that the father is quite old and in poor health. It is speculated that his son, Javier, is in line to take over."

"That's interesting. I know of Javier, but I didn't think he was ready to take control of the empire."

"Why do you say it that way, with all that doubt?" questioned Carolyn.

"The guy's a playboy. He's spending his wealth, not contributing to it."

"His father's failing health must be forcing his hand."

"I know that Klaus Panzer and Dean Kellerman are also Board members. The mole's documents included profiles on both men."

"What did they have to say?" asked Carolyn.

"Panzer is a real disciplinarian with a strong German heritage. He's the self-appointed leader and sees to it that the Board bends to his will. He has two daughters, one who is involved in the business, and a younger one, who is not."

Donovan asked, "Does the Agency know the full membership of the Board?"

"No, but there may be even more members," said Carolyn.

"I have a plan to find out what's next," said Diegert.

Both agents looked at him as he sat on a stool at the linoleum counter.

"I know someone who can get access to Javier Perez. Her name is Fatima Hussain. She's an agent for the Board, and she has a history with Javier."

"You mean you want her to spy on her ex?"

"Fatima has a son who is held by the Board. She's denied access to him unless she serves as an operative."

"She's being blackmailed," offered Carolyn.

"I plan to acquire her son and convince her to infiltrate Javier's place and steal intel to share with us in exchange for her son."

Both agents were quiet for a moment, and then Donovan said, "Interesting, but there are so many holes in your perforated plan that I can't see the possibility of success."

"You don't know the personalities," said Diegert. "I know what Fatima is capable of, and I also know she will do anything for her son."

Carolyn spoke up. "You're suggesting kidnapping a child and holding him hostage to force his mother to extract information from an ex-boyfriend that you're not even certain has valuable intel."

"Alright, I can see your hesitation, but it makes sense that Javier should take an active role in this process as an up-and-coming Board member. You two can shoot holes in my plan, but I'm telling you that it'll work and we'll stop whatever attack is coming to the United States, and neither of you have a better plan to do that."

Carolyn and Donovan looked at each other with exasperated bewilderment.

***

Blevinsky was pleased to find the Board's mole in the FBI was already in Detroit. Special Agent Stanley Talbot had been immediately dispatched to Detroit and was active in the investigation. Blevinsky informed him of the kill order on Diegert and told him of the incident at Station 1300. Talbot arrived at the police station and was informed that Jim Donovan had been seen leaving with the assassination suspect. Talbot found Donovan's contact info in his Bureau smartphone and activated a GPS app to find Donovan. Accompanied by his two junior agents, Steven Peterson and Andrew Gates, the special agent began following the trail to Donovan's location.

At 2113 Locust Circle, Carolyn Fuller was taking notes and trying to make sense of everything that a man she knew and trusted had told her, along with what the admitted assassin of the president had to say. She made it clear to Donovan that the risks they were taking were huge, and the penalties permanent. Donovan agreed with her, but based on his experiences, Diegert was telling the truth and cooperating when he could've easily killed them and escaped. Carolyn continued to struggle with accepting everything she was told.

As Talbot turned the tan Chevy Malibu onto the abandoned Locust Circle, he informed his agents, "Lock and load boys, these people are armed and dangerous. We take them dead if we have to."

"Yes, sir," replied Peterson and Gates as they checked their weapons.

While the three occupants of 2113 Locust Circle sat contemplating their situation, a vehicle emerged on the security camera screen. The car doors opened, and three agents stepped out of the vehicle. The driver of the car spoke into a PA system. "Attention, Agent James Donovan. I am FBI Special Agent Stanley Talbot, and we're here to assist you. Please reveal yourself and allow us to help you."

"It's a hit squad," said Diegert. "The FBI wouldn't send so few agents."

Looking somewhat doubtful, Donovan replied, "You're getting paranoid, the Bureau is on a skeleton staff tonight. They're here to help us."

Carolyn said nothing but nodded at the man in whom she believed. Donovan opened the side door and stepped into the driveway. Diegert and Carolyn watched the security camera's feed on her laptop. Donovan stepped into the field of view in front of the car. He had his hands raised, and although they couldn't hear the conversation, Diegert and Carolyn could see that Donovan and Talbot were talking. Suddenly Talbot drew his weapon and shot Jim Donovan three times.

The senior FBI agent fell to his knees and collapsed on his side as his life poured out in a large puddle of blood on the driveway. Carolyn was shocked, but Diegert grabbed her hand and bolted for the garage. They escaped through the rear door of the garage and ran through the backyards of the unoccupied houses of Locust Circle.

Talbot and his agents entered the kitchen through the side door. They cleared the rooms and returned to the kitchen. The laptop continued to project the scene on the driveway with Jim Donovan's dead body. Talbot stepped to the garage door and saw the back door of the garage wide open. "Alright, we're on a rabbit hunt. Let's cover both sides of the street. Keep your comms open."

Diegert and Carolyn were crouched under a deck in the backyard of a house two doors down from 2113. He signaled for her to remain silent by placing a finger perpendicular to his lips. It was important to listen and determine if the three agents were sticking together or spreading out.

With a hand signal, Talbot directed Gates to take the west side of the street. He indicated that Peterson should start searching the east. Both agents proceeded as directed.

It was a dark night with only a crescent moon. The backyards, having been neglected for several years, possessed both the trappings of human inhabitants—patio furniture, picnic tables, swing sets—and the consequences of unmanaged growth—fallen limbs, layers of leaves, and tall grass. Fences were also an obstacle, and the chain-link variety was especially difficult to detect on this opaque night.

Diegert and Carolyn listened as Agent Peterson clanged into the fence that surrounded the yard. He climbed over the barrier and proceeded with his weapon drawn. Beyond the deck they were hiding under was a swimming pool filled with algae-laden water covered in a rotting layer of leaves. Diegert watched the shadows extending in front of Agent Peterson as he passed between the deck and the pool. Carolyn was field trained as a CIA agent but inexperienced. Fear jangled her nerves as she struggled to keep her composure. The tension of this life-and-death game made it very difficult for her to keep from crying out.

Diegert, on the other hand, knew how to play this game well. He wanted to see how good Agent Peterson was at cat and mouse. Diegert definitely felt he was in the role of the feline. After Peterson passed their hiding spot, Diegert stepped out and crept behind him. He reached out and struck the agent on his elbow, flexing the arm and drawing it back. With his other arm, he placed a chokehold on Peterson's neck. He swept down the right forearm forcefully, stripping the gun from the FBI man's hand. The pistol dropped to the pool deck. Peterson's reflexes were good; he rotated his torso and drove his elbow into Diegert's abdomen, delivering several painful blows. Diegert hung on, twisting Peterson's arm behind his back. The FBI agent kicked Diegert in the shin and stomped on his foot, sending searing pain through the bones of the metatarsals. This maneuver forced Diegert to reposition his footing, which slackened the chokehold.

Peterson grabbed Diegert's hand and pried it loose, releasing the hold and freeing his airway.

Carolyn watched the battle in front of her, shocked at the speed and violence of the two men. She saw the pistol by the side of the pool and retrieved it but remained under the deck. Peterson was now able to pivot and turn into the hold Diegert had on his right arm. Anticipating Peterson's move, Diegert held the man's hand tight and kicked his opponent's knee with a lateral blow. The kick produced a snapping crack as the ligaments in the vulnerable joint gave way to the precision force. Peterson cried out and fell to his right. As he collapsed on the crippled knee, Diegert hit him in the jaw with a palm heel strike. The blow awkwardly twisted Peterson's neck, compressing his brain stem, making consciousness difficult to maintain. The FBI man was still able to see and perceive, but motor control of his body was failing. Diegert grabbed him by the lapels of his gray G-man suit and flung him into the brown-green water of the neglected pool. The sudden immersion into the cold water was startling; it forced Peterson to find his footing and stand up. Diegert descended the pool steps, entering the water up to his waist. Peterson was wiping pond scum from his face when he heard Diegert moving toward him. The agent faced his tormentor, who unexpectedly splashed two handfuls of filthy water into the eyes of the G-man. Capturing the moment, Diegert grasped Peterson's throat with his right hand. Placing his right leg behind the injured leg of the agent, Diegert kicked it out from under him while forcefully pushing his upper body under the water. Peterson's hand clamped on to Diegert's arm while his other arm reached up and out of the water and pounded on Diegert's chest. Diegert increased the pressure on Peterson's throat while the determined man threw several ineffective blows. Diegert grabbed the flailing right hand of his adversary, hyperextended the wrist, and held it out away from an effective strike zone. The surface of the water convulsed from the struggling movements of the desperate man held below. Diegert knew it would be over soon, and he steeled himself for the inevitable conclusion.

Peterson's mind was frantically racing through a million thoughts as his neurons fired survival sequences that failed to change their deteriorating physiologic state. The final image projected on the mind's eye of the dying agent, as water-replaced air in his lungs, was the beautiful sight of his young wife, Sarah, dressed in sexy lingerie smiling at him in the doorway of their bedroom.

Diegert saw a large bubble of air break the surface of the water as the thrashing subsided and the tension in Peterson's arm disappeared. Diegert gently lowered the arm to the water and released the throat of his lifeless foe. The body calmly floated in the murky fluid. Diegert exited the pool.

"Oh my God, are you OK?" exclaimed Carolyn.

Diegert raised his finger to his lips and made a hand gesture, indicating that two more agents were still active. Carolyn composed herself while Diegert began searching the ground for something. She tapped him on the shoulder and held up Agent Peterson's pistol. Diegert nodded and took the weapon. He was surprised it was a Viper 9 mm, not the Glock 23, standard issue for the FBI. They exited the yard through the northern gate, moving away from the safe house and toward the entrance to Locust Circle. Entering the next yard, Diegert found a storage shed in the back corner of the property. The shed had a concrete floor and a wood frame, while the walls and roof were made of aluminum. Carolyn and Diegert entered the structure. The building did not have electricity, so as Diegert searched in the darkness, Carolyn turned on her phone's flashlight. There was an old lawn mower, a rolled-up garden hose, hand tools hanging on a rack, and shelves with typical things for the maintenance of a backyard. When he discovered an enticing combination of items, Diegert realized he could take the fight to the agents by drawing them into a trap.

In a whisper, he explained to Carolyn what he planned to do.

"Shh, just listen. I'm going to mix this bag of fertilizer with the gas in this can and ignite it with this extension cord. You will draw the agents into the building before I blow it up."

Carolyn followed him through the bomb-making part of the plan, but a look of doubt resided on her face in response to the second part of the plan. Reading her emotions, Diegert stepped to the back corner of the shed and, without much effort, pressed out an aluminum panel, creating a backdoor exit. Using hand signals, he pointed at her and gestured that this was her exit.

"When the bomb is ready, I want you to scream outside as loud as you can. Then come in here and bang on the walls, exit out the back, and run."

She looked at him with fear and suspicion, but he didn't acknowledge it. He smiled at her, patted her on the shoulder, and got to work.

He first took a three-tined hand rake and ripped open the bag of fertilizer that lay lengthwise on a shelf. He then jammed one of the metal tines from the hand rake into the receptacle end of the extension cord. This combined piece of equipment was then buried into the bag of granulated ammonium nitrate. A rusty coffee can on a shelf contained old nails, screws, small hinges, and other bits of metal hardware. The can's contents were dumped on top of the fertilizer. Diegert opened the gas can and poured gasoline into the fertilizer, making sure it penetrated into the depth of the bag and thoroughly mixed with the granules. The smell of gasoline permeated the shed and made Carolyn feel sick.

Holding up the three-pronged plug, Diegert whispered, "I'm going to the house to find an exterior outlet to plug this in." Pointing to her wristwatch, he told her, "In four minutes, you scream long and loud. Leave the door to the shed open. Bang on the walls like you're in a fight, then go out the back and run like hell." He waited for her reply . . . she seemed puzzled but then looked directly into his eyes, nodding her head.

Diegert tied off a section of the extension cord so it wouldn't pull out of the fertilizer. On a shelf, he found a hose nozzle spray gun and put it in his pocket. He exited the back of the shed and made his way to the rear of the house, rolling out the electric cord behind him.

Carolyn sat in the shed looking at her watch and feeling like four minutes was a very long time to be alone with Diegert's improvised explosive device. The nausea from the gas was getting worse, and she wanted to get the hell out of there. She realized, though, that she shouldn't rush her actions since the agents could be some distance away. Finally, the fourth minute passed, she cleared her throat, opened the shed door, and stuck her head outside. Like an actress auditioning for a horror movie, Carolyn let out a high, piercing scream. She screamed again and again before ducking back into the shed.

Diegert heard it. Talbot and Gates heard it as well. Over their comm unit, Talbot, who remained at the safe house, instructed Gates and Peterson, "Converge on the sounds to the northeast of your original position."

"Copy," Gates replied, and moved toward the house from which the sounds were emanating. Cautiously, he rounded the corner of the house and heard a struggle coming from a small shed in the corner of the yard. He heard another scream from inside the shed before it went silent. With his gun extended, he crossed the overgrown lawn. Diegert was crouched on the back deck next to an electrical outlet, ready to insert the plug. Gates stepped to the side of the shed's entrance and quickly peered in to determine if the space was clear. He flipped on his mini Maglite, illuminating the shed's interior. When Diegert saw the flashlight's beam, he inserted the plug, sending electricity across the lawn. It sparked when it hit the fork, igniting the fertilizer-and-fuel mixture, creating an explosion that ripped the building apart while dispersing ten thousand pieces of Gates's body all over the abandoned backyard.

Carolyn had underestimated the force of the explosion. She was struck by both the heat surge and a piece of aluminum shrapnel, which gashed her right shoulder. Stunned and bleeding, she moved along the hedgerow toward the street.

Chapter 18

An unexpected explosion of such magnitude shook Talbot as he turned to see the night sky of Locust Circle lit up by an intense fireball. He immediately put out a call to his agents, which got no response from either of them. Proceeding cautiously down the street, he needed to investigate the situation.

Stepping onto the street from the yard where the explosion had occurred, he saw a woman who appeared disoriented. Talbot closed on her quickly, grabbing her from behind and taking her down to the ground. She struggled, but he quickly had her hands bound behind her in flexi cuffs. Carolyn screamed from the pain in her shoulder. Talbot could see the injury, and he forced a second scream when he lifted her by the injured arm.

Diegert had pulled the plug and crept south along the back of the house. He heard Carolyn scream and continued in the direction of her painful shrieks. At the corner of the garage, he could see Talbot in the street tormenting Carolyn Fuller. Talbot shouted, "Diegert, get your ass out here now or this pretty lady pays in pain."

The belligerent FBI agent stood at the edge of the driveway scanning the area for Diegert's movement.

"Throw out your gun or I shoot her in the leg."

"Alright," shouted Diegert. "Here it is."

He tossed the hose spray gun out onto the dark driveway, where it landed with a loud clatter.

"Now you walk out real slow."

"I can't. . . I'm injured, I can't walk."

"Bullshit, fuckin' crawl out onto the driveway."

"Fuck you, you dishonest prick."

"Ha—look who's insulting who."

Diegert crawled slowly and convincingly onto the pavement of the driveway.

In the darkness, Talbot could just barely see Diegert appear on the driveway from around the corner of the garage. He walked up the driveway with Carolyn as a shield in front of him. When he was halfway up the driveway, a motion sensor triggered two bulbs, which flooded the asphalt with blindingly bright light. Carolyn ducked down from the brightness. Talbot let go of her, shielding his eyes with his left arm. Diegert had Agent Peterson's pistol ready and used the moment of illumination to fire a bullet, which hit Talbot's shoulder. The shot spun him to the right, and Diegert fired again. The force of the second projectile opened the FBI agent's cranium, and his brains spilled out when his big body fell back on the blacktop.

Diegert ran over to Carolyn and guided her out of the light and over to the edge of the driveway. He stepped over to Talbot's supine corpse and slipped his smartphone out from his jacket pocket. Crossing back to Carolyn, he looked at her wound and put some pressure on it. "Come on, Donovan has a first-aid kit in his car."

Walking back to the safe house, Carolyn began, "That's it? You just killed three men and now we walk away and bind our wounds?"

"What do you want me to do? Call the police so another hit team can be sent? Those guys weren't going to arrest us; they were going to kill us. Now I'm going to fix you up, and then we're getting the hell out of here."

"I've just never seen people killed like that before. I've been with the agency a long time, but I've never fired my weapon. It's just so sudden."

Diegert held the door for her as she stepped into the safe house. He set her in a kitchen chair and left to retrieve the first-aid kit from Donovan's car. In the trunk, Diegert found a change of clothes. His clothing was saturated in cesspool sludge, stinking like raw sewage. Back inside he changed his clothes and cleaned himself up before tending to Carolyn's injured shoulder. The wound was through the skin but not the muscle. The kit contained a local anesthetic and a fully threaded suture needle. "I'm going to stitch your cut."

Diegert injected the pain-blocking agent, and when she was numb to the touch, he sewed up the gap between the edges of skin. He covered the wound with antibacterial ointment and bandaged it up.

"Thanks," said Carolyn as she looked up into Diegert's eyes.

"Thank Jim; he's the one with the kit."

Carolyn rose from her seat and stood close to Diegert. "I want to thank you. Not just for the stitches but for everything you did tonight. I wouldn't have survived if-"

Carolyn's voice ceased. Her tears choked off her words and she began to cry. She leaned into Diegert as the sobs burst forth from her. Diegert held her and felt his own sadness, which had been building since Romania. The men he killed in the tournament, the hit in Germany, the president of the United States—and now his Mother was in the hands of Crepusculous. He felt the grief well up in him like the bubble of air from Peterson's lungs. Even though he wanted to hold it in, it had to come out. He wrapped his arms around this warm and vulnerable woman. He wanted to protect her while he also revealed his vulnerable side. Tears filled his eyes as the eyes of dying men played across his mind. The windows to the soul, whose light he had extinguished, now made him feel the pain he had inflicted not just on their bodies but on their psyches, their families, and their friends.

Carolyn was crying and sobbing, but she was quite bewildered when she felt Diegert crying and bellowing with the greatest anguish and despair she had ever witnessed in a man. The two of them filled the house with sounds of emotional turmoil. Carolyn couldn't support his weight, and they collapsed to the floor. They held and hugged, fully clothed, each lost in their private world of grief, shared but not revealed.

Carolyn's negative energy gradually dissipated, but Diegert was still releasing the pain he held inside. Carolyn found herself compassionately soothing the grieving man. She stroked his head and wiped his tears. She kissed his forehead and told him it was going to be OK. Her ministrations eased Diegert back from the tortured place to which his mind had traveled. He stopped crying and returned her caresses. They gently stroked one another on the head, face, and neck. Their bodies were entwined, hips pressed against one another, the pressure fueled by a primal urge. It was Diegert who was afraid of what might happen next between two adults in an emotionally charged moment. He reasoned that what might feel satisfying right now could compromise their survival. Always pragmatic when in danger, he knew they had to leave this place now. He avoided looking into her eyes; he also did not want to see her moist lips so close. He moved his hips away from hers, yet he could feel the heat of her body radiating between them when he separated from her.

Carolyn was aroused and confused. She was afraid she had misconstrued the emotional closeness for something more. She was attracted to this man and was experiencing a sexual desire that now felt awkward and out of place. She knew they were still threatened and had to leave right away. Still she felt his erection against her, and the feeling filled her with lust. She was both dispirited and grateful when Diegert said, "We gotta go."

Chapter 19

Dick Chambliss stood in a hallway of the headquarters of the Detroit Police Department reading a printed copy of the ballistics testing performed on the gun found in the holster of Alexi Strakov. The bullets matched those, which had killed President Peter Carson. This revelation changed the thinking about who was guilty of assassinating the president. A review of his background revealed that Strakov was an international freelance operator, sought for questioning in several high-profile killings in Europe. The focus on Diegert was still active, but authorities were divided and the public was now being fed conflicting stories. When this information began disseminating, Blevinsky had to move quickly to purge any records that connected Strakov to the Board. His fail-safe program dropped Strakov like a bag of garbage in a skyscraper's chute. The moment he presented a possible liability, he became a piece of discarded refuse.

Dick Chambliss called a conference with the FBI, CIA, and DPD. The absence of Jim Donovan and Carolyn Fuller made the meeting practically useless. The chief of police treated the Secret Service man like a houseguest whose dog had just taken a crap on the living-room carpet. He was furious that the security was so slack that the most important and imperiled man in the world was shot in his front yard. Detroit would never recover from the damage this would create for the city's reputation. He wanted to know how the Secret Service was going to publicly take the blame for this colossal failure. Chambliss didn't anticipate the public-relations attack. He dismissed the chief's concerns as shortsighted and unpatriotic. The two men left the meeting without even discussing the investigation; their animosity only further entrenched.

***

Untangling from each other and getting up off the floor was an awkward moment for Diegert and Carolyn. They both felt like embarrassed teenagers who'd experimented with carnal passion and now wanted to be as far away from each other as possible. All the regret with none of the joy.

"We've got to get out of here, and I have to find a way across the Canadian border."

"I can help you with that."

Diegert looked at her quizzically.

"I do work for the CIA—and espionage is our business. I've got what we need to cross into Canada."

"And you'd help me?"

"At this point, you're all I've got to figure this out. And I'm not letting you out of my sight."

Outside, Diegert had to pull Donovan's body across the driveway so Carolyn's car could exit the garage. She looked through the car's window at her friend's body being carefully but lifelessly dragged through a puddle of his own blood. The harshness of this business started to weigh on her again. Diegert came to the driver's side window. Carolyn gestured with her thumb to the back of the car. Diegert rolled his eyes and stepped to the rear. Carolyn popped the trunk and joined

Diegert, who was feeling claustrophobic looking into the cramped and uncomfortable luggage space.

"Just a minute," said Carolyn before she ran back into the house. A moment later, she returned with two couch cushions. She placed them in the trunk, and with an enticing flourish of her hand, invited Diegert to climb in. She closed the compartment and double-checked to make sure the magnets securely held the Ontario plates to the trunk lid.

Carolyn took Highway 75 to the Ambassador Bridge. US customs was performing an exit check before vehicles were allowed to cross. With her Canadian passport, windshield registration sticker, and Ontario plates, all she had to do was be polite and she would pass for a resident of the northern neighbor returning home from a business conference. Traffic moved at the expected but annoying crawl. Once lined up to cross the border, there was nothing to do but observe her fellow motorists. Diegert tried to sleep, but he was afraid he might not wake up, since a lot more exhaust fumes permeate the trunk than the cabin of a car. When Carolyn was second in line for the customs agent, she carefully watched the car in front of her. The car had Michigan plates and two male travelers. It was driven by a European-looking man with a salt-and-pepper beard. His passenger had brown skin, jet-black hair and a beard, but mostly he looked like he hadn't recently shaved. The agent took their documents, and after some time, another agent arrived with a sniffer dog who was allowed to circle the car. After the benign canine inspection, the agent asked the men to open the trunk. Carolyn could see the men were objecting to this request, and it looked like they were refusing to comply. Two more agents came to the scene, one standing by the passenger door, while the other took a position by the opening of the driver's door. The motorists were shouting and gesticulating inside the car, which only made the agents place their hands on their weapons. Carolyn was feeling the tension. As an intelligence agent, she could see the warning signs that concerned the customs agents, and the jerks in the car weren't making things any easier. Finally, the lead agent directed the car to drive to the inspection area. Two of the agents escorted the car behind a concrete wall, where the situation would be resolved without public observation.

Carolyn pulled her car up. The agent with the dog stood next to the primary agent, who asked Carolyn for her passport. While inspecting the document, he asked, "Where do you live?"

"Dutton, Ontario."

"The reason for your visit?"

"A business conference."

The dog rose from his seated position and began enthusiastically wagging his tail. The agent looked surprised to see his canine partner behaving like a happy puppy. He leaned forward to Carolyn's window and asked, "Ma'am, do you have a dog?"

"Not in the car, but I do at home."

"OK, thank you. He's still young," said the agent, referring to his dog. "He has a great nose for contraband, but he still gets excited when he smells another dog or someone with whom he wants to make a friend."

Carolyn looked up at the agent and just smiled.

"Is she OK, Mick?" he asked his human partner.

Handing back her passport, the primary agent said, "Yeah, you're all set."

Carolyn crossed the bridge, breezed through Canadian customs, and drove to a dark lot in a public park and let Diegert out of the trunk. As he stretched his body, he said, "I'll never volunteer to ride in a trunk again."

"You're here and you're free, so don't complain. What happens now?"

"Now?" He paused. "I've got to get to Montreal where my fake documents will get me on a flight to London."

"I'm coming with you."

"What?"

"You're still a wanted man, and even though there is some truth to what you've told me, you still shot the president. I helped you leave the United States, but I am not letting you fly off to Europe without me."

"Well good, because I had no idea how I was going to get to Montreal, but I want to ride in a seat this time."

***

Thermobaric bombs destroy with their initial explosions and then continue to kill people by consuming oxygen with super high temperatures. If you survived the explosion, asphyxiation from lack of oxygen would kill you. The Board planted nine bombs in nine cities in the United States. Only Klaus Panzer and Aaron Blevinsky knew the cities and the exact locations within those cities. Javier Perez, who was supposedly in charge of the operation, did not even bother to ask Blevinsky which cities were targeted. The bombs were timed to go off in simultaneous triplets. Each group of three was separated by one hour. The plan was to have the United States attacked nine times within three hours. The inflicted damage to infrastructure and transportation would cripple areas of the country. The chaos and confusion brought about by the disruption of communication would create disinformation and uncoordinated emergency responses. The multiple attacks on a wide variety of communities would create psychological fear and eviscerate America's sense of security. Americans would become refugees in their own homes. They would experience the ravages of war on their own soil like never before. Panzer was completely convinced that America would implode. The devastation would be too great for the weak fabric of the gluttonous nation. In its anemic state, the country would no longer be able to call itself the greatest nation on earth; instead, it would have to face the consequences of its decline. The overweight, in debt, morally bankrupt nation would, Panzer believed, turn on itself and fracture into battling tribes loosely associated along regional lines. Even these groups, though, would have such vast ideological differences that it was possible that the country—that was all about "me"—might very well degenerate into small warrior groups geared for survival like in a post apocalyptic dystopia. He could only hope it would be so, because his plan for dominance would be most effective in a society fractured into a multi-conflict civil war.

Blevinsky was getting impatient waiting for a status report from Talbot. He wanted current information, and hopefully good news, to give Panzer when he asked for an update. He texted Talbot: *Status report?*

***

While traveling east toward Montreal on Highway 401 with Carolyn, Diegert felt Talbot's phone buzz. Aaron Blevinsky's name popped up with a request for a status report. He replied, *We have Diegert. What action do you want taken?*

Blevinsky was ecstatic when he got Talbot's text. He replied, *Terminate him and send me a photo.* Diegert was not surprised by the answer, but he was surprised at how much the terse words hurt. Blevinsky had never been a friend, but he'd been like a coach. Diegert wanted the balding man's approval for the missions he completed. To be so completely and fatally rejected left him with a feeling of failure. He replied to Blevinsky, *Yes, sir.*

Diegert looked up from his texting and asked Carolyn to pull over at the next exit.

A tractor route into a hayfield provided the privacy they needed. Diegert lay on the ground, tilting his head to the side in the most uncomfortable and unnatural position he could manage. Carolyn took his picture. Reviewing the image, Diegert convinced himself he looked pretty dead. Carolyn told him to drive the car. By the time they got back to the 401, Carolyn had Diegert's image in her computer and was editing the photograph with a photo app so the assassin really looked dead. She made his skin pale, darkened under the eyes, and added a touch of jaundice. Dribbling out the nose and smeared at the corner of his mouth, Carolyn added blood, which gave the impression that Diegert's death was a violent one. She showed the image to Diegert, who asked, "Is that my future?"

"I hope not."

***

When Blevinsky received the photo, he was as happy as a kid was on Christmas morning. He published the image on the Web, announcing that Special Agent Stanley Talbot of the FBI had killed the assassin in a violent gun battle. Talbot's bravery and dedication to the investigation were to be commended, and the American people should be proud of this Federal law–enforcement agent.

***

When Carolyn read Blevinsky's posting, she was glad they were already past Toronto on their way to Montreal's Mirabel International Airport.

"How much do you make?" Diegert asked Carolyn as she drove through the night.

"You mean, what's my annual salary?"

"Yeah."

"Why do you want to know that?"

"Because I wonder what all this is worth to you?"

"Eighty-two thousand dollars a year, but that is not why I do this job."

"Why, then?"

"This will sound stupid to you but patriotism, loyalty, service to others."

"Did you get that out of a Marvel or a DC comic?"

"Shut up, you're in no position to judge me. You shot the leader of the free world, killing a great man. You've disrupted the entire country, and except for crying on the floor, I don't see a smidge of this weighing on your conscience. I don't think you're feeling this enough."

"Conscience: Right or wrong? Innocence or guilt? I couldn't consider these with the decision I had to make."

"Had to make? Or chose to make? You did not have to kill the president. You were alone and could've aborted the mission. You can't tell me there isn't a place in your heart that says that was wrong."

"A decision has to be assessed within the context of the situation. You think you understand this, and me. You have no idea, which surprises me, since I thought the CIA was better than that. The obvious and the easy always have to be investigated more thoroughly. Isn't that true?"

"You wanna convince me this was necessary, somehow unavoidable? Why did you pull the trigger?"

"That was the mission."

"Bullshit, you're hiding behind that. Why didn't you change the course of history and let the president live?"

Diegert didn't reply as he swiped the screen of his phone. His thoughts were swirling with a confused sense of need to have Carolyn understand his actions while also wanting to remain in control of his problems.

Carolyn grew impatient. "You have to answer my question; you're not getting a pass. You tell me why you shot the president."

Diegert scrolled through images on his phone until the picture of his mother, gagged with a gun at her head, appeared on the screen. With trembling hands, he looked at the image.

Through a shaky, choked-up voice, Diegert said, "I'm going to show you why I shot him. Pull over; I'm gonna drive."

Diegert took the wheel with Carolyn next to him as they got back on the highway. Diegert's phone lay on the center console.

"Look at my phone."

Carolyn examined the screen, then said, "Who is she and who's holding her?"

"She's my mother, and Crepusculous has her. That image popped up on my screen as the president took the stage. If I didn't shoot him, she would be raped, beaten, and killed. That was my dilemma."

Carolyn grew silent. She hung her head, ran her hand through her hair, as she sighed.

"Then I guess you've got more than one reason to be going after them."

"Damn right."

"Where is she now?"

"I don't know, but they still have her. They could be doing whatever they want to her."

Diegert slammed his fist on the dashboard.

"OK, OK, I'm sorry to have asked, but let's stick to our plan, because I think it will help you find her."

"You really think so?"

"I do."

"You know, I didn't tell you about this before, but I didn't pull the trigger on the gun that shot the president."

Carolyn turned her head, peering at Diegert with a don't give me that bullshit look.

"I swear to God. That gun was equipped with a remote sensor so someone else could fire it. You must've heard of this kind of technology?"

Carolyn nodded, but the doubt never left her eyes.

"I've heard of remotely operated weapons, but I've never seen them demonstrated or worked on a case in which they were involved."

Diegert continued, "When I saw it was the president, I decided I couldn't go through with it. After my mom's picture showed up on my phone, I had to point the gun in his direction, but I couldn't pull the trigger. The instant I failed to act, the gun fired automatically. Crepusculous controlled it."

Carolyn's doubt softened just a little, but she was confused about something. "You mean you didn't know the target was the president beforehand?"

"No. Everything for the mission was on a need-to-know basis. I was instructed where to go, what to wear, and what weapon to bring, but nothing else. Crazy, eh?"

"It's a little bit hard to believe, but it also makes sense if you're sending someone to do a job for which you're afraid they're not fully committed."

"It's total deceit and manipulation."

"So you really didn't kill him, you're an agent whose been used and was then targeted for elimination."

"I'm still targeted for elimination," said Diegert as he scanned Carolyn's face for some clue that she believed him. Her expression was dispassionate.

"I planted the remote-controlled gun on Alexi Strakov's body."

"And who is that?"

"Strakov was the leader of the Crepusculous tactical team. He was one big, mean motherfucker they sent to kill me after I killed the president."

"But that's not what happened, correct?"

"I killed him when he attacked the police station where I met Jim Donovan."

Carolyn put her head down and stroked her forehead as she recalled the death of her friend from the FBI and tried to keep Diegert's story straight.

Diegert continued, "By putting the gun on him, I started a disinformation campaign to make it look like he did it."

She pulled her head up and gave him a sidelong glance.

Diegert jumped in. "Look, Strakov was a very bad guy, and he deserves to be pegged as the president's assassin. He's going to be found dead with the gun in his possession, and when they search his background they'll find out he's an international assassin with multiple prior crimes."

"So you're OK with someone else taking the blame for what you did?"

Diegert thought for a moment as they progressed north on the 401, passing a tractor-trailer loaded with Canadian logs headed to a lumber mill. "If I'm identified as the president's assassin, my life is over, but if a man whose life is already over is seen as the assassin, then I am free to leave this violence behind and live a peaceful life. So, yeah, I'm OK with that."

"I don't exonerate you from the president's death. Even if I believe all that you've told me, you still entered the United States with the intention to kill someone, and that makes you a criminal."

Her words chilled Diegert's marrow. Was she going to turn on him here in Canada? Was she reconsidering helping him? Calling him a criminal, was she now going to be a cop? Diegert looked up as they passed under the sign indicating they were 2 kilometers to the Prescott Exit off the 401. It was open, desolate country; there would be dirt roads running into big fields separated by woodlots. He could do her; dump her, and just drive away, preserving his freedom. He looked at her, feeling a dark menace rising, but the thought made him sick. He felt regret and guilt for just thinking about it. The conflict was clouding his decision, and the exit, veering off to the right, was now visible.

Carolyn's words broke his frustration. "I think the fact that you are a criminal is actually going to be very useful to us.

Diegert twisted his head in surprise at what Carolyn had just said. He tweaked the wheel to the left, keeping the car on the highway.

Carolyn went on to say, "I can't promise a miracle, but there's a mechanism by which I can use you in the investigation."

"How? What do you mean?"

"At the CIA, we deal with bad people all the time. The little fish leads us to the big fish; that's how we topple large organizations. We call these little fish special field assets or SFAs."

Now Diegert's face was filled with doubt as he asked, "So when you catch the big fish, do you go back and take out the little fish too?"

"Yes, sometimes. But if the little fish continues to be useful and doesn't commit more crimes, we'll work with 'em for years, and they're never arrested."

"You think I could be one of those?"

"It's the mechanism by which I can justify what we're doing. But you better produce something big on Crepusculous."

Diegert thought about working for the CIA. It would be even cooler that the Special Forces, which was what he'd secretly hoped he would be able to do while in the Army. Now that that was never going to happen, perhaps this would be better. "Does it come with a salary?"

Carolyn looked at him in utter disbelief. "You don't get paid. You're not an employee. You're a double agent, a mole, an inside man who dishes on the organization in which you are embedded. The CIA is not going to hire you, but they aren't going to arrest you either, as long as you cooperate and provide good intel."

"Oh."

"You're not an agent, you're an asset, and your position within Crepusculous is what makes you valuable. You get it?"

"Yeah, but it's really no different than what we're doing right now."

"Correct, only I have to submit a profile and request permission to designate you as an SFA."

"If you submit a profile on me, they'll say either arrest him or shoot him."

"Actually, assets are most helpful in the early stages of an investigation before things become entrenched. It wouldn't be unprecedented to request this now."

Through the windshield, Carolyn saw a sign indicating a rest stop in five kilometers.

"If I'm hungry, you must be too," she said. Diegert nodded with enthusiasm. "OK, let's stop and eat."

As Diegert drove into the rest area, Carolyn directed him. "Drop me at the entrance and go fill up the gas, then park over there by those semis." She pointed to a dark, distant area of the parking lot where tractor-trailers sat. "I'll bring the food."

"Yeah, but you don't know what I want," said a petulant David Diegert.

"Too bad, you'll eat what I bring." She flung the door open and bolted out of the car.

Diegert put on his baseball cap and kept his head down so the gas cam wouldn't catch his face. After parking the car on the edge of the lot away from the building but not too close to the trucks, he took a piss in the weeds. Waiting for Carolyn in the car, he thought maybe he should just drive away. He still had impulses to run, to be alone, to be independent, but he realized all she'd have to do is call in the license plate and he'd be pursued. No, he would not run from her; she seemed to want to work with him to battle Crepusculous and help him get his mom back. Although it was hard for him to trust her, and believe she trusted him, he was going to have to ride this out. The passenger door opened, and Carolyn climbed in holding white paper bags exuding the warmth and greasy aroma of deep-fried fast food. Diegert smiled as he popped french fries into his mouth before taking big bites of a cheeseburger. With his mouth still full and smiling, he said, "You chose well."

Carolyn's Caesar salad wrap came with an apple.

Sitting in the car with the interior lights on, Carolyn was able to look at Diegert's face. She wanted to see his eyes while they spoke. Diegert sucked up soda through his straw.

"You gotta stop doing the dirty work of liars and untouchable thieves."

Diegert turned to her but kept drinking through the straw.

Carolyn continued, "When you work for the CIA, even as an asset, you work to protect people, and that's a purpose worth the risk."

Diegert nodded his head as he took another bite.

"Killing people must be a burden on your conscience. You do have one, don't you?"

Diegert chewed as he considered his answer; he felt she was reaching deep inside him, asking him to reveal his darkness, but he swallowed and looked her square in the eyes when he said, "I have a conscience. I feel the pain of my actions, but I've also had little choice under the circumstances in which I've been forced to kill."

"That sounds like an excuse."

"It's an explanation. I have killed to keep from being killed. I have killed in order to remain free. You've been the benefactor of these actions, and I wonder how you deal with the weight of it on your conscience?"

"Don't turn this back on me. I have a code and clearance sanctioned by the CIA. If I ever kill someone, it'll be in the line of duty under the rules of engagement associated with a mission."

Diegert allowed a smirk to curl across his lips. "Well, I hope every encounter you have fits within your rules, because every time I've pulled the trigger, there were no rules to guide me." He reached into his bag and gobbled a handful of fries.

"You need to develop your own code, David. You can't wield deadly force with no personal code. How do you decide if it's right or wrong to kill someone?"

Feeling pressed like never before, Diegert responded, "I don't shoot women or children, and the targets I've taken out were all guilty of crimes."

Carolyn locked her eyes on him as she chewed a bite of her wrap. With a measured tone, she asked, "And what was the president's crime?"

"Hey, I already told you I didn't shoot him."

"OK, no women or children, and you'll only shoot criminals."

"Right, that's what I've done and will continue to do."

"I'm going to make sure you do, David. I'm going to make sure you live up to that pledge."

Diegert pulled his gaze away from her and looked out onto the parking lot. He felt ambivalent about his pledge because a promise to act in a very specific manner was a promise he knew he'd be unlikely to keep. A loud slurp reverberated through his cup as he sucked the last of his soda.

Back on the road, Carolyn pulled out her computer and began typing up a profile and permission request for Diegert to become a special field asset.

As the miles persisted, Diegert thought about betraying the people at Headquarters. They were not trustworthy people. They were murderers, hackers, and unethical scientists pumped up on corporate power. It would be honorable to take them down, close the shop, and end their unique type of terror. Diegert figured his crimes would be justified if he now used his position to reveal and destroy the secrets of Crepusculous. Isn't the hero the one who put himself in danger to help others? Wasn't that what he'd been doing? Helping Carolyn and the CIA stop Crepusculous from destroying America would certainly be the work of a heroic person. Diegert began to see himself and the things he'd been doing from a different perspective. Instead of seeing a sad failure, clawing his way through survival, he began to realize that he was in a unique position to thwart the dark intentions of a criminal enterprise. If a poor boy from Minnesota could stop an evil empire from destroying the United States, then he should do so without fear or hesitation. Diegert caught himself from allowing his thoughts to go overboard when the theme from *Rocky* started playing in his head. Nevertheless, he had a lot to think about and the time to do it as the road to Montreal stretched out in front of him.

After passing the exit for Route 416 to Ottawa, the agrarian countryside of central Ontario gave way to the granite outcroppings of the Canadian Shield. Diegert was impressed with the cliff faces formed by the demolition of mountains of granite. Rock had been cleared to make the road, and the debris was crushed and dumped into the swampy hollows to level the bed upon which 830 kilometers of asphalt had been laid, creating Highway 401.Carolyn had been typing for nearly an hour.

"David, what unit of the Army were you with?"

"You better not tell them that."

"Look, I'm trying to make you look good, and I don't have a lot to work with. What was the unit?"

"1st Cavalry out of Fort Hood, The First Team."

"Your rank?"

"Private first class."

"OK, you know your Strakov theory might just be working. I've been monitoring a CIA information site, and Strakov's record is convincing certain people that he is a much more likely suspect than you. One of the assistant directors went so far as to say, "A dead bird in the hand is better than one on the wing.""

"His legend will grow with this crime," thought Diegert out loud.

"It's a long way before you're cleared, but that was a clever move to plant the gun on him."

"Well, that's a trick I learned from my brother; he was always pinning the blame on me."

Carolyn smiled and chuckled. "My brothers were always joshing around with each other. My older brother would set up my younger brother, and Mom would fall for it every time. Patrick would come out smelling like roses, while Michael took the heat and got in trouble. I developed my powers of observation watching those two."

"Sounds like fun. What about the rest of your family?"

Carolyn closed her computer and slid it back into its case as she turned in her seat to face Diegert. A comforting smile lit up her face, and a warm glow started to rise in her cheeks.

"OK, so my two older brothers, Patrick and Michael. They're both married. Pat has three kids, two boys and a girl. Mike has a son and a daughter. I have a younger sister, Laura. She's twenty-eight and, like me, not yet married. Boy, do we get it all the time about why aren't we married yet."

"Why aren't you?"

"That's another story. My dad's a dentist and my mom runs the office. They've worked together as long as they've been married. We just celebrated their forty-year anniversary. We kids sent them on a cruise through the Caribbean, and they had a great time. My parent's marriage is like the ideal. I want a relationship like they have, and it's hard to find, but I'm lucky to have a great family; they're the rock of my foundation."

Glancing over at her throughout her story, Diegert could see the pride and happiness her family inspired. The disappointment and dysfunction of his own family hung in his mind like an all-day rain cloud.

"What about you? Tell me about your family."

Diegert glanced over with a wan smile and turned back to concentrate on the white lines zipping past the car, saying nothing.

"So tell me some more about your brother," persisted Carolyn.

Diegert scratched the back of his head and ran his fingers through his hair. He wondered if he should lie and make his family sound nice. Carolyn had something about her, though; he didn't want to lie to her. Diegert was usually very suspicious of anyone who made him feel this way, but it had been a very long time since he'd felt the beginnings of a sense of trust.

"My brother, Jake, is a drug dealer. He's short, fat, and loud. He's my dad's favorite, and he uses that fact to his advantage on a daily basis. He makes sure my life is as miserable as he wants it to be. I have never trusted him the whole time we were growing up."

Carolyn's smile and jovial expectation faded. "I'm sorry to hear that."

"Well, you're going to love this. My dad is a drunk. He has a tow-truck business in northern Minnesota, which makes no money. He hates me, but at least he has a reason. The man's never been a father to me, and I will be glad if I never see him again."

"Gee, that's harsh. You said he had a reason not to like you; what do you mean by that?"

"That would be my mother. She's tall, beautiful, half white, half Ojibwa Indian."

"Yeah, yeah, I saw the picture on your phone. In spite of the dreadful circumstances, I could see she's a beautiful woman."

"Her beauty is exotic, but it has never been anything but trouble for her. She's emotionally crippled and struggles with a lack of confidence. Her self-esteem is assaulted on a regular basis by my dad, who treats her like a domestic slave. She works her ass off waitressing at a local diner where she's happy to put in extra shifts just to avoid being home. The two of them are financially dependent on each other, but they live on opposite sides of an emotional canyon with jagged rock walls that are a hundred feet high."

"I still don't see why he should hate his own son."

"Because I'm not."

"What?"

"I'm not his true son." Diegert let that statement hang in the air. As he watched her struggle to re-enter the conversation, he could see the CIA investigator in her want to ask the probing questions. This was not an interrogation, though, and she did not pursue the question. Diegert recognized her dilemma and offered the answer.

"My mom got knocked up through an illicit affair, but they stayed together and the bastard son was tolerated but never accepted or loved by Tom Diegert."

Diegert looked her way, and Carolyn caught his eyes and held his gaze. She started to nod very slowly, and Diegert felt that simple gesture carried more meaning than any other communication he'd ever had on this topic. That comfort, that sense of acceptance and belief she seemed to have in him, was a feeling he couldn't recall with anyone else. Part of him wanted to stop the car and run away, the other part wanted to drive forever with Carolyn and leave the real world behind.

"You love your mom, though."

"Yes, I do. She's the one person I can count on to help me, and who loves me no matter what. I hate the fact about how I was conceived, but I love that she didn't give up on me. I know she sacrificed and struggled to raise me as best she could."

Carolyn's warm smile broadened to hear this man speak so reverently and respectfully of his mother in spite of being the product of a passionate transgression.

"You're part Ojibwa, then, that's cool."

Diegert shot her a look as sharp as shattered glass. "No. Definitely not cool."

The silence amplified their distance on this topic as Carolyn was unable to disguise her surprise. "I'm sorry, I mean, having a different culture as part of your heritage is very interesting."

"Oh, fucking bullshit. Different cultures tend to hate each other, especially when one invades and dominates the other. People think racial prejudice is only in the South, but that's because they haven't spent time in the North. The Indians and the white people do not get along, and a half-breed is an affront to both sides. I was abused by both cultures; that's how fucking interesting it was growing up as a *halfsy* in Broward Minnesota."

Carolyn sat silently, keeping an eye on him with a sidelong glance. Diegert stewed in his anger over his biculturalism, gritting his teeth and knotting up his jaw muscles. He eventually spoke again.

"Look, I'm sorry to go off on you, but you hit a nerve, and I have a lot of baggage from the past."

"Yeah, I can tell. Don't you want to let that go? Wouldn't it be better to move beyond it?"

The perplexed look on Diegert's face pleaded for further explanation.

Carolyn continued, "We all have bad experiences from the past. Growing up, you have to experience some bad things so you can tell the difference and find your place on controversial issues. Now, granted, it sounds like your situation was especially bad, but you're an adult now. Don't you want to move past your childhood?"

Diegert said nothing; he just nodded.

"I remember learning about the Ojibwa people in school," offered Carolyn. "They are very spiritual, with . . . I think, seven principles by which they live."

"The seven gifts of the Anishnabe: love, respect, bravery, honesty, humility, wisdom, and truth."

"Whoa! That's impressive. If you can commit those to memory, can't you incorporate them into your life? I gotta believe good things would happen if you did."

"That's easier said than done."

"Everything's easier when only said. In Quantico, we ran five-mile obstacle courses that made a Tough Mudder look like a day in the sandbox. They wanted us to push ourselves through adversity and find the determination to never give up."

Diegert countered saying, "At Fort Benning, we ruck sacked ten miles a day for seven days, slept on the ground, and avoided an op force the entire time."

"I'm not trying to say who's tougher, and I know you can withstand pain, but living by principles is also tough. But it produces good things just like difficult training."

Diegert looked at her as she waited for him to respond. He reached under his collar and pulled his amulet out from under his shirt. The seven colored beads strung on both sides of the medallion caught Carolyn's eye. Diegert told her, "Each bead represents one of the seven gifts, and the medallion has an inscription on the back."

He pulled the necklace over his head and handed it to her. She received it with delicate care in her open hands. The leather was soft and warm; it retained the heat from Diegert's body. The dark bottom half of the circle contrasted with the white top half, and the human foot that traversed both halves almost seemed to be in motion. Carolyn turned the amulet over and saw the inscription.

"This is written in Ojibwa."

"It says: "A man must travel through darkness to find the light.'"

"So that's what you're doing? Seeking the light? Traveling through darkness and killing people along the way?"

"Kind of a twisted vision quest, eh?"

"More like a criminal quest. You've got to get a focus and follow a principle or you'll never even find the light switch. As a field asset, you can help us because you're already in there with the criminals."

"Don't forget the criminals are trying to kill me."

"You're still in their dark world, but maybe fighting them will help you find that light."

Carolyn handed him back the necklace. Diegert clutched it in his hand.

"You're a complicated and conflicted man, David Diegert."

"Yeah, I've heard that one before."

"You have skills and abilities that the agency trains men for years to develop, yet you have no guiding principles to discipline your actions. You're like a wild mustang, strong and fast but unable to be of any good in a civilized life."

Diegert looked over at her, fighting the urge to neigh like a horse. He held up the amulet, saying, "I want out of the darkness, and I'm humble enough to ask for your help finding the light."

Carolyn's expressionless reaction left Diegert wondering if she believed him or doubted his sincerity.

"Alright, David, you're on. I want you to come out of the darkness, but you'll have to follow my lead to the light; I can't force you to go."

Diegert strung the necklace over his head and left it hanging outside his shirt. "I'm with you."

"How much farther to Montreal?"

"About forty miles."

Carolyn tilted the seat back and rolled up her jacket on the headrest, turning away from Diegert to take a nap.

Diegert thought about the seven gifts. He'd memorized them but rarely considered their meaning. Carolyn got him to contemplate the role of the gifts in his life. He thought of humility and how one must recognize that there is much you do not know and be willing to be taught. Honesty, defined as the habit of being truthful. The truth for Diegert was not always clear; it was dependent on the situation.

Bravery, though, brought his thoughts to an uncomfortable place. He wanted so much to believe he was brave. He thought he was brave when he went on missions by himself behind enemy lines and battled attackers without any help, but the Ojibwa definition was not about individual heroics. Ojibwa beliefs on bravery dealt with the fact that you are terrified that you are not good enough and that others will find out. Bravery is to look at your innermost self and face the fact that you consider yourself unworthy and then find the way to true inner strength and acceptance.

Unworthy and not good enough were two feelings Diegert knew very well. How could he not, since this was all he felt from the time he was a little boy, bashed about by his father and brother. Feeling that he was a valuable person was a figment of vapor. He had no context in which to place such a concept, yet he was beginning to realize that without a belief in one's own worth, it was impossible to see the value in anyone else. Now he had to find a sense of self-worth and value while escaping from several law enforcement agencies and stopping Crepusculous from carrying out the rest of its plan.

Chapter 20

Making her way through London's Heathrow Airport, Fatima saw the image of a dead David Diegert on a television in one of the terminal's pubs. She gasped out loud, startling the people around her when the grisly image registered. David was dead. Her student, her pupil, her protégé was now deceased and pilloried in the worldwide media, hung up like big game to bleed out. She was overcome with the despair she felt for the loss of someone she had grown to admire and respect. That callous image of his injured face was disturbing, but a hopeful thought took form that perhaps Diegert was pulling a ruse and might not actually be dead. The indifference and delight with which people were celebrating his death left Fatima feeling conflicted.

***

Carolyn bought tickets to Heathrow on an Air Canada flight under a Canadian identity as Marnie and Ian Taylor from Chelsea, Quebec. Carolyn provided Diegert with a disguise from the espionage kit in her car. With the skills of a theater makeup artist, she had turned his hair gray and given him a beard and mustache. The look matched the Canadian passport she fashioned for him, and Diegert couldn't believe how well the change in appearance worked as he cleared customs for the London-bound flight.

They waited together in the terminal for the flight to board. "We need to rent a place, preferably one outside the city."

Carolyn opened her laptop and found a site featuring cottages in the English countryside. "This one's only twenty minutes from central London."

"OK, rent it for the whole week. Then rent a car, and we'll be ready."

"Are we still going to kidnap that kid?"

"We are liberating him and returning him to his mother."

"You can convince yourself of whatever you want, but it's not right."

"Look, I'm an expert at convincing myself of things."

Over the PA, their flight was called for boarding. Diegert stood up with his bag and could see the doubt in Carolyn's face. "I'll see you in London."

As he walked to the gate, Carolyn wondered if his statement was one of hopeful expectation or a question. She sat for a few moments, realizing she could end this right here. She could skip the flight, report him to authorities, and have him taken into custody right now. His arrest would fulfill her CIA obligations. But then she thought of the bigger plan Diegert was determined to stop, and she realized she could save many more Americans by helping him stop whatever was happening. What she had to deny was that any of this was being done because she was attracted to him. She had to convince herself that any desire for David Diegert was delusional and not the motivation for her actions. She got up and boarded the flight.

***

The assistant director of the FBI in charge of national investigations was Madeline Anderson, a fifty-four-year-old seasoned agent who was director of the West Coast Division of the Bureau for nine years before taking the national position. Dick Chambliss had her on a secure Skype call, and the polite levelheaded Secret Service officer was summarizing for the FBI the problems as he saw them.

"We are not in charge of this investigation. We're being overrun with unsubstantiated media that is broadcasting unconfirmed information as evidence. We are reacting to these things rather than conducting an investigation as we all know we should."

"What do you see as our primary issues at this time?" asked the perturbed assistant director, who was not used to being dressed down about the operation of the Bureau.

"We need clarity on several issues; the report of the David Diegert/Matthew Wilcox character being dead; the location of Agent Talbot, from whom we need an official statement; and the identity of the dead man with the gun that shot the president? These are all issues which have risen from social media but need to be cleared by authorities."

Chambliss observed Anderson lower her face and scratch her forehead. He continued.

"Simultaneously, we need to interview the supervisors on the scene for Eagle Talon Security who handled the outer perimeter and review all available video surveillance within one square mile of the president's address. We need eyes and information so we can understand the conditions at the time of the shooting."

Having listened to his summary, the assistant director stated, "Dick, I will personally direct this investigation, and I will update you each hour."

Chambliss replied, "Thank you, this is the most substantial crime of our lifetimes. We want to get it right."

***

Sitting in the deep leather chair in the London office of his friend and fellow Crepusculous partner Dean Kellerman, Klaus Panzer couldn't take his eyes off the image of David Diegert's dead face. Mysteriously, there was something familiar about his features that were welling up memories so faded that Panzer couldn't tell if they were figments or actual recollections.

"Really, Klaus, it is a bit morbid the way you're transfixed by that gruesome sight."

"Forgive me; I'm a bit preoccupied with this man's death."

"Diegert was a cheeky bastard. He was the one who single-handedly rescued Andrew Cambridge from the Baltic Mob." After deeply inhaling and swallowing another aromatic sip of his brandy, Kellerman continued, "Perhaps we'll be able to find another one like him soon."

Panzer turned to look at the screen again, and the instant his eyes were on it his brain went to work trying to match that image with one of the millions and millions of memories stored in his cortex. Not being one who tolerated unresolved issues, Panzer secretly hoped that Diegert was not dead so he could confront the man and determine the source of his conjecture.

Chapter 21

At Heathrow, Carolyn and Diegert moved through customs without incident and secured their rental car. As Diegert drove to the cottage, an exasperated Carolyn muttered under breath, "Damn it."

"What's wrong?"

As she looked at her phone screen, Carolyn explained, "Back in Montreal, I sent my request for you to be classified as a special field asset."

"They're not buying it."

"No. In fact, they insist I arrest you immediately and call in FBI agents to take you into custody."

"They still think we're in the US."

"Well, I didn't give them any reason to think otherwise."

"So we proceed just the same as if they had said yes. I'm a CIA asset, and I'll act like one."

"If you don't, the message authorizes me to use deadly force."

Her statement shocked him back to the harsh realities of what they were doing. "All right, then, let's hope it doesn't come to that."

Arriving at the cottage, they found the little house well-appointed and comfortable. The bathroom was clean and stocked with thick, soft towels.

"Look, I've had to smell you for the last thirty-six hours, and it's time for you to get rid of the gray hair and fake beard. Hit the shower, would ya?"

When a sniff of his armpits producing a wrinkled nose, Diegert nodded and began peeling the beard off as he headed to the bathroom.

Carolyn opened the computer and connected to the internet. She was searching maps of the area to get her bearings. As she looked up from the screen, she noticed light emerging from the short hall that led to the bathroom. The volume of light told her the door to the bathroom was still open. She knew she should be polite and stay where she was, but the curiosity was too great— besides, she should check and make sure David didn't need anything. She stepped toward the hall quietly, and as she neared the corner, she could see through the open door. In the mirror, she saw Diegert drop his black combat pants and pull down his underwear. His buttocks were reflected, and she reacted to the strong-looking muscles of his ass with a gulp in her throat. David kicked his clothes into a pile and turned around to face the mirror. Carolyn was able to secretly see his entire body in the mirror's reflection. Diegert was fit, muscular, and handsome. The long scar on his thigh looked nasty, and he had bruises on his ribs, which he turned toward the mirror to inspect. He winced as he pressed on the darkest areas of injury. His abdomen was lean, rippled, and without fat. The muscles converged from his hips down to his crotch where his penis hung.

Diegert spun away from the mirror and turned on the shower, adjusted the temperature, and stepped in. Carolyn stood there with all intentions of going back to the computer, but she lingered, drawn to the possibility her mind couldn't let go. She knew Diegert was a criminal, but his mission was redemptive. She hadn't been with a man for so long, and no man she had ever been with had a physique like his. The masculine frame and muscular contours created erotic images in her mind, which were arousing her body. The hug and cry, and the memory of his body on the safe house floor, converged with her thoughts to produce a flow within her. She stepped to the threshold of the bathroom, and the sound of the cascading water pulsed in her brain like the coursing of her blood. Crossing in, she removed her shoes, unbuttoned her blouse, and undid her pants. With her outer garments on the floor, she looked in the mirror and the reflection of him moving behind the translucent shower curtain, his form tantalized her to remove her bra and panties. Feeling bold and fully aroused, she slid the shower curtain back, surprising Diegert with her naked body.

He stopped rubbing the soap between his hands and stepped back, making room for her to step in. She locked her gaze onto his eyes and loved the way his lids pulled back. She smiled at him and giggled a little as the water splashed on her back and ran over her shoulders, dribbling off her nipples. She leaned her head back under the showerhead to wet her hair. With her eyes closed and her face turned up to the ceiling, she could feel Diegert's eyes inspecting every inch of her. She exercised regularly to keep her thirty-two-year-old body in top shape. She needed to not only qualify for the CIA fitness standards, but she was an avid cyclist and swimmer. She knew her athletic curves drew admiring looks from appreciative guys.

Soaking her hair darkened her brunette locks, which she smoothed away from her face as she opened her eyes and looked at Diegert. She reached a hand out and tenderly caressed his injured ribs. He tensed as she touched the painful bruises but relaxed when he felt how gentle she was. She made a sad pouty face that told Diegert she was sympathetic to his pain. Looking deeply into each other's eyes, they brought their bodies together in a close embrace. The feel of skin on skin under the flow of warm water was delightful to both of them, and they stayed like that for several quiet minutes. Carolyn began stroking Diegert's body, running her hands up his back, down over his buttocks, and onto the back of his thighs. Likewise, Diegert caressed her body, following the flow of water over the contours of her hips, back, and thighs. Their mutual exploration aroused and excited them both.

Carolyn was relieved to find that Diegert was a patient lover, which made her feel safe and more erotic. She turned her face to his, and they kissed deeply and passionately. They were both overtaken by the lustful feelings that blossomed when their mouths touched. As their bodies pressed tightly against each other, their passion found an undulating rhythm. Soon Diegert lifted Carolyn, and she positioned his shaft inside her. The two lovers celebrated the pleasure they felt in their strong fit, bodies, following their passion to a climactic orgasm that left them both shuddering, satisfied, and momentarily exhausted.

When Carolyn's feet returned to the bathtub floor, she leaned in against Diegert, and they hugged each other warmly while they relaxed in their sexual denouement.

"That was wonderful," said Carolyn.

"I think we both needed that."

She hugged him tighter and pressed her face into his shoulder. She then looked up at him, saying,

"Honestly, I stepped in here for the sex, but I didn't know it would be that good."

"You're a beautiful woman, and I appreciate your boldness. It was good for me too."

Reaching for a bottle of shampoo called Botanical Bouquet, Carolyn started washing her hair.

Diegert coughed.

"What's wrong?"

"That stuff smells really floral."

"Floral! Well, I think it's nice. It's the only shampoo in here, so you used it already, didn't you?"

"Well, yeah, but only because there was no other choice."

"I think maybe deep inside you like Botanical Bouquet," teased Carolyn.

"Yeah, I like it so much I'm getting out of here right now."

Diegert pulled the curtain, climbed out, dried himself, and left to get dressed.

Carolyn rinsed her hair and stood in the hot water contemplating the complications of what she had done. It had felt so good, but as the passion subsided, she knew it was so wrong in so many ways.

Chapter 22

All four Board members of Crepusculous were visible on the video screen as Klaus Panzer began to address them from his London Office. "This is an auspicious day when Crepusculous will assert its strength. The work to make this second phase of our plan a success has been done, and we will now commence."

Dean Kellerman, Julio Perez, and Chin Liu Wei sat in front of keyboards in their respective offices awaiting the signal for the simultaneous initiation of the greatest plunge in value the New York Stock Exchange had ever seen. The simultaneous initiation was necessary to bypass fail-safe software that would automatically shut down the stock exchange when massive movements were attempted. The Board controlled 20 percent of the value of the stock market. This was accomplished through the holding of many subsidiaries and diversified portfolios, as well as hedge funds and amalgamated property funds, that it's reach and penetration was unseen by regulators. Additionally, they had corrupted significant people in the Security and Exchange Commission. The dishonest regulators needed only to be slow at responding. The initial action would precipitate a cascade of panic selling so that the majority of the losses wouldn't be directly associated with the Board's actions but rather only instigated by them.

In an earlier meeting, Julio Perez had asked about the wisdom of this act, and he was told that the end product of this action would have all the currency in the world under the control of Crepusculous. Mr. Wei's fears were similarly allayed when he was reminded that China already embraced several forms of digital currency, all of which were pegged to the dollar. Digival would replace all of them and keep happy all the customers already convinced of the convenience of digital currency.

Klaus looked at the three pairs of eyes on the screen and the lights at the bottom, which would indicate that the member had actually pressed the "Enter" key, and said, "Gentlemen, let's change the world."

All four "Enter" keys were simultaneously depressed at eleven thirty a.m., Eastern Time, and the transactions put into play removed 20 percent of the value of the New York Stock Exchange. The clamor was immediate; people were both frantic and completely dumbfounded as the proverbial rug was yanked out from under them. Brokers and traders, fund managers and regulators, watched as the irrational become reality. The wealth they had so painstakingly worked to build vanished into the ether. The regulatory delay allowed the exchange to free-fall for thirty-five minutes before all trading was halted. In that period of time, the Board had grabbed all their marbles and gone home. Wall Street was awash in confusion as money men tried to figure out what just happened. Business journalists started reporting before they really knew what had taken place.

Suspicions and possibilities were broadcast as probabilities. Computer glitches were blamed, which gave people immediate hope that the glitch would be fixed and everything would return to normal. Terrorism was reported, and the NYPD Emergency Services Unit was dispatched to see if guys in cool uniforms with automatic weapons could change the situation. The chairperson of the Securities and Exchange Commission, Katherine Smithfield, was called from a meeting and informed of current events. She reviewed the list with her subordinates of all the stop action procedures they had and was assured they had all eventually been enacted. The president, who was meeting with her cabinet restructuring the government, was informed of the crash, forcing her to change the focus of the cabinet meeting.

Presidential staffers compiled statistics of the impact while projecting possible ramifications for both the economy and national security. To the president, this disaster so close to the assassination was starting to look like an act of economic terrorism. As the hours passed, the blogosphere predicted economic Armageddon and the end of the world as it was known. The president had to make an appearance and send a calming message. From the Rose Garden, President Stanwix told the American people, "We have suffered an unprecedented drop in the value of the stock market. All Federal officials involved in the regulation and management, of not only the market but the entire economy, are working on nothing but figuring out what happened and how we can move forward. I want the citizens of the United States to know that the full efforts of the Federal government are working to understand this event and secure our economy and our nation. Many of you, like me, are still caught in the emotional shock wave of the loss of Peter Carson. I hope you find in his legacy the strength and resolve that inspires me to face this challenge with determination and fortitude. For most of you, your day-to-day personal finances are separate from the stock market, and thus you still have funds at your disposal to continue your lives. I ask you to reflect on that fact and remain calm and civil while we figure this out and report back to you. Thank you for your time and attention. God bless the United States of America."

The panic removed 60 percent of the value of the NYSE, producing a drop in the Dow Jones Industrial Average of 80 percent. The Dow dropped from 18,567 to 3,113. The evaporation of wealth exceeded the drop that had triggered the Great Depression of the 1930s, and the public was angry that technology was not able to stop the run. People were dismayed at the possibility that they may have actually lost all their investments: retirement funds, pension plans, and college tuition accounts. With the presidential assassination still an open wound, this disaster was nothing short of a saline rub on raw flesh. The sun was going to rise tomorrow, but for many Americans, that was the only thing of which they were certain.

***

"I have Hamni's address," stated Diegert. "If we're there in two hours, we'll arrive during a shift change, and I can extract him. Here, you can study the map."

Carolyn looked at the map with the route to the address where Hamni resided and could see that it wasn't far. The place was called St. James Home. The website described it as a home for children with developmental needs.

"What kind of needs does Hamni have?" she asked.

"I don't know."

"Maybe I should be the one to pick him up."

"You think so?"

"I don't think you're someone the staff would trust or Hamni would feel secure with. It's all about you being a tough guy; people don't instinctively trust you."

"Well, OK, but take my phone, there's a convincing video of Fatima you can use."

As they drove through London, Carolyn read a newsfeed on her phone. "My God, the New York Stock Exchange just crashed."

"Really? How much?"

"They aren't sure, but a lot. It says here more value was lost than in 2008, and that this could be worse than the 1929 crash that started the Great Depression."

"It's phase two," said Diegert. "Crepusculous is behind it. They're destroying the US economy. We better hurry."

The staff of St. James Home changed shifts at six p.m. after the children had their evening meal. The dining hall was connected to the residence halls by interior walkways, but when the weather was nice, the children could also get there by walking through the sylvan grounds of the 110-year-old facility. Today was a beautiful, sunny day. Carolyn walked through the wrought-iron gate after showing the guard her British driver's license. Once inside, she reviewed the picture of Hamni that Diegert had lifted from Fatima's phone. Dressed in business casual attire, she walked the grounds carrying a briefcase.

A line of children emerged from the dining hall, but the expected enthusiasm of running and shouting was replaced with shuffling gaits, awkward faces, and hands occupied by nervous ticks as the children walked on the concrete paths. No adults appeared until three exited pushing wheelchairs. Scanning the children, Carolyn didn't see Hamni. Only after all the rest of the children emerged did a boy and a girl slowly step out into the warm autumn weather. The boy had black hair and very dark eyes. His skin was a dark-olive complexion and he walked with a stiff upright gait with his head held high like an ostrich scanning the Serengeti. Carolyn recognized him in an instant and initiated her plan.

Approaching Hamni was a tricky first step. Carolyn smiled at the adults pushing the wheelchairs as she passed them. She was friendly yet purposeful, which gave the adults a sense that she seemed to know what she was doing. Hamni's observant mannerism was just that, a habit without the expected outcome; he would, in fact, not make eye contact with anyone.

"Hamni," said Carolyn . "I'm here to take you to go visit your mother."

The boy listened but did not respond. Carolyn pulled out her smartphone and played the video Fatima had sent Diegert. The video was a selfie of Fatima saying, *"Hey, I know you're facing some tough decisions, but I . . . believe in you. I look forward to seeing you soon."*

When Hamni saw his mother's face and heard her voice, he immediately got so excited he began gesticulating and vocalizing in ways that surprised Carolyn. His actions also drew the attention of the staff. The three adults, two women and a man, stopped pushing the wheelchairs and looked back at Hamni's expressions and the woman who was speaking to him.

"Can I help you?" asked the man, who was of Middle Eastern descent.

"Yes, thank you," said Carolyn. "I'm here to pick up Hamni, because his mother is in the hospital and she wants to see him. She told me it was important for Hamni to be told of this first. Can you direct me to the control desk where I can sign him out?"

All three of the staff members looked at Carolyn quizzically as she waited for directions. Hamni was excitedly looking at the picture of his mother on Carolyn's phone and anxiously pulling on her sleeve. The Middle Eastern man was torn between escorting them and abandoning the child in the wheelchair.

"Hamni knows where to go. He is a very smart boy; he'll take you to Gibson Hall."

"Gibson Hall?" Carolyn repeated as Hamni led her away by the sleeve. "Thank you," she said as Hamni waved to the staff, who returned to pushing the wheelchairs and gossiping.

The control desk was staffed by Mildred Faber, who could see that Carolyn had the right papers from the hospital indicating that Fatima was admitted and requested Hamni's release to come visit. Diegert had forged these documents on the flight.

"The last thing I'll need," said the efficient Miss Faber, "is your ID."

Carolyn was so very grateful for the time she had invested in putting together her CIA alternative documents package, which was always in the trunk of her car. She handed Miss Faber her British driver's license, and when it was returned, she walked out holding Hamni's hand.

Diegert pulled up as they exited the front gate of St. James. When they got back to the cottage, Diegert called Fatima.

"Hello," she answered.

"This is David."

"Diegert?"

"Yes."

"What about being dead?"

"A gross exaggeration. I used an opportunity to throw Blevinsky off my trail. Please don't divulge my survival?"

"I won't. Where are you?"

"First, I want to thank you for the video message you sent me. I really appreciate what you said, and it certainly was exactly what I needed to get me through this ordeal."

Fatima felt a sudden softness in her heart that hadn't been there for a long time.

"You're welcome. I could see that Crepusculous turned on you, and I thought you were probably feeling betrayed. I want you to know I wasn't in on the betrayal."

"You know, when you said you believed in me, that really meant a lot and helped me out. Thanks."

"So where are you?"

"I'm in London."

"London! Where? How did you get here? That's amazing!"

"Right now, I'm in Shetland, but, Fatima, I have someone with me. Get ready to receive a picture."

Pointing his phone at Hamni, he said, "We're going to send your mum a picture, OK?"

Hamni didn't actually look directly into the camera, but his face was unmistakable. Diegert sent the picture to Fatima. Her voice came through the phone like an acidic flame.

"I am going to kill you, David Diegert. I am going to see your life end. What are you doing with Hamni? He has special needs, and if you have him out of his home environment for long, he won't be able to handle it. You idiot, what are you doing?"

"Fatima, I want you to believe in me like you said you did. I know Crepusculous has plans."

Fatima screamed her interruption.

"Crepusculous! Fuck them—what are you talking about? You've made a terrible mistake, and Hamni is going to suffer. I'm gonna hurt you so bad, Diegert. This is not a game; you have violated my family."

"Fatima, please hear what I have to say."

"I'm going to hear what you have to say, and then I'm going to kill you anyway."

"Crepusculous plans to attack the United States. I don't know exactly how, but it is going to be big and we need to stop them."

"Oh great, now we're heroes saving the whole damn world, and you've kidnapped my son in the process. This makes absolutely no sense!"

"Fatima, I believe Javier Percz has critical information about the next phase of the attack."

"Phase—what phase?"

"The assassination of the president, the stock market crash, those were phases one and two, and the next phase will be bigger, affecting more people."

"So fucking what? What are you asking me to do?"

"I want you to infiltrate Javier's place and acquire intel about what's next. We need to know what the plan is so we can interrupt it."

"You're acting on a hunch. You have no evidence that Javier knows anything about this."

"You're right, but it makes sense. Javier is going to inherit his father's seat. This is the biggest thing Crepusculous has ever done. It makes sense that the up-and-coming guy would have an important role to play."

"OK, I see it makes sense to you, but it could be totally wrong, and you're forcing me to do something or else you're going to hurt Hamni."

"I'm asking you to get information from Javier, and I'll reunite you with Hamni. You can have the mother-child relationship you've been wanting for so long. He is free of Crepusculous and wants to be with you. Call me back after you've got information from Javier."

Diegert ended the call and turned to Hamni. "Your mum has been delayed. We're going to stay here while we wait for her. OK?"

Hamni's wondering eyes avoided Diegert's face as he started swaying his head back and forth.

"You're a real bastard, you know that?" said Carolyn.

"Yeah, more than you know."

Chapter 23

"Now that Diegert's dead, what do you want me to do with his mother?" Blevinsky asked Panzer. Leaning back in his leather chair, the German tapped his phone against his chin.

"I want her here in London," he told his chargé d'affaires.

"Excuse me," replied Blevinsky. "Did you say London, sir?"

"Yes, I want her here in London and held in comfort. She's not to be mistreated."

On the other end of the phone, Blevinsky was mouthing a litany of silent curses as he had to figure out the logistics of yet another complication in this circus of disasters. Back on the phone, he replied to Panzer, "Yes, sir, I'll inform you of her arrival."

"Good man, Aaron, thank you."

***

Fatima dressed in her black operations outfit. The clothes fit snuggly and were made of Kevlar-reinforced fibers, so they were tough and resistant to tears, abrasions, and bullets. She wore a belt with pouches for necessary items like trank spray, extra ammo, incendiary devices, and formed explosives. Hung over her shoulder was a thirty-foot length of super strong, ultra-light climbing line. Sneaking into Javier's place would involve a stealth entry and quite likely some rough encounters for which she would be well prepared with her Beretta M9 on her hip.

The Perez town house was surrounded by a high wrought-iron fence and patrolled by two guards at night. Under the cover of ten p.m. darkness, Fatima found access by zipping across the power lines, scaling the wall, and dropping onto a balcony from the roof. The balcony serviced an unoccupied bedroom on the third floor. Fatima picked the lock and stepped inside. She crossed the room and entered the hallway. She recalled that Javier had an office on the second floor. She crept to the staircase and waited at the top of the stairs to be certain no residents saw her descent. Going down the stairs left her feeling very exposed, but she saw no one and moved very quickly. The office door, as she remembered it, was big and made of dark mahogany. She turned the knob, stepped inside, and closed the door behind her. She stood quietly, letting her eyes adjust to the dim light that filtered in from the street through the sheer curtains in front of the French doors that led to the office's balcony.

Fatima approached the desk located in the middle of the room. She stepped around to the chair, which faced the room's entrance. She slid out a keyboard from under the desk's surface, and a monitor screen rose up out of an inlaid slot in the desk. Fatima inserted her hacking device into a USB port while the computer was booting up.

The office's motion detection system was designed to be disabled by an arriving inhabitant who submitted the proper code in the keypad within the top right-hand drawer of the desk. If the code was not submitted within two minutes, a silent alarm was sent to the company in charge of security. Fatima had been in the office for more than two minutes, and the security guards were converging on the office. Two of them met at the office door. Another accessed the office balcony from an adjacent room. A fourth guard went to Javier's room to be certain he was unharmed.

When the guard entered Javier's room with his key card, he interrupted the *Kama Sutra* lessons Mr. Perez was receiving from Anisha and Geeta, two mocha beauties from New Delhi. "Hey, what the hell's this?"

"Sir, there's been an intrusion to the premises. I'm here to ensure your safety."

The two guards at the office door were informed by the security company that a single female intruder could be seen on the office camera. The surveillance system was equipped with an audio broadcast capability, over which the security guard at the company headquarters was able to speak to Fatima.

"Attention, you are intruding on this property and must surrender."

The sudden voice startled Fatima, who had just begun to hack into the login encryption. Her jolting reaction was visible on the camera and almost humorous if the company was not supposed to stop people long before they got this far.

"Security guards will enter the office to arrest you. Please submit peacefully."

Fatima pulled her device out of the USB and fired her pistol at the entrance door. The hard wood splintered as bullets passed through, leaving large exit holes. The guards wisely remained to the sides of the door behind thick walls.

Fatima grabbed a statue of a beautiful naked woman from Javier's desk and threw it through the French doors. The smashed glass became a jagged portal through which Fatima stepped out on to the balcony. The street below would allow her to escape, but before she had a chance to tie her rope, she was hit with forty-two hundred volts of Taser-induced electricity. The two wires fired into her by the guard on the balcony conducted so much voltage that Fatima was completely immobile under the electric assault. Her muscles were no longer able to function as the electricity disrupted her motor neurons. When the tazing stopped, she collapsed and was quickly handcuffed and taken back in the building.

"Suspect is in custody," the guard in Javier's room heard over his communication unit.

"What's going on?" asked Javier.

"They have the intruder in custody."

"I want to see the guy. Don't take him away before I get to see him."

"Sir, it's a woman."

"Then I definitely want to see her."

Javier, dressed in a robe and wearing sandals, marched to the second-floor office. He strode into his private study and saw three armed guards and Fatima Hussain wearing handcuffs. He stood quietly for a minute before saying, "Leave the intruder with me. Please close the door and stay in the hallway."

The guards hesitated and looked to one another for direction.

"I know this is unusual, but please, do as I ask."

Mr. Perez seemed calm and relaxed, and they would be right on the other side of door, so the guards acquiesced to his request and left him in the office with the intruder.

Javier looked at Fatima and saw that she was quite uncomfortable. "What are you doing here? What are you trying to steal?"

Fatima gave no reply.

"You can see I have upgraded the security since you broke in eight years ago. I have better security guards as well. You impressed me last time you trespassed into my home, but this time, you rudely interrupted something I was enjoying."

Fatima remained silent, but her eyes were riveted to Javier as he walked to the desk, typed on the keyboard, and dimmed the red lights on the surveillance camera.

"If you're not going to talk, then I'm just going to have you taken to jail to be prosecuted."

"I'm here because of our son," shouted Fatima.

Javier's glare receded slightly.

"He's been kidnapped and is being held by the man who assassinated the president of the United States."

"What?"

"You heard me."

"Yeah . . . but it's a little far-fetched to believe."

"Oh, is it? Crepusculous ordered the assassination of the president, then turned on the assassin and tried to kill him, but he survived and he's pissed and wants to know what's next. What is the next phase of the Board's plan? What is going to happen to the United States?"

Fatima, with her hands still in cuffs, stepped up and shouted in Javier's face. "You know . . . and so he took Hamni from St. James and forced me to break in here to find out what's next."

Fatima fell silent as tears welled up in her eyes and sobs tried to escape her throat. "I need you to help me. I need you to help get our son back. I know you don't think of him as your son, but he is, and he needs your help."

Javier looked at this woman and thought about the extraordinary efforts she had made to help her son. He thought about the time he visited St. James and watched

Hamni. It hurt inside to be such a neglectful father. His own father had always done so much for him. Javier realized that all he did was take. He never gave to anyone, especially of himself. He was insular, selfish, and quite lonely. Here was this woman who knew what it meant to care about someone and put herself in danger just to improve the life of a little boy he could so easily care for if he only would. These thoughts were like a dam breaking, a great release of pressure that had been denied for far too long. Javier Perez needed to grow up and take responsibility for his life, his son, his family, and right now was the moment it was going to happen.

He stepped over to the computer and brought up a file that described the Board's plan for America. He had never fully read it, but he knew the answer Fatima wanted was there. He also knew that the second right-hand desk drawer contained, in a locked box, the device necessary to initiate the next phase of the plan. "Look at this."

Fatima stepped over to the desk. She read the screen and learned that Crepusculous planned to attack nine US cities with thermobaric bombs. The bombs were already in place, and detonation was triggered by a single-source device. The device's signal was sent via a dedicated satellite, and single source meant the signal could not be interrupted, intercepted, or corrupted.

Fatima looked at him. "Where is that device?"

"When I tell you, I want you to guarantee that you and Hamni will come live with me."

Fatima's eyes widened as she gasped at this request. She stepped back from the desk, shaking her head, saying, "I can't believe you just said that while I'm still in handcuffs."

Javier walked to the office's entrance and was disappointed to see that the door had bullet holes through it. He stepped out into the hall and returned with the handcuff keys. Fatima rubbed her wrists after the metal binds were removed. "Thanks," she said.

With Javier standing just behind her and to the right, she kicked him in the shin and drove his head onto the desktop. She grabbed his right shoulder, turned him to his back, and pinned him to the desk by the throat.

"I'm to believe that after all the shit you've put me through for the past nine years that you've had some kind of epiphany and you now want to be a family man? But first you're going to blow up the United States!"

Fatima put her weight on his throat, and the additional force made him squirm. She lifted off and let him breathe.

She got close to his face and said, "You had better choose your next words very carefully, because I could still kill you and get out of here."

She released him and stepped back. Coughing and sputtering while drawing big breaths of air, Javier rolled on the desktop and twisted into a seated position on the desk. After a few more breaths, he began, "I can see why you're upset, but I've been thinking about this for a long time. I just haven't acted. I've come to realize that the wealth I live within steals the ability to recognize the difficulties of others."

Fatima crossed her arms in front of her, rolled her eyes, and looked away.

"But going and watching Hamni and seeing his difficulties . . . he has made me feel it. I could feel his struggle and perseverance, because he is my son. I want to help him, but I need your help to do that. Fatherhood should be so natural, but I need help to be a good Father, and that's what I want to do with you, learn to be a good father."

Javier became very emotional while he spoke; he kept sniffling as tears drained into his nose. Fatima looked at him but did not uncross her arms.

"You want to start acting like a good man? Where is that device? Give it to me."

Javier pulled out the second drawer on the right, unlocked the metal box, and removed a satellite phone. He handed it to Fatima.

"There is just one preprogrammed number; just turn it on, press send, and all the bombs in the US will detonate according to the plan."

Fatima looked at the phone and held it up between them, saying, "This is going to get our son back."

Chapter 24

Hamni found the cottage, and the people, and the food, and the routine all so unfamiliar. He knew things would be different whenever he saw his mother, but she understood his needs and made him comfortable wherever they were. These people were not doing that, and he was getting anxious. Hamni first began to rock back and forth in his chair. He then stood up in front of the big picture window that faced the road. He placed his right foot in front of his left and rocked back and forth from one foot to the other while he looked out the window as if searching for something. He began vocalizing, saying, "Hun-goo, hun-goo," over and over with an escalating crescendo until he screamed out loud, leaning all his weight forward on his right foot while elevating his left behind him. After emptying his lungs into a high-pitched, piercing scream, he put his foot back on the floor and started the whole process over again. He repeated the pattern several times as Diegert and Carolyn watched with perplexed amazement at the intense behavior of this little lost boy. Looking at Carolyn, Diegert said, "Do something."

"Like what?"

"I don't know. You're a woman—comfort him." Diegert turned to walk out of the room. "Calm him down."

Carolyn followed Diegert, saying, "Look, I'm not the babysitter here. Taking him was your idea; he's your responsibility."

"Well, I don't know what to do with him."

"Neither do me."

The crash of breaking glass jolted both of them out of their argument. They were drawn back to the front room where Hamni stood with a gash on his forehead from a jagged shard he had created when he had smashed his head through the window. He was still rocking back and forth, but now he had blood pulsing out of his head and streaming down his face. The room was quickly becoming a crimson mess, splattered with hemorrhaging fluid. Carolyn stepped forward and grabbed Hamni, who struck back at her and started screaming. She struggled with him while blood sprayed all over her. Diegert ran to his duffle bag, and from an internal zippered pocket retrieved a small aerosol can.

He returned to the front room to see Carolyn covered in Hamni's blood and struggling with the small boy, who possessed the crazed strength of a grown man. Diegert stepped up to the two of them, placing his hand over Carolyn's nose and mouth. He sprayed Hamni in the face at close range, and within seconds, the boy was unconscious. "I should've done that a long time ago," said an exasperated Diegert.

Carolyn felt Hamni go limp in her arms, and she took him to the kitchen, placing him on the table. Diegert grabbed a towel from the rack, tore it in half, and put pressure on the gash. "Go to the bathroom and find whatever first aid you can, and I need a needle and thread."

Carolyn passed through the front room on her way to the bathroom where she encountered a very nervous but inquisitive overweight middle-aged woman who must've lived close by. With a startled reaction to the blood-drenched appearance of Carolyn, the woman steeled herself to ask, "Oh dear God . . . do you need help, love?"

Carolyn didn't hesitate. "Yes, our son has special needs and he has just injured himself by smashing the window. Do you have a first-aid kit with a needle and thread?"

The bewildered woman gathered her thoughts and repeated, "Needle and thread—first aid. I will be right back, love."

The woman waddled away as fast as she could. Carolyn went to the bathroom and grabbed a roll of toilet paper and another towel and found a small box of old Band-Aids. She looked at herself in the mirror and saw what a hideous sight she was. That woman certainly was a caring person to have not turned and run away. She splashed water on her face and rubbed it on a towel, leaving a bloody smear on the cotton cloth. She rummaged in the cupboard under the sink but found nothing useful. She walked back through the front room just as the neighbor returned with a plastic first-aid case and her sewing kit. Carolyn took them both. "Thank you so much. Please don't consider me rude, but could you wait out here? My husband is a doctor, and he will be able to treat our son with these."

Carolyn continued to the kitchen; over her shoulder, she said, "What a tough start to our vacation."

Diegert had kept constant pressure on the wound, and the bleeding was stopping. The gash was right at Hamni's hairline about two inches in length, but the tension of the skin had caused it to spread to about an inch and a half in width. Looking at the items Carolyn had brought with her, Diegert exclaimed, "Holy shit, you found these in the house?"

"No."

Carolyn opened the first-aid case and handed Diegert a sterile gauze pad and some antiseptic fluid. He began washing the wound. Carolyn opened the woman's sewing case and found the typical things used to mend and sew clothes. She threaded a needle with some plastic thread that resembled fishing line. She handed the needle to Diegert, who said, "It's a good thing I tranked him, because this is going to hurt."

With quick, even strokes, Diegert had the wound edges back in contact. He tied the sutures tightly so the cut no longer bled. The dressing was preceded by an application of antibiotic ointment, and although a typical bandage for a wound like this would've wrapped around the small boy's head, Diegert sufficed to cover it in a sterile gauze pad and tape it in place. Carolyn stepped in and washed all the blood off the boy's face, hands, and arms. His clothes, as well as hers, were covered in blood.

Carolyn closed up the sewing kit and the first-aid case and returned to the front room. The neighbor was outside on the front steps. "Thank you again so very much; you are very kind. I'm sorry for the frightening appearance of the situation."

"It's all right, love. Many people suffer with the needs of family members."

Carolyn handed the kit and the case back to the helpful woman.

"Is there anything else you need, love?"

"His clothes are rather . . . distasteful, and his luggage was lost on the flight. You wouldn't happen to have any clothes for a small boy, would you?"

"Just a minute, love, I think I may have something."

Back in the apartment, Diegert washed his hands and was drying them when his phone went off. "Hello," he answered.

"Crepusculous has at least nine thermobaric bombs set to go off in US cities, and they are all tied to a single-source detonation device that I have in my possession."

Fatima's icy voice sizzled over the phone and cut through Diegert's cochlea, searing into his brain a fearful realization of the consequences of Hamni's injuries. He needed to gather his wits quickly. "You got this from Javier?"

"Yes."

"How do I know it's authentic?"

"You don't . . . how do I know Hamni's alright? I don't. We have to trust each other, because we've both got what the other wants."

"OK, let's arrange the exchange. I'll send you GPS coordinates in an hour."

"Alright, but if Hamni is harmed, I will kill you and blow up the United States."

Diegert disconnected the call.

The neighbor returned to find Carolyn sweeping the broken glass from the sidewalk in front of the house. She handed Carolyn a paper bag. Carolyn opened the bag and withdrew a pair of soccer shorts and a numbered jersey. She looked at the woman, who, with a wan smile, said, "It's Manchester United. I bought it for my grandson's birthday."

"Oh, that's so sweet . . . We couldn't take it."

"Yes, love, you are in need, and I can get another set."

"Well, then, you must let us pay you for it."

"No, love, I will not take money from those in need."

"Thank you so much. Your kindness is truly so very touching."

The gentle woman patted Carolyn on the forearm and turned to walk back to her house. Over her shoulder, she said, "Just see to it your son becomes a fan of Manchester."

Chapter 25

"We've got to go," said Diegert impatiently. "We've got to go meet Fatima in London."

"Right now?"

"Yeah, what have you got there?"

Carolyn slid the clothes out of the bag. "From the neighbor."

"You stole them?"

Shoving the clothes back in the bag, Carolyn replied, "No, there are actually kind people in this world. A generous neighbor gave them to me because we need them. If you will excuse me?"

Diegert stepped to the side and Carolyn went to dress Hamni.

***

When Fatima put her phone down, Javier said, "You let him dictate the meeting place."

"It's not important. We have to be ready to take Hamni back safely."

"You're sure he has him?"

"I called St. James earlier, and they admitted Hamni left the premises with a woman."

Javier scratched his head and ran his fingers through his thick black hair. Fatima addressed him sternly, "Don't attempt anything that will put Hamni in jeopardy. Diegert is resourceful and ruthless, but I know he will give us our son in exchange for the device."

"You believe that because you want to believe it."

"Yes, I do," said the very quick and highly agitated woman, who then kicked Javier in the hip and twisted his arm around his back as she took out his knee from behind, pressing his face to the floor.

"You want to show me you're a changed man, you show me by making our son a priority."

She stepped up and away from him. He rolled to his side, saying, "You know it's only because you're a girl that I let you do that to me."

"Yeah right. Go get me a gun from one of your guards and then lock them in their office. I don't want any heroics endangering Hamni."

***

Diegert and Carolyn changed into their last set of clean clothes while Hamni was now wearing a number-ten jersey for the Manchester United Football Club. The young lad was still unconscious, and both Diegert and Carolyn were grateful for that. While Carolyn drove, Diegert searched Google Maps for a suitable meeting place.

"When we get the device, I take custody of it," said the CIA agent.

"You're going to turn it in to the agency?"

"By turning it in, I have a chance of making a deal for leniency."

"You're going to arrest me?"

"I suggest you turn yourself in. The hunt for you will continue, and it will go international. Once that happens, the stakes get higher and your chances of survival plummet."

"I've been hunted before."

"I don't think you understand the intensity with which you will be pursued. But I also don't want to see you dead."

"You think you can get me a lenient deal?"

"I don't know. Maybe we can appeal for a commutation of the death penalty and negotiate the charges you'll face."

"Maybe, but I hope they appreciate the fact that we stopped the US from being destroyed. Hey, turn left here."

Carolyn pulled the car onto the street to her left. Diegert explained, "This is Mackenzie. It connects to Remington, and it's on Remington that I've found what I'm looking for."

***

When Blevinsky's ID appeared on Panzer's phone, the wealthy German activated the speaker. "Is she here in London?"

"Yes, sir, the Gulfstream landed a short time ago. She will occupy the secure suite at the Royal Ambassador Hotel."

"Excellent. Thank you, Aaron."

"Will you be seeing her, sir?"

"I'll inform you of what you need to know."

"Of course, sir."

***

"Park here," instructed Diegert. Carolyn pulled into a vacant lot whose pavement was crumbling into gravel. The weeds weakened the surface by seeking the soil beneath the cracks. The whole neighborhood was devoid of inhabitants. The buildings were undergoing rehabilitation. Each old structure had scaffolding rising up the sides and tarps wrapping the outside, keeping the weather from the interior construction work. The reclamation of these buildings would one day produce a gentrified community of new residents. It wasn't too hard to imagine this place having a cool future, but right now the conditions reminded Carolyn of Detroit decay.

"Now here's the plan. I'm going to find a location in that building."

Diegert pointed to the building across the street that had a large external foyer overgrown with weeds.

"I plan to access an upper floor that's open enough to give me a sight line back to here. I will draw her up to me. Fatima won't allow the exchange until Hamni is secured. So she will come back down to the car. You will be concealed in the dark, out of sight, and when I signal you on your phone, you'll unlock the car with the remote. Once Fatima has Hamni, she will leave and we'll have the device."

"Why this elaborate plan to get her up to the work site?"

"She may very well have an additional attack plan or a Crepusculous hit team in play with her. I want to spread things out and keep her guessing about Hamni's location. This way neither of us has to actually be there when she gets him back."

Nodding her agreement with a look of doubt, Carolyn capitulated to his plan.

"I'm going to find my place in the building, then I'll send my GPS coordinates to Fatima and wait."

"I just stay down here?"

"Keeping Hamni calm and quiet is critical to the plan."

"Well, we've really had no success with that."

"Here," Diegert said, extended his hand and giving Carolyn the can of Trank.

"I'm not spraying him with that again."

"You might have to."

Again expressing an indignant sense of surrender, Carolyn took the tiny aerosol can.

"This whole thing is crazy. You're hoping your manipulations work, but if they don't, then what?"

"Look, stopping people with criminal intent always involves craziness. You know that. When this is all over, the US will be safe, and you and I . . . can take another shower."

"With Botanical Bouquet?"

"I sure hope not."

Diegert stepped out of the car and disappeared around the corner of the building across the street.

* * *

Fatima's phone chirped and she opened the message from Diegert. The GPS coordinates indicated a location in the Brentwood district on Remington Avenue. "Come on, Javier, it's time to go."

* * *

After waiting ten minutes, Carolyn checked on Hamni again. He was unconscious, but he looked like he was peacefully sleeping with his seat belt on and his head leaning against the sidewall of the car's interior. His dark-brown shoes and black socks did not complement the striking red of his Manchester United soccer suit. She opened the car door and stepped out into the soft rain that fell from the dark sky. Not far from the edge of the parking lot was a hedgerow of overgrown bushes that fronted an overhanging roof. Carolyn concealed herself behind the thick foliage and began to shiver, as the wet evening grew cool. She tested the remote, confirming that the car remained within the key's operating range. For having such a seemingly simple role, Carolyn was very tense.

Chapter 26

On Remington Avenue, Diegert had chosen the sixth floor of this building under renovation. The floor was completely gutted, only the studs and the construction materials remained. The wiring, plumbing, and ductwork were all being upgraded and only a few bulbs, hanging in protective cages, provided what light there was. Diegert walked to one of the window spaces. They were all devoid of glass and had plastic sheets hanging over them. He drew back the plastic and could see the car in the lot where he had left Carolyn. Crossing the building to the opposite side, he looked out, anticipating Fatima's arrival. He'd purposefully given her directions that wouldn't have her passing the area where the car with Hamni was parked.

The silver-gray Mercedes was a bit garish, but it didn't surprise Diegert. The car parked alongside the deserted street, and Fatima stepped out. Her sleek, lean figure was familiar, and he could see her face in the streetlight. Fatima lifted a leather hood over her head against the rain. Diegert called her cell. When she lifted her phone to her ear, he said, "Sixth floor of the building across the street on your right."

She disconnected, turned her head, and looked directly at him. She began walking toward the building, and when Diegert saw her enter, he stepped over to the stairwell to greet her arrival. Diegert observed her ascent up the stairwell, which was the only entrance to the floor. She was still wearing the black leather hood of her coat. Her pants were black and tight and tucked into sturdy but fashionable leather boots. She stepped off the last step and crossed to the center of the floor. "I don't see my son," began the woman who sought to control the situation.

"You do have the device?"

"You don't get to see it until I see my son."

"Hamni is so cute. You never told me what a darling little boy he is, and he's incredibly smart."

"Shut up. What's your plan?"

"Did you know he could play chess? He took two straight games off me."

"Stop talking about him. Where is he?"

"He's safe and secure and nearby."

From the stairwell, another figure rose from the hole in the floor. The dark-haired man crossed the top stair and stood in front of the stairwell, removing his black leather gloves. Diegert's gaze projected from his dark eyes like that of a cornered panther. Fatima said, "Javier has the device. He will give it you when I have Hamni."

"This sucks, you untrustworthy bitch."

"You're telling me. Now where is he?"

"You two are very tense. Let's just calm down for a moment," said the handsome Spaniard. Diegert's weariness lost none of its intensity. Fatima continued to watch his every move. Javier Perez continued, "I've heard some interesting things about you, Mr. Diegert. I've been told you're the best killer of men in the world. This, of course, was delivered as a warning, not a compliment. I appreciate the world's finest things. It has been my life's experience to be surrounded by only the best in the world. Food, cars, yachts, clothing . . . entertainment—always the best. But an experience I have not had is to be in the presence of the best assassin in the world!"

Diegert looked at him and felt like the panther was now in a zoo cage.

"You killed the president of the United States and got away with it. Here you are!"

Javier removed his black leather jacket, revealing a fine white linen dress shirt under a black leather vest. He wore black denim jeans, and his ankle high boots were also black.

"The cunning, the grit, the willingness to kill, you must feel like a powerful predator, choosing how and when your victims will die and watching their lives end at your direction. Now that's a powerful experience I have never had."

"Will you shut up. Let's exchange the device and get our son back," barked an impatient Fatima.

Diegert raised his eyebrow and looked into Javier's eyes. He saw the mounting displeasure of a man who was not used to taking orders from a woman. Diegert wanted to see if he was going to make the mistake of not listening to Fatima.

"Hamni's in a car," said Diegert. Pointing behind him, he continued, "Look out this window. You will see a car in the lot below."

"You left him in a car by himself?" Fatima threw the plastic out of the way, thrusting her head out the window.

"He's secure. It's locked."

Turning away from the window, Fatima's fury erupted. "God damn it, that's not good enough for him.

God damn you, Diegert. You should know he can't be left alone."

"Then give me the device, and the two of you can go get your son."

As Diegert finished his statement, his sight fell directly upon Javier, who cringed at the mention of his shared parenthood with Fatima.

"Give me the device, and I'll remotely unlock the car for you."

***

Hamni opened his eyes and blinked a few times. He felt a slight chill. The rain on the car windows made what little ambient light there was diffuse and heavily shadowed. He scratched his ear and realized he wasn't dreaming. He realized he didn't recognize anything. He looked at the clothes he was wearing and didn't recognize them either. He was quiet for another moment, and then a scream burst out from him that expressed all the fear and anxiety of a boy dependent upon routine to make order of the scattered world in his brain.

Being all alone in unfamiliar surroundings was extremely frightening. He struggled with the seat belt. When he finally unclipped it, he was unaware of the automatic retraction and felt the strap was trying to re-bind him. He fought with the belt until it snapped out of his hand, freeing him to the full space of the car's interior. He pulled on the door handle, but it was locked. He began rocking back and forth chanting his personal mantra, "Hun-goo, hun-goo," with escalating intensity. From her place in the bushes, Carolyn could hear the muffled chant and see that he was moving. When he first smacked his head into the window, Carolyn was startled by the tremendous force thrust into the glass by this already injured boy. She fingered the canister of Trank as she approached the car.

***

"Alright," said Fatima. Directing her instructions to Javier, she said. "I'll call you when I get down there. The exchange will be simultaneous."

"OK," answered the wealthy playboy.

Fatima descended the staircase and made her way to the ground floor. She had to walk a block to get to the other side of the building where Hamni was waiting for her in the car. She flipped the hood over her head against the rain.

Javier continued to speak with Diegert on the sixth floor. "As I was saying, taking a man's life must feel incredible."

"It's a feeling of power like no other, Javier. It's the power of life. It's not based on wealth or family position or anything material. It comes from your inner strength and personal resolve."

"Yes . . . I can imagine it does. You know, you and I are alike in many ways."

With a doubtful smirk on his face, Diegert replied, "I don't think I see it that way. Give me the device and call Fatima."

"In due time."

"Now."

Diegert stepped forward with his hand out and his look hardening into his fight face. Javier shifted into a defensive stance. Diegert advised him, "I don't think that's a good idea."

"You won't be the first guy I've had to beat down. I can't get away with fucking over two hundred women a year without pissing off some husbands and boyfriends. Bring it on, you wuss."

Diegert lowered his center of gravity and widened his base of support as he circled around Javier in a clockwise direction. The Spaniard rotated, keeping his eyes locked on Diegert's. The assassin struck first. He jabbed with his right and kicked with his left. The jab failed to distract. Javier reacted to the left leg kick with his right, striking Diegert in the thigh, forcing him to spin to keep from falling. Knowing he was vulnerable while his back was turned on his adversary, Diegert rapidly repositioned himself to face Javier.

"The best in the world! That's who my tae kwon do teacher was. Master Kim Le Pac. Now I get to see if my black belt is a match for the world's best assassin."

Stepping away and rising out of his ready stance, Diegert said, "If you got all that on me, then I guess we're done here and your son is going to die."

Diegert pulled from his pocket the keys to the car. "The car is rigged, and the detonator is tied to the remote. This way I get rid of Fatima as well."

"No!" shouted Javier, and Diegert threw the keys across the room into the darkness. The assassin closed quickly with a flurry of punches to the head and neck as the Spaniard struggled to regain his defensive stance. It surprised Diegert how well this wealthy pretty boy weathered the blistering punishment. Diegert attempted to deliver a fatal blow, but Javier fended off the most deadly strikes while reestablishing his fighting position. His face was battered and the corner of his mouth was bleeding, but there was still plenty of fight in him.

***

Hamni remained in the back seat on the driver's side. His head was bleeding again after striking the window. Carolyn opened the rear passenger door, and the instant illumination frightened the boy, whose wide eyes met Carolyn's. She smiled and hoped he would recognize her. He did not. He screamed, backing away from her, pressing himself against the locked door.

"Hamni, relax. Shhhh, settle down. It's OK. It's OK."

Her words were ineffective, and the boy continued to scream. Carolyn raised the can of tranquilizing spray, hesitating because she was unsure if he would overdose from another blast.

The force she felt on the belt of her pants was not only surprising but incredibly strong. The back of her head smacked on the doorframe as she was pulled out of the car and flung onto the wet ground. She looked up to see a black-clad figure with a hood. Fatima knelt down, pressing her thumb on the trachea of Carolyn's throat. The pressure was extremely painful and made it difficult for Carolyn to breathe. Fatima had her full attention. "Give me the keys."

Carolyn removed the keys from her pocket and handed them over. The angry mother stood up and pointed her Sig Sauer P320 at Carolyn, who raised her hands and sought to make eye contact with the face under the hood. Fatima, from the angry place in her soul and hidden beneath her dark shroud, fired into the right side of Carolyn's chest.

Hamni froze when he heard the shot. His next sight, though, was his beautiful, loving mother pulling a hood off her head, revealing a smiling, comforting face, one he knew so well and longed to be with every day. The confused and bewildered boy thrust his arms out and embraced his mother like he did no other person in the world. He was excited, exhausted, and so very happy to be with her. Fatima hugged the boy, kissed him, and was so relieved to have him back. She held him tight and released all the anxiety she had been feeling for his safety. She looked at his head bandage and the sports uniform and was disappointed the woman outside would not be answering questions. She belted Hamni in the front seat, and with the joy of being reunited with her child, drove away from the Brentwood neighborhood.

****

Drawing short, painful gasps, Carolyn lay motionless in the rain soaked parking lot. The iron-tinged taste of blood came to her mouth as she coughed globs of crimson mucous from her lungs. Instinctively, she turned her head to the side before losing consciousness while staring through the shafts of asphalt splitting weeds.

Chapter 27

Javier bounced on his feet and danced in a circle as he cleared his head and got back in the fight. "Sex and violence both stimulate the same part of the brain," shared the man who was testing Diegert. "So fighting is a lot like sex. It's best one-on-one. It's an adrenaline rush, the outcome is uncertain, and there is both pleasure and pain."

Eyeing his adversary for damage from the earlier attack, Diegert replied, "Well, I can't wait to fuck you."

As the two combatants warily eyed each other seeking an advantage, Javier stepped in and struck Diegert's jaw with a quick right jab. Simultaneously, Diegert plunged a powerful right jab into Javier's abdomen. The strike doubled over the Spaniard. Diegert grabbed the back of his enemy's head and powerfully drove Javier's face into his flexed knee.

Javier collapsed on the floor. Diegert moved toward him to search for the device. With his right leg, Javier whipsawed the assassin's left leg, toppling him backward to the floor. Javier found a jagged shard of wood. With blood streaming down his face, the desperate son of a billionaire charged Diegert. From his supine position, Diegert kicked Javier in the hip. As Javier fell forward to the ground, he stabbed Diegert in the thigh. The pain from the impaled piece of wood seared Diegert's leg muscles. Diegert rolled toward Javier and punched him in the temple. The blow cracked Javier's skull and wrenched his neck. Diegert pulled the wooden spike out of his leg and grabbed a handful of powdered grout from a nearby bag. Javier regained his footing and came at Diegert, who was now on one knee. As Javier approached, Diegert threw the grout into his face. The dusty material coated Javier's eyes, nose, and mouth. It mixed with the blood on his face, becoming an adherent paste. The Spaniard gasped, breathing in even more of the dust. He then coughed in an uncontrollable spasm. Diegert rose up, grabbed Javier's right arm, twisted it behind his back, and drove him forward into a hanging sheet of plastic. He wrapped the plastic around Javier's head, kicking out his legs, forcing him to suffocate. Diegert applied force with fatal intent.

Javier retrieved the satellite phone from his vest pocket. With the push of one button, he activated the phone's initiation code. He held the phone aloft and Diegert saw the screen light up with green letters: "ACTIVATED—00:30." Javier tossed the phone across the open space. Diegert saw the phone on the far side of the room and realized he couldn't finish off Javier and stop the phone from detonating the United States. Releasing Javier, Diegert raced over to the phone. The screen indicated that there were nineteen seconds remaining. Diegert, recognizing the satellite phone as similar to the one on the *Sue Ellen*, entered the shutdown code. The screen went black. It remained black for a very tense moment before red letters appeared on the screen: "D . . . E . . . - . . . ACTIVATED."

Diegert looked back to the hanging plastic, but Javier was gone. Bruised and bleeding, with a deep wound in his leg, Diegert shuffled to the window, pushing back the tarp to see that the car was gone and Carolyn was lying on the ground in the rain.

Descending the stairs as fast as his injured body could go, he struggled to run around the block to where he had left her. Diegert knelt beside her, turned her head and gently stroked her cheek and forehead. Carolyn's eyes opened and she spat out a mouthful of bloody phlegm. Diegert held her face and looked into her frightened eyes. He held her head as Carolyn gasped for breath in ragged, guttural jolts.

"That bitch . . . shot me."

Running his hand underneath her, Diegert felt no exit wounds.

"It didn't go through, so you're gonna live."

"It . . . doesn't . . . feel that way."

On her phone, Diegert dialed nine-nine-nine. He gave the dispatcher the address and left on the GPS signal for them to follow.

Carolyn clutched Diegert's arm. "Give . . . me . . . the device."

"Shh, just relax, the ambulance is coming."

"Give it to me," croaked Carolyn.

Taking off his jacket, rolling it up, and placing it under her head, he said, "You need to stay calm and relax."

"Don't make a fool . . . of me . . . for trusting you," said Carolyn, rolling to her side and grabbing Diegert's arm.

"Don't worry, I'll keep the device safe," said Diegert as he looked over his shoulder in the direction of the wailing sirens.

Tightening her grip on his forearm, Carolyn commanded, with as much force as she could muster, "Don't leave."

"I've got to."

"Don't abandon me," said Carolyn as she succumbed to her failing strength, rolled onto her back, and let her head sink into Diegert's coat.

"I won't, I'm your asset."

"I should never have trusted you."

Squatting next to her, Diegert pulled the sat phone from his pocket and began striking the keys. "Listen, I'm turning on the GPS tracker on the sat phone." Continuing to type on the keys, he said, "I'm creating an access code in order to turn the GPS on, and I'm hiding the code so that anyone who tries to turn off the GPS won't be able to, so the phone will continually broadcast its location."

"So what?"

"Wait." Diegert picked up Carolyn's phone. "I'm placing the number of the sat phone into your phone, and you'll be able to track the phone's GPS signal twenty-four seven. You'll always know where I am."

"Just give me the device."

"I can't do that. I'm going deep into Crepusculous. I'll be an even more valuable asset. We'll bring them to their knees."

Carolyn's breaths became shorter, and she could no longer speak. Her eyes though shone with the fire of frustration as she helplessly watched Diegert stand up as the ambulance arrived. He moved off into the shadows, watching as the paramedics ran over to Carolyn. As they worked on her, a thought flashed in his mind: Had he found his Sue Ellen? When he was sure she was getting proper treatment, he disappeared into the night with the power to destroy the United States in his pocket.

Chapter 28

Shuffling into the night, Diegert used his belt as a tourniquet around his leg to reduce the flow of blood. Moving along a deserted concrete walkway beside the River Thames, Diegert searched the satellite phone's history, retrieving two numbers from the trash bin that had not yet been permanently deleted. Conference calling both numbers, he steeled himself for the confrontation.

"Hello," came the hesitant but familiar voice of Blevinsky.

"Hallo," came a distinctly German voice he had never heard before.

"Gentlemen, this is David Diegert. Based on the caller ID, you should be aware of the device in my possession. I know what this is programmed to do, and I know how valuable it is to you. The only way you get this back is to release my mother."

"You're in no position to be making demands," shot Blevinsky.

"Wait a moment," interrupted Panzer. "Mr. Diegert, I am very impressed with your determination. You seem to have the ability to return from the dead," said the German lightheartedly.

"I'd be happy to see if you could pass that test."

Chuckling uncomfortably, Panzer replied, "Perhaps another time. We can however arrange for you to see your mother. Aaron, would you please assist our young man's reunion? I look forward to making your acquaintance shortly, David." Panzer disconnected. Blevinsky got Diegert's cell phone number and sent him directions to the Royal Ambassador Hotel. Diegert demanded, "I want to speak to my mother."

"Alright."

Diegert grew tense during the wait. What if this was a trap? What if she was injured? What would he do with her once they were free?

"David?"

"Mom, are you OK? Where are you?"

"I'm fine, I'm in a very fancy apartment at some fancy hotel."

"Are they hurting you?"

"No, but they won't let me leave. The men have guns."

"Mom, I'm on my way to come get you."

"David, it's not safe. Does this have anything to do with the money you sent me?"

"Mom, I know you're scared and this is serious business, but it's not about that money. I'll try to explain when I get there. I won't be long."

"It's not safe, David, you shouldn't come."

Blevinsky disconnected Diegert from his mother and connected him to a conference call with the guards at the Royal Ambassador. "Gentlemen, when Mr. Diegert arrives, you're to treat him with nothing but courtesy and respect. Is that understood?"

"Yes, sir," said several voices simultaneously.

"Alright, men, disconnect." When all the guards had hung up, Blevinsky spoke just to Diegert. "I don't care how you did it, but I'm not happy you're back in Europe."

"Not only Europe, Aaron, but London, and your boss has to be wondering why his operations manager isn't on top of it, when I'm calling him from the single-source detonation device for your elaborate plan. Fuck you, Blevinsky."

It was a long walk on an injured leg, but he found the private entrance for the penthouse at the Royal Ambassador. The guard on the street patted him down for a weapon but made no attempt to take his phone. Inside the entrance, he was directed to the private elevator, which he rode with a guard straight to the top of the hotel. The elevator doors slid open, revealing the interior of the penthouse with its rich décor and luxurious furnishings.

A guard greeted him as he stepped off the elevator into the foyer of the penthouse apartment. "If you would please follow me, Mr. Diegert."

His limping gait put an ache in his hips while he left bloody footprints every step of the way. The guard stood before wide double doors and slid one of the panels into the wall. Diegert watched as the door retracted into its pocket, revealing his mother standing in the middle of the room. She smiled when she saw her son, but her facial expression passed through surprise and shock before revealing horror. Diegert looked down at himself to realize his pant leg was soaked in blood, his boot covered in a crimson sheen, while his thigh was encircled by a cinched-up belt. His shirt was torn and dirty, his face bruised, his hair a mess, and his hands smeared with blood. Denise Diegert's gape-mouthed inability to speak led Diegert to begin. "Mom, I'm alright. The leg will be fine." While his body shook from the blood loss, he held his hands out to her. She rushed across the room, wrapped her arms around him, and held on tight. Diegert melted into her, with a sense of relief to have found her safe and unharmed. She pulled back from him, feeling his weakness as the blood loss depleted him. "David, you need a doctor."

The guard at the door interjected. "Mrs. Diegert, a doctor has been called and will be here in seven minutes."

"Seven minutes?"

Looking at his phone screen, he said, "Yes, ma'am."

"David, you've got to lie down."

Leading him to the couch, she said, "What happened to you? Tell me what's going on. I need to know, honey."

Looking at her frightened eyes and stressed face, Diegert said, "Mom, I'm so sorry you're involved in this. These people are dangerous. I don't want to scare you, but we're in deep trouble."

Diegert closed his eyes and drifted into a semiconscious stupor. Denise kneeled on the floor next to him and looked back at the guards with even more suspicion and fear.

Right on time, a doctor arrived with a backpack full of equipment. He ordered the guards to move Diegert into one of the bedrooms. Diegert's wounds were treated, he received an IV transfusion, his thigh was stitched, and he was then cleaned up and dressed in a loose-fitting pair of black pants and a gray T-shirt. The doctor administered a dose of Healix, and soon Diegert was feeling better. When he exited the treatment bedroom, his mother beamed.

"David, you look so much better."

She hugged him and could feel the strength had already started to return to his sturdy frame. They sat together on the couch.

"You were saying we're in danger."

"Oh, Mom, I was delirious. We're going to be fine."

He reassuringly patted her shoulder and squeezed her forearm.

She clutched his hand and locked on to his gaze. "I'm not comfortable with your change of opinion. Why would we now be safe?"

Diegert smiled, seeking a way to get her to relax. He struggled with lying to her but wanted her to be calm and not so concerned. "We're going to be fine because . . ."

As the words stumbled over his lips, the elevator door opened and from it exited a distinguished man with a full head of gray hair and piercing blue eyes set in a handsome face, wearing an impeccably tailored gray suit on his trim, tall body. He walked with a powerful stride that belied his years and quickly carried him into the main room where Diegert and Denise sat. Although he had never laid eyes on this man, Diegert needed no introduction to realize that Klaus Panzer had just entered the room. The bold man exuded confidence; projecting an expectation of getting whatever he wanted simply by exerting his sense of inalienable rights.

Diegert and his mother rose to their feet. Between them and Panzer was a long, rectangular coffee table on which stood a vase filled with soft white baby's breath and a dozen red roses. Diegert observed a change in the look on Panzer's face. The sense of control gave way to an expression of surprised recognition. The man seemed unsettled as he looked at Diegert's mother. Glancing at his mother's face, he saw the same look. She knew this man. These two knew each other, yet they were both stunned to be in one another's presence at this moment.

Neither Panzer nor Denise spoke, but their faces revealed the presence of their history. Panzer stepped to the side, coming around the coffee table to stand before the tall, dark-haired woman. She held his gaze, unblinking with a slight defiance in the set of her chin. "Denise. . . Diegert?" is all Panzer said as he reached for her hand, gently lifting it to his lips and placing a kiss just past her knuckles.

What the fuck? raced through Diegert's head as he watched the man he considered his archenemy fondling the hand of his mother. The protestations clogged Diegert's throat, and his only expression was an open-mouthed look of disbelief.

Panzer broke the silence as he turned to Diegert, saying, "Young man, this may come as quite a surprise to you, but your mother and I knew each other a long time ago. Twenty-five years ago to be exact."

Chapter 29

Standing in the opulent apartment of the Ambassador Hotel, it fell into place in Diegert's mind the instant the words were spoken, but accepting the fact was not so sudden. He struggled with the puzzle piece, unable to place it into the empty hole in his life where a father's love was supposed to fit. The man he had often fantasized about meeting was certainly not standing in front of him. His mother had known all along and never said a word, keeping hidden the name of his real father. Loving her and trusting her were two things Diegert struggled to do simultaneously.

Stepping over and clapping Diegert on the shoulder, Panzer said, "You are the long-lost son I never knew I had."

He was standing right in front of him. With a well-placed strike, he could take him down and end his life within thirty seconds. Diegert looked up at the man whose ice-blue eyes were unsettling yet also strangely calming. The man spoke again. "You are something that can never be bought but which I have wanted for decades."

"How do you know I'm your son?"

Flustered for a moment, Panzer said, "In 1991, your mother was on the catering staff at the Deerfield Lodge where I was a guest demonstrating some of our very best hunting rifles to a group of American sportsmen."

He looked at Denise, who nodded her head.

"I trust her to know."

Glaring at his mother until she turned her eyes to the floor, Diegert struggled to keep himself from lashing out at both of these thoughtless people . . . his parents.

Panzer continued, "I think we both have a lot to process, but I feel like I have been given a gift I never thought I would receive."

"Yeah, well, I feel like I've just been kicked in the head. Only to find out that I've been lied to all my life by the one person I should be able to trust."

Diegert stepped away from Panzer, who crossed back to stand next to Denise.

"You fuck her and walk away leaving her to raise a bastard son with no idea I even exist."

Unaccustomed to being dressed down, Panzer searched for words. "I . . . if . . . if she had contacted me and let me know . . . but I never heard from her."

"Of course not, you shithead, she was a poor country girl married to an alcoholic scumbag who controlled her with deprivation and violence. Why do you think she was attracted to you? Did you even pay her?"

Panzer and Denise looked at each other.

Diegert let them contemplate their actions from so long ago. "I'm a bastard from a free fuck."

Diegert spun away from them and walked to the window. "I can see that both of you don't think about other people." Stepping away from the window and whirling to face them, Diegert raised his voice as he crossed the room.

"Mom, because you're so scared of being abandoned that you're unwilling to be responsible. And you, Klaus Panzer, who the hell knows what you think? But the kind of work I've been doing for you, tells me you don't give a shit about other people." Leaning in close, Diegert said, "I've killed for you."

Panzer replied, "Thank you, son."

With an instant rage, Diegert shoved Panzer in the chest, forcing the trillionaire to stumble backward.

Three guards all drew their weapons and moved in with barrels trained on Diegert.

Denise stepped between them, raising her arms. "Wait, wait, don't shoot." She turned to Diegert and embraced him while speaking in his ear. "I love you, David, more than anything, and I'm sorry for hurting you, but I have always loved you."

"I know, Mom, but I don't know what to do."

Pulling back and looking into Diegert's face through tear-filled eyes, she pointed at Panzer. "He's so rich and powerful; let's see what he can do for us. He could give you a good job."

"I don't think you get what this guy does, Mom."

"I don't care. It cannot be that bad. Look at Jake and Dad; they're both criminals."

"The order of magnitude makes those two look like first-offense shoplifters."

"I'm tired of living poor. I want to live better. I have lived a lousy life while others have walked all over me. Maybe I have to step on somebody to live better. I'm OK with that."

"She's right, you know, son," interrupted Panzer as he waved his hand, directing the guards to holster their weapons. "I can offer both of you opportunities within my organization. Denise, I could see you working in our philanthropic branch making high six figures."

Denise smiled at him. "Six figures?"

Diegert rolled his eyes. "I already work for you."

"Yes, I know, son, but I see an expanded role for you in management. A position that is. . . not so tactical. It would be a promotion."

"See, David, this could be good."

Diegert passed between the couch and the coffee table, bumping the table leg and jostling the vase of roses and baby's breath. Instinctively, he reached out to steady the solid ceramic vessel. He grasped the narrow neck of the vase and swung it like a club into the face of the guard to his left. The flowers and water sprayed across the room as the guard tumbled to the floor with imploded teeth. As the second guard reached for his gun, Diegert threw the vase end over end, striking him in the head. Turning back to his left, Diegert grabbed the first guard's pistol and shot him. He swung to the second guard and shot him as well. The third and final guard came running from the elevator with his weapon drawn. Upon entering the room, Diegert leveled three bullets into his chest, dropping him to the floor.

With the gun still hot in his hand, Diegert cast his sight on Panzer, who now held Denise in front of him with a freshly cut rose stem pressed against her neck.

Diegert smirked. "You're going to stab her with a rose?"

"The end is sharp, and the stem is stiff." He pressed the shaft to her neck, which drew blood and a squeal from Denise. "I'll drive it right through her throat."

Diegert pulled out the satellite phone, dropped it onto the coffee table, and pointed the pistol at it. "You let her go right now."

Panzer's eyes diverted to the phone, and Diegert fired the pistol into the floor, startling the man. With a quick move, Diegert punched Panzer on the jaw, knocking him to the floor, forcing the release of his mother.

Panzer slowly rose to his feet while Diegert picked up the satellite phone.

Denise moved to the side, placing her hand on her neck wound.

Panzer and Diegert faced each other like combatants in a ring. Diegert's pistol made clear his advantage. He spoke first. "So where do we go from here?"

"Remember what I told you: there is a future for you in my organization. You will be successful beyond your wildest dreams."

"That's fucking bullshit."

Diegert lifted the pistol, placing Panzer's face in the iron sights.

Extending his hands and backing away, Panzer said, "Before acting rashly, you should consider all your options."

"Yeah, I will. I could kill you right here." Panzer continued backing up, making his way through the apartment. "I could kill you in the bedroom." Panzer passed the bedroom door. "I could kill you in the bathroom." Panzer stood in the doorframe of the bathroom. "Get in there." Panzer stepped into the bathroom as Diegert stood outside with the pistol steady in his hand.

Panzer pleaded, "Son, I'm the only person on earth who can show you a father's love."

Diegert's steely gaze and fatal focus softened for an instant.

Panzer continued, "Let me share my wealth, power, and love with my one true son. Won't you give me that chance?"

Diegert hesitated but did not lower the pistol as he contemplated his reply. "I can see the wealth and power, but I don't believe in the love."

Keeping his father at the end of his pistol, Diegert reached out and slammed the door. He wedged the door closed with a sturdy straight-backed chair jammed against the knob.

Returning to the main room, he grabbed the medical backpack and dressed his mother's puncture wound.

"David, I'm so sorry I never told you, but I never imagined I would ever see that man again."

Folding her into his arms, he hugged her, saying, "Shah, it's OK."

Breaking into a sob, Denise said, "A mother should never have to share such shame with her son."

Patting her shoulder, Diegert said, "It's OK, Mom. You're the one person in this whole world who I love."

Gazing up at her son, Denise said, "Oh, David, it's good to hear you say that again."

The water of love, sadness, joy, and grief seeped from the windows of their souls, spilled over their lids, and rolled down their faces as they looked at each other with emotions that could not find words. All Diegert's tension and trepidation was giving way to the relief and exhilaration he felt now that he had secured her release. Next, he was going to guarantee her freedom.

Wiping his eyes on his sleeve, he picked up his pistol and said, "Come on, Mom, we're starting new lives. Let's get out of here."

With his arm around her shoulder, they walked over to the elevator. He instinctively placed himself between her and the doors before pressing the call button. While waiting, he thought about how he could take her anywhere she wanted to go and give her a life of comfort and happiness. She, after all the tough times, deserved a peaceful life, and he was excited about making that happen.

The metal panels of the elevator separated, revealing the interior of the cabin and the presence of Pierre and two other men. Diegert's pistol immediately rose, but his hesitation at seeing the one friendly guy from Headquarters cost him dearly when Pierre pulled the trigger on his Taser, releasing forty-two hundred volts of muscle-paralyzing electricity into Diegert's legs and torso. As he fell to the floor, Diegert fired his weapon, but the spasms in his arm sent the bullet harmlessly into the ceiling. He felt all muscular control vacate his body. Looking up, he watched as the two men flexi-cuffed his mom's hands behind her back, covered her mouth with duct tape, and shoved her into the elevator.

Pierre barked the orders, "Hold her in the elevator. You, go find Mr. Panzer."

Convulsing on the floor, Diegert turned his eyes to see Pierre open a small case and extract a syringe. "You're a foolish idiot for taking the hard way to learn how this business works. I'm sorry to do this, but you've forgotten we are servants to the powerful."

The second man returned with Panzer. The gray-haired tyrant stepped over to Diegert, knelt on his chest, and took the satellite phone. He then bent forward, looking straight into the wide eyes of his terrified son, and growled; "Now I will show you a father's love."

As he stood up, Panzer nodded to Pierre, who pressed the syringe into Diegert's thigh. The injection sedated the consciousness of David Diegert, fading his world to black.

THE END

Turn the page for a preview of

Book Three of the David Diegert Series

Code of the Assassin

Available Summer of 2020

Code of the Assassin
Preview of Book 3

CHAPTER 1

BEEP, BEEEEP! In spite of the rain, the asshole rolled down his window to shout, "Get outta the way you bloody little twat." Grimy spray from angry tires doused Mei Ling's moped. Her high wellies and long raincoat deflected the rude splash from a puddle of London rain. The large hood of her coat kept her cigarette dry, each drag illuminating her determined face as she drove through traffic on this drizzly night. At the direction of her Father, Chin Lei Wei, she was to surveil the Ambassador Hotel.

As a Board member of Crepusculous, Chin Lei participated in the control of seventy-five percent of the world's economy. In partnership with three other men, he was part of a secret group of billionaires, orchestrating the most significant economic influence on planet earth. While bracing against the wet chill, Mei Ling thought her father's need for her to be his eyes and ears in London was a blessing and a curse. She had more freedom than she would have had in China, but her assignments carried real danger. Trained in Kung Fu and Wushu, she was capable, not only of defending herself, but killing if an enemy persisted. Killing was not her mission tonight.

Her father had assigned her to conduct espionage, observing activities at one of London's most exclusive hotels.

Distrusting, Klaus Panzer, the most powerful member of the Crepusculous Board, Mr. Wei sent his daughter to report on the occurrences at the Ambassador. With absolute trust, he relied on her ability to observe while remaining unseen and unrecognized as a child of Crepusculous. Unlike the privileged offspring of the rest of the wealthy board members, she worked to preserve the empire, although this assignment felt like subterfuge. The multi-paneled door of the hotel's underground garage retracted. Through the opening, a black Mercedes S550 slipped sinuously into the rain. Following the sleek sedan, a black panel van lurched onto the road, speeding off in the opposite direction. Mei Ling started her moped and followed the lithe, luxurious car.

*****

Denise Diegert, David's mother, sat petrified in the back passenger seat of the van. The plastic zip ties were restricting the blood flow to her hands, while the duct tape over her mouth forced her to breathe through her nostrils. Her seat belt held her in place, yet she could turn to see David lying unconscious on the floor of the van. What was her son doing in London? She was shocked to see him when he appeared in the penthouse of the Ambassador. He was supposed to be in Afghanistan. Frazzled at having been kidnapped, forced unto a private jet and flown all the way to London, Denise was told nothing about why this was happening and who was giving the orders. Then David showed up at the hotel,

followed moments later by Klaus Panzer, a man she
hoped never to see again her entire life. Panzer had raped
her years ago, unknowingly leaving her pregnant and
never contacting her. He was David's father, but she
never reached out to him. He forced her to have sex with
him for his own gratification; he was never going to help
her. She raised David in the home of her husband, Tom
Diegert, who figured out he was not this child's father.
He let the boy stay, but made his life a living hell,
denying him love, acceptance and support. In the
penthouse, she saw Panzer's men inject drugs into David,
who now lay unconscious on a dirty sheet, stinking of
motor oil. She tried not to cry, but she loved him so
much, and to her he was still that curious, inquisitive little
boy who loved to go on nature walks, camping trips, and
long canoe paddles. David was so enthralled with the
natural world; he was happy and carefree whenever he
was with his mother on an outdoor adventure. Because
of Panzer, he now knew the shame she had hidden from
him his entire life. He was the bastard son of the world's
richest man. She never wanted him to know for fear of
losing him. She always thought if Panzer knew what a
special boy his son David was, he would take him from
her, just as he took her body for his pleasure that night.
Powerful men do whatever they want to poor people like
her. She loved David and never wanted him raised by the
selfish, overbearing brute who raped her, even if he did o
possess tremendous wealth. It eviscerated her heart to
have to admit to David that Klaus was right when he put
it together and forced her to confirm that he was David's
father. The secret erupted from her with just a slight nod.
This awful secret was supposed to be tucked away
forever with her, and taken to her grave. Staring at her
son, whose breathing came in raspy gasps while his head

rolling back and forth, as the van sped down a freeway. Her tears streaked the duct tape before dripping off her chin. Denise feared for both of them as they were being driven to wherever Klaus Panzer had ordered his men to take them.

The Mercedes crawled with the traffic making it easy for Mei Ling to keep pace. The dark windows, however, made it impossible for her to see inside the vehicle. Klaus Panzer sat comfortably in the soft leather seat. He adjusted his sleeves and smoothed his thick gray hair. From his breast pocket, he extracted a satellite phone. With this single device, he possessed the capacity to instigate a series of thermobaric bombs planted in a dozen US locations. These bombs, combine heat and force to produce a super-hot, explosive impact, which ignites oxygen in the air creating death through flaming asphyxiation. The chemistry of the bombs is extremely stable allowing them to lie in place for long periods of time, remaining undetected, yet capable of being activated by a remote signal. Each charge was strategically placed to disrupt a critical piece of infrastructure, disabling transportation, communication, banking, energy distribution, food, and water supply and ultimately governmental authority. Panzer, through his private espionage wing of Crepusculous, set up the unprecedented attack on America. The country would be severely hampered for months. It was 9/11, times twelve all within twelve hours. From the back seat of the Mercedes, Panzer input the code, which would set off the first set of explosions and initiate the entire cascade. Mei Ling saw the blinker illuminating the right side of the black sedan, the car was moving onto the expressway ramp. She leaned her moped to the right, gunning it along the shoulder passing all the cars including Panzer's. Even though Panzer's original plan had someone else inputting the code, he had the sequence of numbers and letters memorized. Now that David Diegert had confounded the original plan it was going to have to be Panzer who ignited the hellacious destruction he had planned for America. "464748DAZ," Panzer typed on the phone's keyboard. He waited for confirmation that the signal was received by his private satellite orbiting five hundred miles above the earth. The green word; ACTIVATED did not appear.

Mei Ling arrived at the base of the expressway ramp to see two police vans swerve into position. The first cut in front of Panzer's car, while the second moved in behind trapping the Mercedes. From the vans, black-clad operators with helmets and submachine guns swarmed Panzer's vehicle. Panzer re-entered the activation code, with no response. His driver asked, "How should I proceed?" In a moment of silence, Panzer was uncharacteristically flustered, yet he had the clarity of mind to realize that Diegert must have re-programmed the satellite phone so it would not accept the activation code. His plans were foiled, and now a London SWAT team surrounded his vehicle. Panzer initiated the phone's failsafe mechanism sending a self-destructive charge through the circuitry destroying all the data. A thick plume of acrid smoke rose from the disabled device. Panzer opened the car's roof allowing the smoke to escape and the rain to enter. The SWAT team braced as the belch of smoke exited the car's roof. As he closed the roof and brushed the rain from his suit, Panzer instructed his chauffeur, "See what they want." As the chauffeur stepped out of the car, electrodes pierced his legs and torso. The jolting charge of a taser sent the man crashing back against the car, striking his head as he crumpled to the rain-soaked pavement. Through the window next to him, Panzer peered directly into the barrel point of an H&K MP5. The jacked-up operator's face was obscured by his black goggles, but his intent was clear. In spite of the threat, Panzer opened the door, stepping out into the rain; he rose to his six-foot, four-inch height. Droplets beaded up and rolled off the expensive fabric of his custom-tailored suit. The armed operators kept their guns trained upon him, but they did not subdue him. Klaus Panzer's regal bearing commanded respect even under extremely tense conditions.

A pair of detectives exited their car and approached Panzer's, looking at each other with restrained concern. The first wore a beige raincoat and a beat-up fedora. The taller of the two wore a green coat with a belt sashed tightly around his waist. His umbrella was black. They stepped past the armed operators and were immediately addressed by Panzer. "Unless you insist, I do not believe handcuffs are necessary."
"Shut up and put'em out," said the detective in the beige coat. Snapping the cuffs on Panzer's wrists, he allowed the distinguished man's arms to remain in front of him.

*****

Mei Ling watched as Panzer was led to the detective's car and placed in the back seat. Two officers loaded the unconscious chauffeur into the back of the limousine before climbing in, one behind the wheel. The first van pulled forward, then the Mercedes, followed by the detective's car with Panzer. The second van took up the rear position as the four-vehicle armada streaked up the entrance ramp, merged into the high-speed traffic, disappearing from the young lady's spying eyes. Fortunately, Mei Ling captured the event, which occupied less than three minutes, on her cell phone.

*****

Denise noticed the sign for London Polytechnic University as the van drove through the South entrance, crossed campus on Academic Drive and pulled up to a garage door on the backside of a large building.. The van sat quietly as Denise read the sign identifying the building as Culhane Hall. The garage door opened allowing the van into the building. Once inside, the doors closed.

London Polytechnic University or LPU, as most people referred to it, is a major technical university serving London since 1945. The University, built as part of the reconstruction following World War II, offers degrees in engineering, computer science, communications, medicine, and nursing as well as psychology, business, and finance. The basic sciences are represented by Departments of Biology, Chemistry, Physics, and Biotechnology specializing in nanotechnology. The University was founded by the Panzer family. The fact that the school was being built with "German" money was kept quiet in the late 40's when the planning and initial construction occurred.

For Klaus Panzer and Crepusculous, the University was the perfect place to hide in plain sight. Panzer's father designed the structures so there were unseen parts of campus from which clandestine operations could be conducted. Deep underground, in a labyrinth of secured facilities, Panzer maintained a vast network of labs, training facilities, and barracks where specialized personnel were housed and prepared for missions to support the Board of Crepusculous. It was a private paramilitary, functioning right below a bucolic campus dedicated to the open mind, the freedom of thought and the betterment of humanity. Panzer loved the contradiction and was proud of the seen and unseen capabilities of LPU.

Denise was taken from the van and released into comfortable, but secure, quarters. Her binds were removed, and she was allowed to shower and get into clean clothes before being served a fresh meal. David was slid out of the van onto a gurney, taken to medical, placed in a hospital bed and restrained. He remained unconscious while Dr. Clarissa Zeidler monitored his medical care.

*****

Panzer eyed the two detectives as the car made its way onto the expressway. He opened with, "Introductions please?"

The detective in the beige coat turned. "Shut up and don't say anything more."

The man in the green coat, who was driving, said, "I'm Agent Theodore Jackson with MI5. People call me Ted."

Reluctantly the other spoke, "I'm Detective Robert Morrow of the London Criminal Investigation Division. You do not have to say anything, but, it may harm your defense if you do not mention, when questioned, something which you later rely on in court. Anything you say may be given as evidence."

"May I place my one phone call?" asked Panzer.

"But of course," oozed Detective Morrow's sarcastic reply.

Panzer placed a text to the head of his legal team instructing him to track his GPS and meet him at the resulting police station. Choosing to exercise his right to remain silent, Panzer said nothing more. Looking through the rain-streaked windows, he found himself fuming at the clever actions of David Diegert.

Diegert lay in a medical bed, twitching like a dreaming dog. He imagined himself naked, lying on his back, strapped to a block of ice floating in a tumultuous sea, buffeted by torrents of cold wind from a dark foreboding sky. The ice chunk rocked as massive waves splashed frigid water over him. Snow fell in windswept sheets, the cold sting of each flake torturing Diegert's bare skin. Twisting and turning, tightened his restraints, preventing him from curling into a heat-preserving ball. He shivered with violent spasms as his body desperately attempted to generate warmth. Shaking uncontrollably, and hit by yet another wet wave, he looked up to see the clouds converging into a funnel. Was he in a snowbound tornado? The funnel cloud descended, coming right at him. Helplessness radiated from his gut as the cold power of the sky hit him with full force. From the dark center of the funnel, a face emerged. A cold gray face of a man with sharp cheekbones, icy hair, and judgmental blue eyes. The voice of Klaus Panzer chilled Diegert with an icy blast. The words, icicle daggers penetrating his heart.

"Now I will show you a father's love."

The threatening phrase intensified Diegert's shivering as the cold force of the icy grip of Klaus Panzer clamped on to his soul. The gray face rose above him, yet the cold blue eyes remained locked on his. Thunder boomed, and lightning crackled across the sky as cold wind preceded Panzer's next words. "You are my one true son. You will now see what that means to me." The words entered Diegert's ears like ice picks, with meaning as obscure as the sun in the dark gray sky. As the funnel pulled back up into the clouds, Diegert awoke when one last clap of snow thunder rolled across the expanse of his chilling nightmare.

Opening his eyes, Diegert was relieved to find he wasn't strapped to an iceberg but lay in a bed. Scanning the room, he could see he was in some kind of a medical facility. The room was light aqua green with installations on the wall for gas ports and lights that would flash in case of emergency. The bed had sturdy rails on both sides. Diegert was covered in a white sheet and one thin blue blanket. He laid there without attendants, other patients or the noises one would expect in a busy hospital. When he attempted to lift his hand, the restraints became apparent. Both wrists and ankles were encircled in soft lamb's wool with a solid brass buckle holding together the two ends of strong leather binds. There was a glowing red button next to his right hand, which he pressed. He received no feedback and pressed it a few more times. His patience was practically worn out, when a person finally appeared through the curtain draping the entrance to his room. Lifting his head, Diegert saw a young woman whose unsmiling face brought no cheer to the room. She looked at him, not with concern, but responsibility. Her glasses were round, rimmed in flat black, her brown hair pulled back into an efficient ponytail. Over aqua blue scrubs she wore, a thin white cardigan, which she drew, closed while wrapping her arms around her midsection, minimizing her breasts. From what Diegert could see, she needn't bother with such modesty.

"How can I help you?" she asked.

"Where am I?"

"I'm responsible for your medical care. I can't provide you with information." She turned and pulled back the curtain as she exited.

"Hey wait…come back here."

With her body already on the other side of the curtain, she moved the fabric from in front of her face. "Yes."

"I'm thirsty."

"My monitor indicates that your fluid level is within normal limits. Your IV is providing all the water your body needs."

Diegert followed her eyes to the tube inserted into his arm. "Well fuck that, my throat's dry."

The rudeness of Diegert's reply deepened the frown on her face. "I'll turn up the volume of your IV fluid from my computer." She snapped the fabric of the curtain closed disappearing from view.

"Hey come on, don't get all pissed off. I just want a drink of water. Hey! Come back."

She did not come back. Diegert watched the drips of his IV, and sure enough, the rate of flow did increase. He spent time trying to move as much as his four-point restraints would allow. His immobility brought back recollections of the past few hours when he had confronted Klaus Panzer to rescue his kidnapped mother.

He had succeeded. He and his Mom were exiting the Penthouse, leaving Panzer locked in the bathroom. As the elevator opened, Diegert's surprise to see a trusted friend caused him to hesitate long enough to be tazed and drugged, his mom, cuffed and gagged. Now, again, he had no idea where she was and what was happening to her.

****

Inside the police station, the detectives questioned Panzer.

"Are you involved with any terrorist organizations?" asked Detective Morrow.

"What makes you think that?" replied Panzer.

"Just answer the question," grumbled Morrow.

Detective Jackson interjected, "We've received intelligence implicating you in a terrorist plot. Can you tell us why such an accusation would be directed at you?"

"I believe it has to do with certain business rivals who feel they will gain an advantage by smearing me. I'm sorry such outrageous behavior ensnared you, gentlemen."

"Will you identify these business rivals for us?" Agent Jackson held eye contact with Panzer.

Panzer blinked and turned away. "I prefer to handle my own business issues. These rivals need to learn how to conduct themselves. That is a lesson I can share with them without inconveniencing you."

"It's our job to make sure people operate within the law."

"Interesting…" said Panzer. "I think of your job as beginning when someone breaks the law."

Morrow grunted. "Our job gets interesting when someone breaks the law." He held up the disabled satellite phone.

"We found this in your limousine."

Panzer gazed at the charred remains. "That device has been destroyed. A very unfortunate occurrence given the valuable contact data it possessed."

"What kind of data?" pushed Morrow.

"Business contacts, for people with whom I conduct commerce. However, it did contain proprietary data which exists nowhere else, now gone forever."

Leaning forward, Morrow said, "Yeah… that's the kind of stuff we're looking for."

"Well I hate to disappoint you," Panzer gestured toward the melted mass, "but I'm afraid you'll find nothing useful on that lump of plastic."

Panzer's lawyers arrived at the Police Station dressed in Kiton suits with dramatic red ties. He smiled when he saw the determination on their faces. The detectives saw their legal representatives, in low budget rack wear, casting disappointed frowns.

The Crepusculous lawyers went right to work addressing the allegations and making arrangements. No charges were filed, and a receipt was issued for the burned-out satellite phone. As he exited the building, Panzer stopped to speak with Morrow and Jackson. "Thank you for your service, I appreciate your professionalism."

Morrow replied through gritted teeth, "Next time you're spending the night in jail."

Jackson, with a calmer tone, said, "When dealing with your business rivals, remember that enforcing the law is our job." He handed Panzer his business card.

Panzer examined the card. "I will see to it that the Police Benevolent Association receives a donation."

"Don't bother," said Morrow.

"We always appreciate the public's support," replied Jackson.

With his driver sufficiently recovered, Panzer was back in the limousine and on route to his townhouse. He called Javier Perez, connecting to the playboy's voice mail. *"This is Javier, if we have made love in the past; you are a very fond memory. If we have not, please leave your number. Chow."*

The seductive message only pissed Panzer off. He shouted, "Meet me at my townhouse as soon as you get this message. Zip up your pants and report to me immediately."

****

Javier saw the name on his screen and was not at all surprised by such a brusque demand. Being the son of Julio Perez, the man who represented one-fourth of Crepusculous, came with responsibilities. Javier judiciously avoided responsibility his whole adult life, preferring to enjoy the wealth, easily seducing women with his handsome face. That face, however, currently was battered and bruised from a violent encounter with David Diegert. Javier had possessed the satellite phone detonation device but lost it to Diegert in a vicious fight. In spite of being an accomplished martial artist and doing some damage to Diegert, Javier's blackened eye, split cheek, and fat lip revealed the outcome of his battle with the world's best assassin.

Along with his father, the other members of Crepusculous included Chin Lei Wei, the Englishmen Dean Kellerman, and Klaus Panzer, who was arguably the most influential of the four. Javier knew he would have to comply with Panzer's demand, so he dismissed a curvaceous Czech exchange student from his room at his London Townhouse and contemplated how he would manage the undoubtedly intense interaction that awaited him.

Javier, at first, paid little attention to the plan Klaus Panzer had devised to destroy the value of the US dollar. When he discovered the action included bombing a dozen US cities, he realized Panzer was going too far. Javier knew he wasn't well respected within the Crepusculous Board, but he also knew that successful economic warfare need not be fought with guns, bombs and mass destruction. He felt he must tell Klaus Panzer to use a more effective tool to devalue the dollar. He was going to have to show the world's most powerful man that he could learn something from the world's most successful playboy.

Mei Ling sent her video of Panzer's limousine being stopped by the police to her father through a secure link Her note said: It took me a while to get to the police station on my moped. Panzer was not there long, as I saw him leaving just as I arrived.
Her father wrote back: Was there any resistance to his arrest? Everything in the video looks peaceful.
Mei Ling replied: There was no resistance, Panzer complied.
Chin Lei replied: Anything else to report?
Mei Ling: A van also left the hotel at the same time as Panzer. It traveled in the opposite direction. I could not follow it, but the license tag was: VS52 CZS.
Chin Lei: Very well, stay prepared for additional instructions.

Mei ling was ticked. That was it? No thank you, just an expectation to do more.

The Wei family was one of the richest in China. Her father's wealth granted him membership on the Crepusculous Board. His position with Crepusculous was unknown to Me Ling, or at least that's what Chin Lei believed. In fact, keeping her in London so she could spy on Panzer was something that Chin Lei did because he had so little trust in anyone outside the family. Expecting her not to learn about the Board when she was tasked with spying on the presumptive leader of the organization, was something only a nearsighted father would believe.

Mei Ling had two brothers, Quiang her older brother and Shing her younger. Both were granted great privileges, especially the older who was heir to the Wei Empire. Living in China, the two boys enjoyed fast cars and county clubs. Like the other sons of Crepusculous, the boys lived like royals. Catered to and privileged, they had no reason to delay gratification. Mei Ling was given a subservient role even though she was smarter, more determined and far more capable than either of the boys. She was glad to be in London and not under the direct eye of her father and his traditional beliefs. The servants in her townhouse would have to cover for her once again as she blew off her curfew and drove her moped to the Rupert Street Bar in Soho for a night of making friends over drinks.

Thank you for Reading

Please post a review on Amazon, or the site of your choice. Your review will let the world know how you enjoyed this story.

A review needn't be long.
A sentence of two is sufficient.

I appreciate your time, effort and energy spent sharing your opinion with other readers.

Thank you.

Bill Brewer

ABOUT THE AUHTOR

Bill Brewer writes to engage his readers. Using imagination and research, he creates compelling characters whom he thrusts into dangerous situations. To thrill his readers, Bill sets a blistering pace and keeps the action coming as the plot explodes across the pages. The story reveals its secrets as the characters experience triumph, betrayal, victory, and loss. While you're reading, look for passages filled with anatomical details that this University Professor of Human Anatomy & Physiology uses to bring realism into his story.

When not teaching or writing, Bill can be found seeking adventure, peace and camaraderie, hiking, biking and paddling near his home in Rochester NY.

SOCIAL MEDIA

Please visit my website and subscribe for e-mail updates.

billbrewerbooks.com

Also, please follow me on

- <u>Facebook</u>: Bill Brewer Books
- <u>Twitter</u>: @Brewer Books
- <u>Instagram</u>: billbrewer434

THRILLEX Publishing

Made in the USA
Middletown, DE
29 April 2020